If on a winter's night a traveller

Italo Calvino was born in Cuba in 1923. He grew up in Italy. He was an essayist and journalist and a member of the editorial staff of Einaudi in Turin. His other novels include *Invisible Cities* and *The Castle of Crossed Destinies*. In 1973 he won the prestigious Premio Feltrinelli. He died in 1985.

By Italo Calvino

The Path to the Nest of Spiders
Adam, One Afternoon*
Our Ancestors*
Difficult Loves*
Marcovaldo*
Cosmicomics
t zero
The Watcher and Other Stories
Italian Folktales
Invisible Cities
The Castle of Crossed Destinies
If on a winter's night a traveller*
Mr Palomar*

available from Minerva

ITALO CALVINO

If on a , winter's night a traveller

Translated from the Italian
by William Weaver

Minerva

A Minerva Paperback
IF ON A WINTER'S NIGHT A TRAVELLER

3 5 7 9 10 8 6 4

First published in Great Britain 1981
by Martin Secker & Warburg Ltd
This Minerva edition published 1992

Reprinted 1992 (three times), 1993 (three times), 1994,
1995 (three times), 1996 (twice)
Reissued 1997
Reprinted 1997

Random House UK Limited
20 Vauxhall Bridge Road, London SW1V 2SA

Random House Australia (Pty) Limited
20 Alfred Street, Milsons Point, Sydney,
New South Wales 2061, Australia

Random House New Zealand Limited
18 Poland Road, Glenfield, Auckland 10, New Zealand

Random House South Africa (Pty) Limited
Endulini, 5a Jubilee Road, Parktown 2193, South Africa

Originally published in Italy under the title
Se una notte d'inverno un viaggiatore

Copyright © Giulio editore s.p.a. Torino 1979
English translation copyright
© Harcourt Brace Jovanovich Inc. 1981

Random House UK Limited Reg. No. 954009

A CIP catalogue record for this title
is available from the British Library
ISBN 0 7493 9923 6

Papers used by Random House UK Limited
are natural, recyclable products made from wood grown in
sustainable forests. The manufacturing processes conform to
the environmental regulations of the country of origin

Printed and bound in Great Britain

For Daniele Ponchiroli

TRANSLATOR'S NOTE
In Chapter Eight the passage from
Crime and Punishment
is quoted in the beloved translation
of Constance Garnett.

W. W.

Contents

Contents

If on a winter's night a traveller

[1]

You are about to begin reading Italo Calvino's new novel, *If on a winter's night a traveler*. Relax. Concentrate. Dispel every other thought. Let the world around you fade. Best to close the door; the TV is always on in the next room. Tell the others right away, "No, I don't want to watch TV!" Raise your voice—they won't hear you otherwise—"I'm reading! I don't want to be disturbed!" Maybe they haven't heard you, with all that racket; speak louder, yell: "I'm beginning to read Italo Calvino's new novel!" Or if you prefer, don't say anything; just hope they'll leave you alone.

Find the most comfortable position: seated, stretched out, curled up, or lying flat. Flat on your back, on your side, on your stomach. In an easy chair, on the sofa, in the rocker, the deck chair, on the hassock. In the hammock, if you have a hammock. On top of your bed, of course, or in the bed. You can even stand on your hands, head down, in the yoga position. With the book upside down, naturally.

Of course, the ideal position for reading is something you can never find. In the old days they used to read standing up, at a lectern. People were accustomed to standing on their feet, without moving. They rested like that when they were tired of horseback riding. Nobody ever thought of reading on horseback; and yet now, the idea of sitting in the saddle, the book propped against the horse's mane, or maybe tied to the horse's ear with a special harness, seems attractive to you. With your feet in the stirrups, you should feel quite comfortable for reading; having your feet up is the first condition for enjoying a read.

Well, what are you waiting for? Stretch your legs, go ahead and put your feet on a cushion, on two cushions, on the arms of the sofa, on the wings of the chair, on the coffee table, on the desk, on the piano, on the globe. Take your shoes off first. If you want to, put your feet up; if not, put them back. Now don't stand there with your shoes in one hand and the book in the other.

Adjust the light so you won't strain your eyes. Do it now, because once you're absorbed in reading there will be no budging you. Make sure the page isn't in shadow, a clotting of black letters on a gray background, uniform as a pack of mice; but be careful that the light cast on it isn't too strong, doesn't glare on the cruel white of the paper, gnawing at the shadows of the letters as in a southern noonday. Try to foresee now everything that might make you interrupt your reading. Cigarettes within reach, if you smoke, and the ashtray. Anything else? Do you have to pee? All right, you know best.

It's not that you expect anything in particular from this particular book. You're the sort of person who, on principle, no longer expects anything of anything. There are plenty, younger than you or less young, who live in the expectation of extraordinary experiences: from books, from people, from journeys, from events, from what tomorrow has in store. But not you. You know that the best you can expect is to avoid the worst. This is the conclusion you have reached, in your personal life and also in general matters, even international affairs. What about books? Well, precisely because you have denied it in every other field, you believe you may still grant yourself legitimately this youthful pleasure of expectation in a carefully circumscribed area like the field of books, where you can be lucky or unlucky, but the risk of disappointment isn't serious.

So, then, you noticed in a newspaper that *If on a winter's night a traveler* had appeared, the new book by Italo Calvino, who hadn't published for several years. You went to the bookshop and bought the volume. Good for you.

In the shop window you have promptly identified the

cover with the title you were looking for. Following this visual trail, you have forced your way through the shop past the thick barricade of Books You Haven't Read, which were frowning at you from the tables and shelves, trying to cow you. But you know you must never allow yourself to be awed, that among them there extend for acres and acres the Books You Needn't Read, the Books Made For Purposes Other Than Reading, Books Read Even Before You Open Them Since They Belong To The Category Of Books Read Before Being Written. And thus you pass the outer girdle of ramparts, but then you are attacked by the infantry of the Books That If You Had More Than One Life You Would Certainly Also Read But Unfortunately Your Days Are Numbered. With a rapid maneuver you bypass them and move into the phalanxes of the Books You Mean To Read But There Are Others You Must Read First, the Books Too Expensive Now And You'll Wait Till They're Remaindered, the Books ditto When They Come Out In Paperback, Books You Can Borrow From Somebody, Books That Everybody's Read So It's As If You Had Read Them, Too. Eluding these assaults, you come up beneath the towers of the fortress, where other troops are holding out:

the Books You've Been Planning To Read For Ages,

the Books You've Been Hunting For Years Without Success,

the Books Dealing With Something You're Working On At The Moment,

the Books You Want To Own So They'll Be Handy Just In Case,

the Books You Could Put Aside Maybe To Read This Summer,

the Books You Need To Go With Other Books On Your Shelves,

the Books That Fill You With Sudden, Inexplicable Curiosity, Not Easily Justified.

Now you have been able to reduce the countless embattled troops to an array that is, to be sure, very large but still calculable in a finite number; but this relative relief is then undermined by the ambush of the Books Read Long Ago Which It's Now Time To Reread and the Books You've Always Pretended To Have Read And Now It's Time To Sit Down And Really Read Them.

With a zigzag dash you shake them off and leap straight into the citadel of the New Books Whose Author Or Subject Appeals To You. Even inside this stronghold you can make some breaches in the ranks of the defenders, dividing them into New Books By Authors Or On Subjects Not New (for you or in general) and New Books By Authors Or On Subjects Completely Unknown (at least to you), and defining the attraction they have for you on the basis of your desires and needs for the new and the not new (for the new you seek in the not new and for the not new you seek in the new).

All this simply means that, having rapidly glanced over the titles of the volumes displayed in the bookshop, you have turned toward a stack of *If on a winter's night a traveler* fresh off the press, you have grasped a copy, and you have carried it to the cashier so that your right to own it can be established.

You cast another bewildered look at the books around you (or, rather: it was the books that looked at you, with the bewildered gaze of dogs who, from their cages in the city pound, see a former companion go off on the leash of his master, come to rescue him), and out you went.

You derive a special pleasure from a just-published book, and it isn't only a book you are taking with you but its novelty as well, which could also be merely that of an object fresh from the factory, the youthful bloom of new books, which lasts until the dust jacket begins to yellow, until a veil of smog settles on the top edge, until the binding becomes dog-eared, in the rapid autumn of libraries. No, you hope always to encounter true newness, which, having been new once, will continue to be so. Having read the freshly published book, you will take possession of this newness at the first moment, without having to pursue it, to chase it. Will it happen this time? You never can tell. Let's see how it begins.

Perhaps you started leafing through the book already in the shop. Or were you unable to, because it was wrapped in its cocoon of cellophane? Now you are on the bus, standing in the crowd, hanging from a strap by your arm, and you begin undoing the package with your free hand, making movements something like a monkey, a monkey who wants to peel a banana and at the same time cling to the bough. Watch out, you're elbowing your neighbors; apologize, at least.

Or perhaps the bookseller didn't wrap the volume; he gave it to you in a bag. This simplifies matters. You are at the wheel of your car, waiting at a traffic light, you take the book out of the bag, rip off the transparent wrapping, start reading the first lines. A storm of honking breaks over you; the light is green, you're blocking traffic.

You are at your desk, you have set the book among your business papers as if by chance; at a certain moment you shift a file and you find the book before your eyes, you open it absently, you rest your elbows on the desk, you rest your temples against your hands, curled into fists, you seem to be concentrating on an examination of the papers and instead you are exploring the first pages of the novel. Gradually you settle back in the chair, you raise the book to the level of your nose, you tilt the chair, poised on its rear legs, you pull out a side drawer of the desk to prop your feet on it; the position of the feet during reading is of maximum importance, you stretch your legs out on the top of the desk, on the files to be expedited.

But doesn't this seem to show a lack of respect? Of respect, that is, not for your job (nobody claims to pass judgment on your professional capacities: we assume that your duties are a normal element in the system of unproductive activities that occupies such a large part of the national and international economy), but for the book. Worse still if you belong—willingly or unwillingly—to the number of those for whom working means really working, performing, whether deliberately or without premeditation, something necessary or at least not useless for others as well as for oneself; then the book you have brought with you to your place of employment like a kind of amulet or talisman exposes you to intermittent temptations, a few seconds at a time subtracted from the principal object of your attention, whether it is the perforations of electronic cards, the burners of a kitchen stove, the controls of a bulldozer, a patient stretched out on the operating table with his guts exposed.

In other words, it's better for you to restrain your impatience and wait to open the book at home. Now. Yes, you are in your room, calm; you open the book to page one, no, to the last page, first you want to see how long it is. It's not too long, fortunately. Long novels written today are perhaps a contradiction: the dimension of time has been shattered, we cannot love or think except in fragments of time each of which goes off along its own trajectory and immediately disappears. We can rediscover the continuity of time only in the novels of that period when time no longer seemed stopped and did not yet seem to have exploded, a period that lasted no more than a hundred years.

You turn the book over in your hands, you scan the sentences on the back of the jacket, generic phrases that don't say a great deal. So much the better, there is no message that indiscreetly outshouts the message that the book itself must communicate directly, that you must extract from the book, however much or little it may be. Of course, this circling of the book, too, this reading around it before reading inside it, is a part of the pleasure in a

Chapter one

new book, but like all preliminary pleasures, it has its
optimal duration if you want it to serve as a thrust toward
the more substantial pleasure of the consummation of the
act, namely the reading of the book.

So here you are now, ready to attack the first lines of
the first page. You prepare to recognize the unmistakable
tone of the author. No. You don't recognize it at all. But
now that you think about it, who ever said this author had
an unmistakable tone? On the contrary, he is known as an
author who changes greatly from one book to the next.
And in these very changes you recognize him as himself.
Here, however, he seems to have absolutely no connection
with all the rest he has written, at least as far as you can
recall. Are you disappointed? Let's see. Perhaps at first
you feel a bit lost, as when a person appears who, from
the name, you identified with a certain face, and you try
to make the features you are seeing tally with those you
had in mind, and it won't work. But then you go on and
you realize that the book is readable nevertheless, independently of what you expected of the author, it's the
book in itself that arouses your curiosity; in fact, on sober
reflection, you prefer it this way, confronting something
and not quite knowing yet what it is.

If on a,
winter's
night
a traveler

The novel begins in a railway station, a locomotive huffs, steam from a piston covers the opening of the chapter, a cloud of smoke hides part of the first paragraph. In the odor of the station there is a passing whiff of station café odor. There is someone looking through the befogged glass, he opens the glass door of the bar, everything is misty, inside, too, as if seen by nearsighted eyes, or eyes irritated by coal dust. The pages of the book are clouded like the windows of an old train, the cloud of smoke rests on the sentences. It is a rainy evening; the man enters the bar; he unbuttons his damp overcoat; a cloud of steam enfolds him; a whistle dies away along tracks that are glistening with rain, as far as the eye can see.

A whistling sound, like a locomotive's, and a cloud of steam rise from the coffee machine that the old counterman puts under pressure, as if he were sending up a signal, or at least so it seems from the series of sentences in the second paragraph, in which the players at the table close the fans of cards against their chests and turn toward the newcomer with a triple twist of their necks, shoulders, and chairs, while the customers at the counter raise their little cups and blow on the surface of the coffee, lips and eyes half shut, or suck the head of their mugs of beer, taking exaggerated care not to spill. The cat arches its back, the cashier closes her cash register and it goes pling. All these signs converge to inform us that this is a little provincial station, where anyone is immediately noticed.

Stations are all alike; it doesn't matter if the lights cannot illuminate beyond their blurred halo, all of this is a setting you know by heart, with the odor of train that lingers even after all the trains have left, the special odor of stations after the last train has left. The lights of the station and the sentences you are reading seem to have the job of dissolving more than of indicating the things that surface from a veil of darkness and fog. I have landed in this station tonight for the first time in my life, entering and leaving this bar, moving from the odor of the platform to the odor of wet sawdust in the toilets, all mixed in a single odor which is that of waiting, the odor of telephone booths when all you can do is reclaim your tokens because the number called has shown no signs of life.

I am the man who comes and goes between the bar and the telephone booth. Or, rather: that man is called "I" and you know nothing else about him, just as this station is called only "station" and beyond it there exists nothing except the unanswered signal of a telephone ringing in a dark room of a distant city. I hang up the receiver, I await the rattling flush, down through the metallic throat, I push the glass door again, head toward the cups piled up to dry in a cloud of steam.

The espresso machines in station cafés boast their kinship with the locomotives, the espresso machines of yesterday and today with the locomotives and steam engines of today and yesterday. It's all very well for me to come and go, shift and turn: I am caught in a trap, in that nontemporal trap which all stations unfailingly set. A cloud of coal dust still hovers in the air of stations all these years after the lines have been totally electrified, and a novel that talks about trains and stations cannot help conveying this odor of smoke. For a couple of pages now you have been reading on, and this would be the time to tell you clearly whether this station where I have got off is a station of the past or a station of today; instead the sentences continue to move in vagueness, grayness, in a kind of no man's land of experience reduced to the lowest common denominator. Watch out: it is surely a method of involving you gradually, capturing you in the story before you realize it—a trap. Or perhaps the author still has not made up his mind, just as you, reader, for that matter, are not sure what you would most like to read: whether it is the arrival at an old station, which would give you a sense of going back, a renewed concern with lost times and places, or else a flashing of lights and sounds, which would give you the sense of being alive today, in the world where people today believe it is a pleasure to be alive. This bar (or "station buffet," as it is also called) could seem dim and misty only to my eyes, nearsighted or irritated, whereas it could also be steeped in light diffused by tubes the color of lightning and reflected by mirrors in such a way as to fill completely every passage and interstice, and the shadowless space might be overflowing with music exploding at top volume from a vibrant silence-killing machine, and the pinballs and the other electric games simulating horse races and manhunts are all in action, and colored shadows swim in the transparency of a TV and in that of an aquarium of tropical fish enlivened by a vertical stream of air bubbles. And my arm might not hold a briefcase, swollen and a bit worn, but might be pushing a square suitcase of plastic material supplied with little wheels, guided by a chrome stick that can be folded up.

You, reader, believed that there, on the platform, my gaze was glued to the hands of the round clock of an old station, hands pierced like halberds, in the vain attempt to turn them back, to move backward over the cemetery of spent hours, lying lifeless in their circular pantheon. But who can say that the clock's numbers aren't peeping from rectangular windows, where I see every minute fall on me with a click like the blade of a guillotine? However, the result would not change much: even advancing in a polished, sliding world, my hand contracted on the light rudder of the wheeled suitcase would still express an inner refusal, as if that carefree luggage represented for me an unwelcome and exhausting burden.

Something must have gone wrong for me: some misinformation, a delay, a missed connection; perhaps on arriving I should have found a contact, probably linked with this suitcase that seems to worry me so much, though whether because I am afraid of losing it or because I can't wait to be rid of it is not clear. What seems certain is that it isn't just ordinary baggage, something I can check or pretend to forget in the waiting room. There's no use my looking at my watch; if anyone had come and waited for me he would have gone away again long ago, there's no point in my furiously racking my brain to turn back clocks and calendars in the hope of reaching again the moment before something that should not have happened did happen. If I was to meet someone in this station, someone who perhaps had nothing to do with this station but was simply to get off one train and leave on another train, as I was to have done, and one of the two was to pass something to the other—for example, if I was supposed to give the other this wheeled suitcase which instead has been left on my hands and is scorching them—then the only thing to do is to try to re-establish the lost contact.

I have already crossed the café a couple of times and have looked out of the front door onto the invisible square, and each time the wall of darkness has driven back inside this sort of illuminated limbo suspended between the two darknesses, the bundle of tracks and the foggy city. Where would I go out to? The city outside there has no name yet, we don't know if it will remain outside the novel or whether the whole story will be contained within its inky blackness. I know only that this first chapter is taking a while to break free of the station and the bar: it is not wise for me to move away from here where they might still come looking for me, or for me to be seen by other people with this burdensome suitcase. And so I continue to cram tokens into the public telephone, which spits them back at me every time. Many tokens, as if for a long-distance call: God knows where they are now, the people from whom I am to receive instructions or, rather—let's come right out and say it—take orders. It is obvious that I am a subordinate, I do not seem the sort of man who is traveling for personal reasons or who is in business for himself; you would say, on the contrary, that I am doing a job, a pawn in a very complicated game, a little cog in a huge gear, so little that it should not even be seen: in fact, it was established that I would go through here without leaving any traces; and instead, every minute I spend here I am leaving more traces. I leave traces if I do not speak with anyone, since I stick out as a man who won't open his mouth; I leave traces if I speak with someone because every word spoken is a word that remains and can crop up again later, with quotation marks or without. Perhaps this is why the author piles supposition on supposition in long paragraphs without dialogue, a thick, opaque layer of lead where I may pass unnoticed, disappear.

I am not at all the sort of person who attracts attention, I am an anonymous presence against an even more anonymous background. If you, reader, couldn't help picking me out among the people getting off the train and contin-

If on a winter's night a traveler

ued following me in my to-and-fro-ing between bar and
telephone, this is simply because I am called "I" and this
is the only thing you know about me, but this alone is
reason enough for you to invest a part of yourself in the
stranger "I." Just as the author, since he has no intention
of telling about himself, decided to call the character "I" as
if to conceal him, not having to name him or describe him,
because any other name or attribute would define him
more than this stark pronoun; still, by the very fact of
writing "I" the author feels driven to put into this "I" a bit
of himself, of what he feels or imagines he feels. Nothing
could be easier for him than to identify himself with me;
for the moment my external behavior is that of a traveler
who has missed a connection, a situation that is part of
everyone's experience. But a situation that takes place at
the opening of a novel always refers you to something else
that has happened or is about to happen, and it is this
something else that makes it risky to identify with me,
risky for you the reader and for him the author; and the
more gray and ordinary and undistinguished and commonplace the beginning of this novel is, the more you and
the author feel a hint of danger looming over that fraction
of "I" that you have heedlessly invested in the "I" of a
character whose inner history you know nothing about, as
you know nothing about the contents of that suitcase he is
so anxious to be rid of.

Getting rid of the suitcase was to be the first condition
for re-establishing the previous situation: previous to
everything that happened afterward. This is what I mean
when I say I would like to swim against the stream of
time: I would like to erase the consequences of certain
events and restore an initial condition. But every moment
of my life brings with it an accumulation of new facts,
and each of these new facts brings with it its consequences; so the more I seek to return to the zero moment
from which I set out, the further I move away from it:

though all my actions are bent on erasing the consequences of previous actions and though I manage to
achieve appreciable results in this erasure, enough to
open my heart to hopes of immediate relief, I must, however, bear in mind that my every move to erase previous
events provokes a rain of new events, which complicate
the situation worse than before and which I will then, in
their turn, have to try to erase. Therefore I must calculate
carefully every move so as to achieve the maximum of
erasure with the minimum of recomplication.

A man whom I do not know was to meet me as soon as I
got off the train, if everything hadn't gone wrong. A man
with a suitcase on wheels, exactly like mine, empty. The
two suitcases would bump into each other as if accidentally in the bustle of travelers on the platform, between
one train and another. An event that can happen by
chance, but there would have been a password that that
man would have said to me, a comment on the headline of
the newspaper sticking out of my pocket, on the results of
the horse races. "Ah, Zeno of Elea came in first!" And at
the same time we would disentangle our suitcases, shifting the metal poles, perhaps also exchanging some remarks about horses, forecasts, odds; and we would then
go off toward different trains, each pushing his suitcase
in his own direction. No one would have noticed, but I
would have been left with the other man's suitcase and he
would have taken away mine.

A perfect plan, so perfect that a trivial complication
sufficed to spoil it. Now I am here not knowing what to do
next, the last traveler waiting in this station where no
more trains arrive or leave before tomorrow morning. It is
the hour when the little provincial city crawls into its
shell again. At the station bar the only people left are
locals who all know one another, people who have no
connection with the station but come this far through the
dark square perhaps because there is no other place open

16

If on a winter's night a traveler

in the neighborhood, or perhaps because of the attraction that stations still exercise in provincial cities, that bit of novelty that can be expected from stations, or perhaps only in recollection of the time when a station was the single point of contact with the rest of the world.

It's all very well for me to tell myself there are no provincial cities any more and perhaps there never were any: all places communicate instantly with all other places, a sense of isolation is felt only during the trip between one place and the other, that is, when you are in no place. I, in fact, find myself here without a here or an elsewhere, recognized as an outsider by the nonoutsiders at least as clearly as I recognize the nonoutsiders and envy them. Yes, envy. I am looking from the outside at the life of an ordinary evening in an ordinary little city, and I realize I am cut off from ordinary evenings for God knows how long, and I think of thousands of cities like this, of hundreds of thousands of lighted places where at this hour people allow the evening's darkness to descend and have none of the thoughts in their head that I have in mine; maybe they have other thoughts that aren't at all enviable, but at this moment I would be willing to trade with any one of them. For example, with one of these young men who are making the rounds of local shopkeepers collecting signatures on a petition to City Hall, concerning the tax on neon signs, and who are now reading it to the barman.

The novel here repeats fragments of conversation that seem to have no function beyond that of depicting the daily life of a provincial city. "What about you, Armida? Have you signed yet?" they ask a woman I can see only from behind, a belt hanging from a long overcoat trimmed with fur, the collar turned up, a thread of smoke rising from the fingers gripping the stem of a glass. "Who says I want to put a neon sign over my shop?" she answers. "If the City is planning to save money on street lights, they certainly aren't going to light the streets with my money! Anyway, everybody knows where Armida's Leather Goods is. And when I've pulled down the metal blind, the street will just stay dark, and that's that."

"That's a good reason for you to sign," they say to her. They address her familiarly, as *tu;* they all call one another *tu;* their speech is half in dialect; these are people used to seeing one another daily year after year; everything they say is the continuation of things already said. They tease one another, even crudely: "Admit it, you like the street dark so nobody can see who comes to your place! Who visits you in the back of the shop after you've locked up?"

These remarks form a murmuring of indistinct voices from which a word or a phrase might emerge, decisive for what comes afterward. To read properly you must take in both the murmuring effect and the effect of the hidden intention, which you (and I, too) are as yet in no position to perceive. In reading, therefore, you must remain both oblivious and highly alert, as I am abstracted but prick up my ears, with my elbow on the counter of the bar and my cheek on my fist. And if now the novel begins to abandon its misty vagueness and give some details about the appearance of the people, the sensation it wants to transmit to you is that of faces seen for the first time but also faces that seem to have been seen thousands of times. We are in a city in whose streets the same people often run into one another; the faces bear a weight of habit which is communicated even to someone like me, who, though I have never been here before, realizes these are habitual faces, whose features the bar mirror has watched thicken or sag, whose expressions evening after evening have become wrinkled or puffy. This woman was perhaps the beauty of the city; even now I feel, seeing her for the first time, she could be called an attractive woman; but if I imagine looking at her with the eyes of the other customers at the bar, then a kind of weariness settles on her, perhaps only the shadow of their weariness (or my weariness, or yours). They have known her since she was a girl, they know everything there is to know about her, some of them may have been involved with her, now water under the bridge, over and done with; in other words, there is a veil of other images that settles on her image and blurs it, a weight of memories that keep me from seeing her as a person seen for the first time, other people's memories suspended like the smoke under the lamps.

The great pastime of these customers at the bar seems to be betting: betting on trivial events of daily life. For example, one says, "Let's bet on who comes first to the bar here tonight, Dr. Marne or Chief Gorin." And another says, "And when Dr. Marne does get here, what will he do to avoid meeting his ex-wife? Will he play billiards or fill in the football-pool form?"

In an existence like mine forecasts could not be made: I never know what could happen to me in the next half hour, I can't imagine a life all made up of minimal alternatives, carefully circumscribed, on which bets can be made: either this or that.

"I don't know," I say in a low voice.

"Don't know what?" she asks.

It's a thought I feel I can also say now and not keep for myself as I do with all my thoughts, say it to the woman who is here beside me at the bar, the owner of the leather-goods shop, with whom I have a slight hankering to strike up a conversation. "Is that how it is, here in your town?"

"No, it's not true," she answers me, and I knew this was how she would answer me. She insists that nothing can be foreseen, here or anywhere else: of course, every evening at this hour Dr. Marne closes his office and Chief Gorin comes off duty at the police station; and they always drop by here, first one or first the other; but what does that signify?

"In any case, nobody seems to doubt the fact that the doctor will try to avoid the former Madame Marne," I say to her.

"I am the former Madame Marne," she answers. "Don't listen to them."

Your attention, as reader, is now completely concentrated on the woman, already for several pages you have been circling around her, I have—no, the author has—been circling around the feminine presence, for several pages you have been expecting this female shadow to take shape the way female shadows take shape on the written page, and it is your expectation, reader, that drives the author toward her; and I, too, though I have other things to think about, there I let myself go, I speak to her, I strike up a conversation that I should break off as quickly as I can, in order to go away, disappear. You surely would want to know more about what she's like, but instead only a few elements surface on the written page, her face remains hidden by the smoke and her hair, you would need to understand beyond the bitter twist of her mouth what there is that isn't bitter and twisted.

"What stories do they tell?" I ask. "I don't know a thing. I know that you have a shop, without a neon sign. But I don't even know where it is."

She explains to me. It is a leather-goods shop, selling suitcases and travel articles. It isn't in the station square but on a side street, near the grade crossing of the freight station.

"But why are you interested?"

"I wish I had arrived here earlier. I would walk along the dark street, I would see your shop all lighted up, I would go inside, I would say to you: If you like, I'll help you pull down the shutter."

She tells me she has already pulled down the shutter, but she has to go back to the shop to take inventory, and she will be staying there till late.

If on a winter's night a traveler

The men in the bar are exchanging wisecracks and slaps on the back. One bet has already been decided: the doctor is coming into the place.

"The chief's late tonight. I wonder why."

The doctor comes in and waves a general greeting; his gaze does not stop on his wife, but he has certainly noticed that a man is talking with her. He goes on to the end of the room, turning his back on the bar; he thrusts a coin into the pinball machine. Now I, who should have remained unnoticed, have been scrutinized, photographed by eyes that I cannot deceive myself I have eluded, eyes that forget nothing and no one connected with the object of jealousy and pain. Those slightly heavy, slightly watery eyes are enough to make me realize that the drama between the two has not yet ended: he continues coming to this café every evening to see her, to open the old wound again, perhaps also to know who is walking her home this evening; and she comes to this café every evening perhaps deliberately to make him suffer, or perhaps hoping that the habit of suffering will become for him a habit like any other, that it will take on the flavor of the nothingness that has coated her mouth and her life for years.

"The thing I'd like most in the world," I say to her, since at this point I might as well go on talking with her, "is to make clocks run backward."

The woman gives some ordinary answer, such as, "You only have to move the hands." "No, with thought, by concentrating until I force time to move back," I say; or, rather, it isn't clear whether I really say it or would like to say it or whether the author interprets in this way the half sentence I am muttering. "When I got here my first thought was: Maybe I achieved such an effort with my thoughts that time has made a complete revolution; here I am at the station from which I left on my first journey, it has remained as it was then, without any change. All the lives that I could have led begin here; there is the girl who could have been my girl and wasn't, with the same eyes, the same hair. . . ."

She looks around, as if making fun of me; I point my chin at her; she raises the corners of her mouth as if to smile, then stops: because she has changed her mind, or because this is the only way she smiles. "I don't know if that's a compliment, but I'll take it as one. And then what?"

"Then I am here, I am the I of the present, with this suitcase."

This is the first time I mention the suitcase, even though I never stop thinking about it.

And she says, "This is the evening of square suitcases on wheels."

I remain calm, impassive. I ask, "What do you mean?"

"I sold one today, a suitcase like that."

"Who bought it?"

"A stranger. Like you. He was on his way to the station, he was leaving. With an empty suitcase, just bought. Exactly like yours."

"What's odd about that? Don't you sell suitcases?"

"I have a lot of this model in stock at the shop, but nobody here buys them. People don't like them, or they're no use. Or people don't know them. But they must be convenient."

"Not for me. For example, just when I'm thinking that this evening could be a beautiful evening for me, I remember I have to drag this suitcase after me, and I can't think about anything else."

"Then why don't you leave it somewhere?"

"Like a suitcase shop," I say.

"Why not? Another suitcase, more or less."

She stands up from the stool, adjusts the collar of her overcoat in the mirror, the belt.

"If I come by later on and rap on the shutter, will you hear me?"

"Try."

She doesn't say good-bye to anyone. She is already outside in the square.

Dr. Marne leaves the pinball machine and approaches the bar. He wants to look me in the face, perhaps overhear some remarks from the others, or only a snicker. But they are talking of bets, the bets on him, not caring if he listens. There is a stirring of gaiety and intimacy, of slaps on the back, which surrounds Dr. Marne, a business of old jokes and teasing; but at the center of this merriment there is a zone of respect that is never breached, not only because Marne is a physician, public health officer or something of the sort, but also because he is a friend, or perhaps because he's a poor bastard who bears his misfortunes while remaining a friend.

"Chief Gorin is arriving later than all the predictions tonight," someone says, because at that moment the chief enters the bar.

He enters. "Good evening, one and all!" He comes over to me, lowers his eyes to the suitcase, the newspaper, mutters through clenched teeth, "Zeno of Elea," then goes to the cigarette machine.

Have they thrown me to the police? Is he a policeman who is working for our organization? I go over to the machine as if I were also buying cigarettes.

He says, "They've killed Jan. Clear out."

"The suitcase?" I ask.

"Take it away again. We want nothing to do with it now. Catch the eleven o'clock express."

"But it doesn't stop here. . . ."

"It will. Go to track six. Opposite the freight station. You have three minutes."

"But . . ."

"Move, or I'll have to arrest you."

The organization is powerful. It can command the police, the railroad. I trail my suitcase along the passages between the tracks until I reach track six. I walk along the platform. The freight section is at the end, with the grade crossing that opens into the fog and the darkness. The chief is at the door of the station bar, keeping an eye on me. The express arrives at top speed. It slows down, stops, erases me from the chief's sight, pulls out again.

[2]

You have now read about thirty pages and you're becoming caught up in the story. At a certain point you remark: "This sentence sounds somehow familiar. In fact, this whole passage reads like something I've read before." Of course: there are themes that recur, the text is interwoven with these reprises, which serve to express the fluctuation of time. You are the sort of reader who is sensitive to such refinements; you are quick to catch the author's intentions and nothing escapes you. But, at the same time, you also feel a certain dismay; just when you were beginning to grow truly interested, at this very point the author feels called upon to display one of those virtuoso tricks so customary in modern writing, repeating a paragraph word for word. Did you say paragraph? Why, it's a whole page; you make the comparison, he hasn't changed even a comma. And as you continue, what develops? Nothing: the narration is repeated, identical to the pages you have read!

Wait a minute! Look at the page number. Damn! From page 32 you've gone back to page 17! What you thought was a stylistic subtlety on the author's part is simply a printers' mistake: they have inserted the same pages twice. The mistake occurred as they were binding the volume: a book is made up of sixteen-page signatures; each signature is a large sheet on which sixteen pages are printed, and which is then folded over eight times; when all the signatures are bound together, it can happen that two identical signatures end up in the same copy; it's the sort of accident that occurs every now and then. You leaf anxiously through the next pages to find page 33, assuming it exists; a repeated signature would be a minor inconvenience, the irreparable damage comes when the proper signature has vanished, landing in another copy where perhaps that one will be doubled and this one will be missing. In any event, you want to pick up the thread of your reading, nothing else matters to you, you had reached a point where you can't skip even one page.

Here is page 31 again, page 32 . . . and then what comes next? Page 17 all over again, a third time! What kind of book did they sell you, anyway? They bound together all these copies of the same signature, not another page in the whole book is any good.

You fling the book on the floor, you would hurl it out of the window, even out of the closed window, through the slats of the Venetian blinds; let them shred its incongruous quires, let sentences, words, morphemes, phonemes gush forth, beyond recomposition into discourse; through the panes, and if they are of unbreakable glass so much the better, hurl the book and reduce it to photons, undulatory vibrations, polarized spectra; through the wall, let the book crumble into molecules and atoms passing between atom and atom of the reinforced concrete, breaking up into electrons, neutrons, neutrinos, elementary particles more and more minute; through the telephone wires, let it be reduced to electronic impulses, into flow of information, shaken by redundancies and noises, and let it be degraded into a swirling entropy. You would like to throw it out of the house, out of the block, beyond the neighborhood, beyond the city limits, beyond the state confines, beyond the regional administration, beyond the national community, beyond the Common Market, beyond Western culture, beyond the continental shelf, beyond the atmosphere, the biosphere, the stratosphere, the field of gravity, the solar system, the galaxy, the cumulus of galaxies, to succeed in hurling it beyond the point the galaxies have reached in their expansion, where spacetime has not yet arrived, where it would be received by nonbeing, or, rather, the not-being which has never been and will never be, to be lost in the most absolutely guaranteed undeniable negativity. Merely what it deserves, neither more nor less.

But no. Instead you pick it up, you dust it off; you have to take it back to the bookseller so he will exchange it for you. You know you are somewhat impulsive, but you have learned to control yourself. The thing that most exasperates you is to find yourself at the mercy of the fortuitous, the aleatory, the random, in things and in human actions—carelessness, approximation, imprecision, whether your own or others'. In such instances your dominant passion is the impatience to erase the disturbing effects of that arbitrariness or distraction, to re-establish the normal course of events. You can't wait to get your hands on a nondefective copy of the book you've begun. You would rush to the bookshop at once if shops were not closed at this hour. You have to wait until tomorrow.

You spend a restless night, your sleep is an intermittent, jammed flow, like the reading of the novel, with dreams that seem to you the repetition of one dream always the same. You fight with the dreams as with formless and meaningless life, seeking a pattern, a route that must surely be there, as when you begin to read a book and you don't yet know in which direction it will carry you. What you would like is the opening of an abstract and absolute space and time in which you could move, following an exact, taut trajectory; but when you seem to be succeeding, you realize you are motionless, blocked, forced to repeat everything from the beginning.

The next day, as soon as you have a free moment, you run to the bookshop, you enter, holding the book already opened, pointing your finger at a page, as if that alone were enough to make clear the general disarray. "You know what you sold me? . . . Look here. . . . Just when it was getting interesting . . ."

The bookseller maintains his composure. "Ah, you, too?

Chapter two

I've had several complaints already. And only this morning I received a form letter from the publisher. You see? 'In the distribution of the latest works on our list a part of the edition of the volume *If on a winter's night a traveler* by Italo Calvino has proved defective and must be withdrawn from circulation. Through an error of the bindery, the printed signatures of that book became mixed with those of another new publication, the Polish novel *Outside the town of Malbork* by Tazio Bazakbal. With profound apologies for the unfortunate incident, the publisher will replace the spoiled copies at the earliest possible moment, et cetera.' Now I ask you, must a poor bookseller take the blame for the negligence of others? We've been going crazy all day. We've checked the Calvinos copy by copy. There are a number of sound volumes, happily, and we can immediately replace your defective *Traveler* with a brand-new one in mint condition."

Hold on a minute. Concentrate. Take all the information that has poured down on you at once and put it in order. A Polish novel. Then the book you began reading with such involvement wasn't the book you thought but was a Polish novel instead. That is the book you are now so anxious to procure. Don't let them fool you. Explain clearly the situation. "No, actually I don't really give a damn about that Calvino any more. I started the Polish one and it's the Polish one I want to go on with. Do you have this Bazakbal book?"

"If that's what you prefer. Just a moment ago, another customer, a young lady, came in with the same problem, and she also wanted to exchange her book for the Polish. There, you see that pile of Bazakbal on the counter, right under your nose? Help yourself."

"But will this copy be defective?"

"Listen. At this point I'm not swearing to anything. If the most respected publishing firms make such a muddle, you can't trust anything any more. I'll tell you exactly what I told the young lady. If there is any further cause for complaint, you will be reimbursed. I can't do more than that."

The young lady. He has pointed out a young lady to you. She is there between two rows of bookshelves in the shop, looking among the Penguin Modern Classics, running a lovely and determined finger over the pale aubergine-colored spines. Huge, swift eyes, complexion of good tone and good pigment, a richly waved haze of hair.

And so the Other Reader makes her happy entrance into your field of vision, Reader, or, rather, into the field of your attention; or, rather, you have entered a magnetic field from whose attraction you cannot escape. Don't waste time, then, you have a good excuse to strike up a conversation, a common ground, just think a moment, you can show off your vast and various reading, go ahead, what are you waiting for?

"Then you, too, ha ha, the Pole," you say, all in one breath. "But that book that begins and then gets stuck there, what a fraud, because it happened to you, too, I'm told; and the same with me, you know? Having given it a try, I'm dropping this one and taking this other, but what a coincidence, the two of us."

Hmm, perhaps you could have coordinated it a bit better, but you have at least expressed the main ideas. Now it's her turn.

She smiles. She has dimples. She is even more attractive to you.

She says: "Ah, indeed, I was so anxious to read a good book. Right at the beginning, this one, no, but then it began to appeal to me. . . . Such a rage when I saw it broke off. And it wasn't that author. It did seem right away a bit different from his other books. And it was really Bazakbal. He's good, though, this Bazakbal. I've never read anything of his."

"Me either," you can say, reassured, reassuring.

Chapter two

"A bit too unfocused, his way of telling a story, too much so for me. I rather enjoy that sense of bewilderment a novel gives you when you start reading it, but if the first effect is fog, I'm afraid the moment the fog lifts my pleasure in reading will be lost, too."

You shake your head pensively. "In fact, there is that risk."

"I prefer novels," she adds, "that bring me immediately into a world where everything is precise, concrete, specific. I feel a special satisfaction in knowing that things are made in that certain fashion and not otherwise, even the most commonplace things that in real life seem indifferent to me."

Do you agree? Then say so. "Ah, yes, that sort of book is really worthwhile."

And she continues: "Anyway, this is also an interesting novel, I can't deny that."

Go on, don't let the conversation die. Say something; just keep talking. "Do you read many novels? You do? So do I, or some at least, though nonfiction is more in my line. . . ." Is that all you can think of? Now what? Are you stopping? Good night! Aren't you capable of asking her: Have you read this one? And this? Which of the two do you like better? There, now you have something to talk about for half an hour.

The trouble is that she's read many more novels than you have, especially foreign ones, and she has an orderly memory, she refers to specific episodes; she asks you, "And do you remember what Henry's aunt says when . . ." and you, who unearthed that title because you know the title and nothing more, and you liked letting her believe you had read it, now have to extricate yourself with generic comments, like "It moves a bit slowly for me," or else "I like it because it's ironic," and she answers, "Really? You find it ironic? I wouldn't have said . . ." and you are upset. You launch into an opinion on a famous author,

30

because you have read one of his books, two at most, and without hesitation she attacks frontally the *opera omnia*, which she seems to know perfectly, and if she does have some doubts, that's worse still, because she asks you, "And the famous episode of the cut photograph: is it in that book or the other one? I always get them mixed up. . . ." You make a guess, since she gets mixed up. And she says, "Why, what are you talking about? That can't be right. . . ." Well, let's say you both get mixed up.

Better to fall back on your reading of yesterday evening, on the volume you are both now clutching in your hands, which should repay you for your recent disappointment. "Let's hope," you say, "that we've got a perfect copy this time, properly bound, so we won't be interrupted right at the climax, as happens . . ." (As happens when, how? What do you mean?) "I mean, let's hope we get to the end satisfactorily."

"Oh, yes," she answers. Did you hear that? She said, "Oh, yes." It's your turn now, it's up to you to make a move.

"Then I hope I'll meet you again, since you're also a customer here; that way we could exchange our impressions after reading the book." And she answers, "With pleasure."

You know where you want to arrive, it is a fine net you are spreading out. "The funniest thing would be if, just as we had thought we were reading Italo Calvino and it turned out to be Bazakbal, now that we hope to read Bazakbal we open the book and find Italo Calvino."

"Oh, no! If that happens, we'll sue the publisher!"

"Listen, why don't we exchange telephone numbers?" (This is what you were aiming at, O Reader, moving around her like a rattlesnake!) "That way, if one of us finds something wrong with his copy, he can ask the other for help. . . . If there are two of us, we have a better chance of putting together a complete copy."

Chapter two

There, you have said it. What is more natural than that a solidarity, a complicity, a bond should be established between Reader and Reader, thanks to the book?

You can leave the bookshop content, you, a man who thought that the period when you could still expect something from life had ended. You are bearing with you two different expectations, and both promise days of pleasant hopes; the expectation contained in the book—of a reading experience you are impatient to resume—and the expectation contained in that telephone number—of hearing again the vibrations, at times treble and at times smoldering, of that voice, when it will answer your first phone call in a short while, in fact tomorrow, with the fragile pretext of the book, to ask her if she likes it or not, to tell her how many pages you have read or not read, to suggest to her that you meet again . . .

Who you are, Reader, your age, your status, profession, income: that would be indiscreet to ask. It's your business, you're on your own. What counts is the state of your spirit now, in the privacy of your home, as you try to re-establish perfect calm in order to sink again into the book; you stretch out your legs, you draw them back, you stretch them again. But something has changed since yesterday. Your reading is no longer solitary: you think of the Other Reader, who, at this same moment, is also opening the book; and there, the novel to be read is superimposed by a possible novel to be lived, the continuation of your story with her, or better still, the beginning of a possible story. This is how you have changed since yesterday, you who insisted you preferred a book, something solid, which lies before you, easily defined, enjoyed without risks, to a real-life experience, always elusive, discontinuous, debated. Does this mean that the book has become an instrument, a channel of communication, a rendezvous? This does not mean its reading will grip you less: on the contrary, something has been added to its powers.

Chapter two

This volume's pages are uncut: a first obstacle opposing your impatience. Armed with a good paper knife, you prepare to penetrate its secrets. With a determined slash you cut your way between the title page and the beginning of the first chapter. And then ...

Then from the very first page you realize that the novel you are holding has nothing to do with the one you were reading yesterday.

Outside
the town
of
Malbork

An odor of frying wafts at the opening of the page, of onion in fact, onion being fried, a bit scorched, because in the onion there are veins that turn violet and then brown, and especially the edge, the margin, of each little sliver of onion becomes black before golden, it is the juice of the onion that is carbonized, passing through a series of olfactory and chromatic nuances, all enveloped in the smell of simmering oil. Rape oil, the text specifies; everything here is very precise, things with their nomenclature and the sensations that things transmit, all the victuals on the fire at the same time on the kitchen stove, each in its vessel exactly denominated, the pans, the pots, the kettles, and similarly the operations that each preparation involves, dusting with flour, beating the egg, slicing the cucumbers in fine rounds, larding the hen to be roasted. Here everything is very concrete, substantial, depicted with sure expertise; or at least the impression given to you, Reader, is one of expertise, though there are some foods you don't know, mentioned by name, which the translator has decided to leave in the original; for example, *schoëblintsjia.*

But on reading *schoëblintsjia* you are ready to swear to the existence of *schoëblintsjia*, you can taste its flavor distinctly even though the text doesn't say what that flavor is, an acidulous flavor, partly because the word, with its sound or only with its visual impression, suggests an acidulous flavor to you, and partly because in the symphony of flavors and words you feel the necessity of an acidulous note.

As Brigd kneads the ground meat into the flour moistened with egg, her firm red arms dotted with golden freckles become covered with particles of white dust with bits of raw meat stuck to them. Every time Brigd's torso moves back and forth at the marble table, her skirts rise an inch or two behind and show the hollow between her calf and femoral biceps, where the skin is whiter, crossed by a fine, pale-blue vein. The characters take on form gradually in the accumulation of minute details and precise movements, but also of remarks, shreds of conversation, as when old Hunder says, "This year's doesn't make you jump the way last year's did," and after a few lines you understand he means the red pepper; and "You're the one who jumps less with every passing year!" Aunt Ugurd says, tasting something with a wooden spoon and adding a pinch of cinnamon to the pot.

Every moment you discover there is a new character, you don't know how many people there are in this immense kitchen of ours, it's no use counting, there were always many of us, at Kudgiwa, always coming and going: the sum never works out properly because different names can belong to the same character, indicated according to the circumstances by baptismal name, nickname, surname or patronymic, and even by appellations such as "Jan's widow," or "the apprentice from the corn shop." But what counts are the physical details that the novel underlines—Bronko's gnawed nails, the down on Brigd's cheeks—and also the gestures, the utensils that this person or that is handling—the meat pounder, the colander for the cress, the butter curler—so that each character already receives a first definition through this action or attribute; but then we wish to learn even more, as if the butter curler already determined the character and the fate of the person who is presented in the first chapter handling a butter curler, and as if you, Reader, were already prepared, each time that character is introduced again in the course of the novel, to cry, "Ah, that's the butter-curler one!" thus obligating the author to attribute to him acts and events in keeping with that initial butter curler.

Our kitchen at Kudgiwa seemed to be made deliberately so that at any hour many persons would be found in it, each intent on cooking himself something, one hulling chick peas, another putting the tench in marinade, everybody seasoning or cooking or eating something, and when they went away, others came, from dawn till late at night, and that morning I had come down at this early hour and already the kitchen was in full operation because it was a different day from the others: Mr. Kauderer had arrived the night before with his son, and he would be going away this morning, taking me in the son's place. I was leaving home for the first time: I was to spend the whole season on Mr. Kauderer's estate, in the province of Pëtkwo, until the rye harvest, to learn the working of the new drying machines imported from Belgium; during this period Ponko, youngest of the Kauderers, would stay with us and acquire the techniques of grafting rowans.

The usual smells and noises of the house crowded around me that morning as if in farewell: I was about to lose everything I had known till then, and for such a long period—so it seemed to me—that when I came back nothing would be as it had been before, nor would I be the same I. And hence this farewell of mine was as if forever: to the kitchen, the house, to Aunt Ugurd's knödel; so this sense of concreteness that you perceived from the very first lines bears in it also the sense of loss, the vertigo of dissolution, and you realize that you perceived this, too, alert Reader that you are, from the first page, when, though pleased with the precision of this writing, you sensed that, to tell the truth, everything was slipping through your fingers; perhaps it was also the fault of the translation, you told yourself, which may very well be faithful but certainly doesn't render the solid substance those terms must have in the original language, whatever it may be. Each sentence, in short, wants to convey to you both the solidity of my relationship with the Kudgiwa house and my regret at losing it, and further—perhaps you didn't realize it, but if you think back you'll see this is exactly the case—the drive to break away from it, to run toward the unknown, to turn the page, far from the acidulous odor of the *schoëblintsjia*, to begin a new chapter with new encounters in the endless sunsets beyond the Aagd, on the Pëtkwo Sundays, at the festivities in the Cider Palace.

The portrait of a girl with short-cropped black hair and a long face had emerged for a moment from Ponko's little trunk; then he immediately hid it under an oilskin jacket. In the bedroom beneath the dovecote, which had till now been mine and from today on would be Ponko's, he was unpacking his things and arranging them in the drawers I had just emptied. I watched him in silence, sitting on my already closed little trunk, mechanically hammering at a stud that stuck out, a bit crooked; we had said nothing to each other after a grunted hello; I followed him in all his movements, trying to be thoroughly aware of what was going on: an outsider was taking my place, was becoming me, my cage with the starlings would become his, the stereoscope, the real Uhlan helmet hanging from a nail, all my things that I couldn't take with me remained to him; or, rather, it was my relationship with things, places, people, that was becoming his, just as I was about to become him, to take his place among the things and people of his life.

That girl . . . "Who is that girl?" I asked, and with an ill-advised movement I reached out to uncover and grasp the photograph in its carved wooden frame. This girl was different from the girls in these parts who all have round faces and braids the color of bran. It was not until this moment that I thought of Brigd; in a flash I saw Ponko and Brigd, who would dance together on the Feast of Saint Thaddeus, Brigd who would mend Ponko's woolen gloves, Ponko who would give Brigd a marten captured with *my* trap. "Let go of that picture!" Ponko yelled and grabbed both my arms with iron fingers. "Let go! This minute!"

"To remind you of Zwida Ozkart," I managed to read on the picture. "Who is Zwida Ozkart?" I asked, and already a fist had struck me full in the face, and already with fists clenched I had flung myself on Ponko and we were rolling on the floor trying to twist each other's arms, knee each other, break ribs.

Ponko's body had heavy bones, his arms and legs hit sharply, the hair I tried to grab in order to throw him backward was a brush as stiff as a dog's coat. While we were clutching each other I had the sensation that in this struggle the transformation was taking place, and when he rose he would be me and I him, but perhaps I am thinking this only now, or it is only you, Reader, who are thinking it, not I; indeed, in that moment wrestling with him meant holding tight to myself, to my past, so that it wouldn't fall into his hands, even at the cost of destroying it, it was Brigd I wanted to destroy so she wouldn't fall into Ponko's hands, Brigd, with whom I had never thought I was in love, and I didn't think I was even now, but once, only once, I had rolled with her, one on top of the other almost like now with Ponko, and she and I were biting each other on the pile of peat behind the stove, and now I felt that I had already been fighting for her against a Ponko still in the future, that I was already fighting him for both Brigd and Zwida. I had been seeking to tear something from my past so as not to leave it to my rival, to the new me with dog's hair, or perhaps already I had been trying to wring from the past of that unknown me a secret to add to my past or to my future.

The page you're reading should convey this violent contact of dull and painful blows, of fierce and lacerating responses; this bodiliness of using one's own body against another body, melding the weight of one's own efforts and the precision of one's own receptivity and adapting them to the mirror image of them that the adversary reflects. But if the sensations reading evokes remain scant compared to any sensation really experienced, it is also because what I am feeling as I crush Ponko's chest beneath my chest or as I block the twisting of an arm behind my back is not the sensation I would need to declare what I would like to declare, namely the amorous possession of Brigd, of the firm fullness of that girl's flesh, so different from the bony solidity of Ponko, and also the amorous possession of Zwida, of the melting softness I imagine in Zwida, the possession of a Brigd I feel already lost and of a Zwida who has only the bodiless substance of a photograph under glass. In the tangle of male limbs opposing and identical, I try in vain to clasp those female ghosts that vanish in their unattainable difference; and I try at the same time to strike myself, perhaps the other self that is about to take my place in the house or else the self most mine that I want to snatch away from that other, but which I feel pressing against me and which is only the alienness of the other, as if that other had already taken my place and any other place, and I were erased from the world.

The world seemed alien to me when in the end I broke

away from my adversary with a furious push and stood up, planting my feet on the floor. Alien was my room, the small trunk that was my luggage, the view from the little window. I feared I could no longer establish a relationship with anyone or anything. I wanted to go find Brigd, but without knowing what I wanted to say to her or do to her, what I wanted to have her say to me or do to me. I headed toward Brigd thinking of Zwida: what I sought was a two-headed figure, a Brigd-Zwida, just as I was double-faced moving away from Ponko, trying in vain with my saliva to remove a spot of blood from my corduroy suit—my blood or his, from my teeth or from Ponko's nose.

And double-faced as I was, I heard and saw, beyond the door of the big room, Mr. Kauderer standing, making a broad horizontal gesture to measure the space before him and saying, "And so I found them before me, Kauni and Pittö, twenty-two and twenty-four years old, with their chests torn open by wolf bullets."

"When did it happen?" my grandfather asked. "We knew nothing about it."

"Before leaving we attended the octave service."

"We thought things had long been settled between your family and the Ozkarts. That after all these years you had buried the hatchet, that the whole horrible business between you was over."

Mr. Kauderer's eyes, which had no lashes, kept staring into the void; nothing moved in his gutta-percha-yellow face. "Between Ozkarts and Kauderers peace lasts only from one funeral to the next, and the hatchet is not buried, but our dead are buried and we write on their graves: This was the Ozkarts' doing."

"And what about your bunch, then?" Bronko asked, a man who called a spade a spade.

"The Ozkarts also write on their graves: This was the Kauderers' doing." Then, rubbing one finger over his mustache, he said, "Here Ponko will be safe, at last."

Outside the town of Malbork

It was at this point that my mother clasped her hands and said, "Holy Virgin, will our Gritzvi be in danger? They won't take it out on him?"

Mr. Kauderer shook his head but didn't look her in the face. "He isn't a Kauderer! We're the ones who are in danger, always!"

The door opened. From the hot urine of the horses in the yard a cloud of steam rose in the icy, glassy air. The stableboy stuck his flushed face inside and announced, "The buggy is ready!"

"Gritzvi! Where are you? Hurry up!" Grandfather shouted.

I took a step forward, toward Mr. Kauderer, who was buttoning up his felt greatcoat.

[3]

The pleasures derived from the use of a paper knife are tactile, auditory, visual, and especially mental. Progress in reading is preceded by an act that traverses the material solidity of the book to allow you access to its incorporeal substance. Penetrating among the pages from below, the blade vehemently moves upward, opening a vertical cut in a flowing succession of slashes that one by one strike the fibers and mow them down—with a friendly and cheery crackling the good paper receives that first visitor, who announces countless turns of the pages stirred by the wind or by a gaze—then the horizonal fold, especially if it is double, opposes greater resistance, because it requires an awkward backhand motion—there the sound is one of muffled laceration, with deeper notes. The margin of the pages is jagged, revealing its fibrous texture; a fine shaving—also known as "curl"—is detached from it, as pretty to see as a wave's foam on the beach. Opening a path for yourself, with a sword's blade, in the barrier of pages becomes linked with the thought of how much the word contains and conceals: you cut your way through your reading as if through a dense forest.

The novel you are reading wants to present to you a corporeal world, thick, detailed. Immersed in your reading, you move the paper knife mechanically in the depth of the volume: your reading has not yet reached the end of the first chapter, but your cutting has already gone far ahead. And there, at the moment when your attention is gripped by the suspense, in the middle of a decisive sentence, you turn the page and find yourself facing two blank sheets.

You are dazed, contemplating that whiteness cruel as a wound, almost hoping it is your dazzled eyesight casting a blinding glare on the book, from which, gradually, the

Chapter three

zebra rectangle of inked letters will return to the surface. No, an intact blank really reigns on the two sides that confront each other. You turn another page and find the next two are printed properly. Blank, printed; blank, printed; and so on until the end. The large sheets were printed only on one side, then folded and bound as if they were complete.

And so you see this novel so tightly interwoven with sensations suddenly riven by bottomless chasms, as if the claim to portray vital fullness revealed the void beneath. You try jumping over the gap, picking up the story by grasping the edge of the prose that comes afterward, jagged like the margin of the pages separated by the paper knife. You can't get your bearings: the characters have changed, the settings, you don't understand what it's about, you find names of people and don't know who they are—Hela, Casimir. You begin to suspect that this is a different book, perhaps the real Polish novel *Outside the town of Malbork*, whereas the beginning you have read could belong to yet another book, God only knows which.

It had already occurred to you that the names didn't sound particularly Polish: Brigd, Gritzvi. You have a good atlas, very detailed; you turn to the index of places: Pëtkwo, which should be a fairly important town, and the Aagd, which could be a river or a lake. You track them down in a remote plain of the north that wars and peace treaties have successively awarded to different countries. Perhaps also to Poland? You consult an encyclopedia, a historical atlas; no, Poland has nothing to do with it; this area, in the period between the two wars, was an independent state: Cimmeria; capital Örkko; national language Cimmerian, belonging to the Bothno-Ugaric family. The "Cimmeria" article in the encyclopedia concludes with not very reassuring sentences: "In successive territorial divisions between her powerful neighbors the young nation was soon erased from the map; the autochthonous

43

population was dispersed; Cimmerian language and culture had no development."

You are impatient to get in touch with the Other Reader, to ask her if her copy is like yours, and to tell her your conjectures, the information you have gathered. . . . You look in your pocket diary for the number you wrote next to her name when you and she introduced yourselves.

"Hello, Ludmilla? Have you seen? It's a different novel, but this one, too, or at least my copy . . ."

The voice at the other end of the wire is hard, a bit ironic. "Look, I'm not Ludmilla. I'm her sister, Lotaria." That's right, she did tell you: "If I don't answer, my sister will be there." "Ludmilla is out. What is it? What did you want?"

"I just wanted to tell her about a book. . . . It's not important, I'll call back. . . ."

"A novel? Ludmilla always has her nose buried in a novel. Who's the author?"

"Well, it's a kind of a Polish novel that she's also reading. I thought we might exchange some impressions. Bazakbal's novel."

"Polish? What sort?"

"Um, it doesn't seem half bad to me."

No, you misunderstood. Lotaria wants to know the author's position with regard to Trends of Contemporary Thought and Problems That Demand a Solution. To make your task easier she furnishes you with a list of names of Great Masters among whom you should situate him.

Again you feel the sensation you felt when the paper knife revealed the facing white pages. "I couldn't say, exactly. You see, I'm not actually sure even of the title or the author's name. Ludmilla will tell you about it: it's a rather complicated story."

"Ludmilla reads one novel after another, but she never clarifies the problems. It seems a big waste of time to me. Don't you have this impression?"

If you start arguing, she'll never let you go. Now she is inviting you to a seminar at the university, where books are analyzed according to all Codes, Conscious and Unconscious, and in which all Taboos are eliminated, the ones imposed by the dominant Sex, Class, and Culture.

"Will Ludmilla be going, too?"

No, it seems Ludmilla takes no part in her sister's activities. But on the other hand, Lotaria is counting on your participation.

You prefer not to commit yourself. "I'll see, I'll try to drop by. I can't promise. Meanwhile, would you please tell your sister I called? . . . But anyway, it doesn't matter, I'll call back. Thanks a lot." That's enough, go ahead and hang up.

But Lotaria detains you. "Look, there's no point in your calling here again, this isn't Ludmilla's place, it's mine. Ludmilla always gives my number to people she doesn't know, she says I keep them at a distance. . . ."

You are hurt. Another cruel shock: the book that seemed so promising broke off; the telephone number that you also believed the beginning of something proves to be a dead end, with this Lotaria who insists on questioning you. . . .

"Ah, I see. Sorry."

"Hello? Ah, you're the gentleman I met in the bookshop?" A different voice, *hers*, has taken over the telephone. "Yes, this is Ludmilla. You have blank pages, too? We might have expected as much. Another trap. Just when I was getting involved in it, when I wanted to read more about Ponko, and Gritzvi . . ."

You are so happy you can't utter a word. You say: "Zwida . . ."

"What?"

"Yes, Zwida Ozkart! I would like to know what goes on between Gritzvi and Zwida Ozkart. . . . Is this novel really the kind you like?"

A pause. Then Ludmilla's voice resumes slowly, as if

she were trying to express something not easily defined. "Yes, it is. I like it very much. . . . Still, I wish the things I read weren't all present, so solid you can touch them; I would like to feel a presence around them, something else, you don't quite know what, the sign of some unknown thing. . . ."

"Yes, in that respect, I, too . . ."

"Even though, I don't mean to say . . . here, too, the element of mystery isn't lacking. . . ."

You say: "Well, look, the mystery, in my opinion, is this. It's a Cimmerian novel, yes, Cim-mer-ian, not Polish, and the title and the author aren't the ones they say. You didn't realize? Let me tell you. Cimmeria, two hundred and forty thousand inhabitants, capital Örkko, principal resources peat and by-products, bituminous compounds. No, this isn't in the novel. . . ."

A silence, on your part and hers. Perhaps Ludmilla has covered the receiver with her hand and is conferring with her sister. She probably has ideas of her own on Cimmeria, that one. God knows what she'll come out with. Be careful.

"Hello, Ludmilla."

"Hello."

Your voice turns warm, winning, insistent. "Listen, Ludmilla, I must see you, we have to talk about this thing, these circumstances, coincidences, discrepancies. I'd like to see you right away. Where are you? Where would you prefer us to meet? I'll be there in a minute."

And she says, calm as ever: "I know a professor who teaches Cimmerian literature at the university. We could consult him. Let me telephone him and ask when he can see us."

Here you are at the university. Ludmilla has announced your visit with her to Professor Uzzi-Tuzii, at his department. Over the telephone the professor seemed delighted to put himself at the disposal of anyone taking an interest in Cimmerian authors.

You would have preferred to see Ludmilla alone some-where, or perhaps to pick her up at home and accompany her to the university. You suggested this to her, over the telephone, but she said no, no need for you to go out of your way, at that hour she would already be in the neigh-borhood on other business. You insisted; you don't know your way around, you're afraid of getting lost in the labyrinth of the university: wouldn't it be better to meet in a café a quarter of an hour before? This didn't suit her, either; you would meet directly there, "at Bothno-Ugaric Languages," everybody knows where it is, you only have to ask. You understand by now that Ludmilla, for all her mild manner, likes to take the situation in hand and de-cide everything herself: your only course is to follow her.

You arrive punctually at the university, you pick your way past the young men and girls sitting on the steps, you wander bewildered among those austere walls which stu-dents' hands have arabesqued with outsize capital writing and detailed graffiti, just as the cavemen felt the need to decorate the cold walls of their caves to become masters of the tormenting mineral alienness, to make them fa-miliar, empty them into their own inner space, annex them to the physical reality of living. Reader, we are not sufficiently acquainted for me to know whether you move with indifferent assurance in a university or whether old traumas or pondered choices make a universe of pupils and teachers seem a nightmare to your sensitive and sensible soul. In any case, nobody knows the department you are looking for, they send you from the basement to the fifth floor, each door you open is the wrong one, you withdraw in confusion, you seem to be lost in the book with white pages, unable to get out of it.

A lanky young man comes forward, in a long sweater.

As soon as he sees you, he points a finger at you and says, "You're waiting for Ludmilla!"

"How do you know that?"

"I realized. One look is enough for me."

"Did Ludmilla send you?"

"No, but I'm always wandering around, I meet this one and I meet that one, I hear something here and see something there, and I naturally put them together."

"Do you also know where I'm supposed to go?"

"If you like, I'll take you to Uzzi-Tuzii. Either Ludmilla has been there for a while already or she'll come late."

This young man, so extroverted and well informed, is named Irnerio. You can call him *tu*, since he already calls you that. "Are you a student of the professor's?"

"I'm not a student of anything. I know where he is because I used to pick up Ludmilla there."

"Then Ludmilla's the one who studies in the department?"

"No, Ludmilla has always looked for places where she could hide."

"Who from?"

"Oh, from everybody."

Irnerio's answers are a bit evasive, but it would seem that it is chiefly her sister that Ludmilla tries to avoid. If she hasn't arrived punctually at our appointment, it is so as not to meet Lotaria in the hall; she has her seminar at this hour.

But you, on the contrary, believe there are some exceptions to this incompatibility between the sisters, at least as far as the telephone is concerned. You should make this Irnerio talk a bit more, see if he really is as knowledgeable as all that.

"Are you a friend of Ludmilla's, or of Lotaria's?"

"Ludmilla's, of course. But I manage to talk with Lotaria, too."

"Doesn't she criticize the books you read?"

Chapter three

"Me? I don't read books!" Irnerio says.

"What do you read, then?"

"Nothing. I've become so accustomed to not reading that I don't even read what appears before my eyes. It's not easy: they teach us to read as children, and for the rest of our lives we remain the slaves of all the written stuff they fling in front of us. I may have had to make some effort myself, at first, to learn not to read, but now it comes quite naturally to me. The secret is not refusing to look at the written words. On the contrary, you must look at them, intensely, until they disappear."

Irnerio's eyes have broad, pale, flickering pupils; they seem eyes that miss nothing, like those of a native of the forest, devoted to hunting and gathering.

"Then would you mind telling me why you come to the university?"

"Why shouldn't I? There are people going and coming, you meet, you talk. That's the reason I come here; I don't know about the others."

You try to picture how the world might appear, this world dense with writing that surrounds us on all sides, to someone who has learned not to read. And at the same time you ask yourself what bond there may be between Ludmilla and the Nonreader, and suddenly it seems to you that it is their very distance that keeps them together, and you can't stifle a feeling of jealousy.

You would like to question Irnerio further, but you have arrived, by some back stairs, at a low door with a sign, DEPARTMENT OF BOTHNO-UGARIC LANGUAGES AND LITERATURES. Irnerio knocks sharply, says *"Ciao"* to you, and leaves you there.

The door opens, barely a crack. From the spots of whitewash on the jamb, and from the cap that appears, over a fleece-lined work jacket, you get the notion that the place is closed for renovation, and there is only a painter inside or a cleaning man.

49

Chapter three

"Is Professor Uzzi-Tuzii in?"

The gaze that assents, from beneath the cap, is different from what you would expect of a painter: the eyes of one preparing to leap over a precipice, who is projecting himself mentally to the other side, staring straight ahead, and avoiding looking down or sideways.

"Are you he?" you ask, though you have realized it can be no one else.

The little man does not widen the crack. "What do you want?"

"Excuse me, it was about some information . . . We telephoned you . . . Miss Ludmilla . . . Is Miss Ludmilla here?"

"There is no Miss Ludmilla here . . ." the Professor says, stepping back, and he points to the crammed bookshelves on the walls, the illegible names and titles on the spines and title pages, like a bristling hedge without gaps. "Why are you looking for her in my office?" And while you remember what Irnerio said, that for Ludmilla this was a place to hide, Uzzi-Tuzii seems to underline, with a gesture, the narrowness of his office, as if to say: Seek for yourself, if you think she's here. As if he felt the need to defend himself from the charge of keeping Ludmilla hidden there.

"We were to come together," you say, to make everything clear.

"Then why isn't she with you?" And this observation, logical for that matter, is also made in a suspicious tone.

"She'll be here soon . . ." you insist, but you say it with an almost interrogative note, as if you were asking Uzzi-Tuzii to confirm Ludmilla's habits, of which you know nothing, whereas he might know a great deal more. "You know Ludmilla, don't you, Professor?"

"I know . . . Why do you ask me? . . . What are you trying to find out? . . ." He becomes nervous. "Are you interested in Cimmerian literature or—" And he seems to

50

mean "or Ludmilla?" But he doesn't finish the sentence; and to be sincere you should answer that you can no longer distinguish your interest in the Cimmerian novel from your interest in the Other Reader of that novel. Now, moreover, the professor's reactions at the name Ludmilla, coming after Irnerio's confidences, cast mysterious flashes of light, create about the Other Reader an apprehensive curiosity not unlike that which binds you to Zwida Ozkart, in the novel whose continuation you are hunting for, and also to Madame Marne in the novel you had begun to read the day before and have temporarily put aside, and here you are in pursuit of all these shadows together, those of the imagination and those of life.

"I wanted . . . we wanted to ask you if there is a Cimmerian author who . . ."

"Be seated," the professor says, suddenly placated, or, rather, again caught up in a more stable and persistent concern that re-emerges, dissolving marginal and ephemeral concerns.

The room is cramped, the walls covered with shelves, plus another bookcase that, having no place to lean against, is in the midst of the room dividing the scant space, so the professor's desk and the chair on which you are to sit are separated by a kind of wing, and to see each other you must stretch your necks.

"We are confined in this sort of closet. . . . The university expands and we contract. . . . We are the poor stepchild of living languages. . . . If Cimmerian can still be considered a living language . . . But this is precisely its value!" he exclaims with an affirmative outburst that immediately fades. "The fact that it is a modern language and a dead language at the same time . . . A privileged position, even if nobody realizes . . ."

"You have few students?" you ask.

"Who do you think would come? Who do you think remembers the Cimmerians any more? In the field of suppressed languages there are many now that attract more attention . . . Basque . . . Breton . . . Romany. . . . They all sign up for those. . . . Not that they study the language: nobody wants to do that these days. . . . They want problems to debate, general ideas to connect with other general ideas. My colleagues adjust, follow the mainstream, give their courses titles like 'Sociology of Welsh,' 'Psycholinguistics of Provençal." . . . With Cimmerian it can't be done."

"Why not?"

"The Cimmerians have disappeared, as if the earth had swallowed them up." He shakes his head, apparently to summon all his patience and repeat something already said a hundred times. "This is a dead department of a dead literature in a dead language. Why should they study Cimmerian today? I'm the first to understand, I'm the first to say it: if you don't want to come, then don't come; as far as I'm concerned, the department could even be abolished. But to come here only to . . . No, that's too much."

"Only to—what?"

"Everything. I'm forced to see everything. For weeks on end nobody comes, but when somebody does come it's to do things that . . . You could remain well away from here, I say, what could interest you in these books written in the language of the dead? But they do it deliberately, let's go to Bothno-Ugaric languages, they say, let's go to Uzzi-Tuzii, and so I'm involved, forced to see, to participate. . . ."

"In what?" you inquire, thinking of Ludmilla, who came here, who hid here, perhaps with Irnerio, with others.

"In everything . . . Perhaps there is something that attracts them, this uncertainty between life and death, perhaps this is what they feel, without understanding. They come here to do what they do, but they don't sign up for the course, they don't attend classes, nobody ever takes an interest in the literature of the Cimmerians, buried in the books on these shelves as if in the graves of a cemetery. . . ."

"I was, in fact, interested in it. . . . I had come to ask if there exists a Cimmerian novel that begins . . . No, the best way is to tell you right off the names of the characters: Gritzvi and Zwida, Ponko and Brigd. The action begins at Kudgiwa, but perhaps this is only the name of a farm; then I believe it shifts to Pëtkwo, on the Aagd. . . ."

"Oh, that can be found quickly!" the professor exclaims, and in one second he is freed from his hypochondriacal fog and glows like an elcctric bulb. "It is unquestionably *Leaning from the steep slope,* the only novel left us by one of the most promising Cimmerian poets of the first quarter of our century, Ukko Ahti. . . . Here it is!" And with the leap of a fish swimming against rapids he aims at a precise spot on a shelf, grasps a slim volume bound in green, slaps it to dispel the dust. "It has never been translated into any other language. The difficulties, to be sure, are enough to discourage anyonc. Listen: 'I am addressing the conviction . . .' No: 'I am convincing myself to transmit . . .' You will note that both verbs are in the present progressive."

One thing is immediately clear to you: namely that this book has nothing in common with the one you had begun. Only some proper names are identical, a detail that is surely very odd, but which you do not stop to ponder, because gradually, from Uzzi-Tuzii's laborious extempore translation the outline of a story is taking shape, from his toilsome deciphering of verbal lumps a flowing narrative emerges.

Leaning
from
the steep
slope

I am becoming convinced that the world wants to tell me something, send me messages, signals, warnings. I have noticed this ever since I have been in Pëtkwo. Every morning I leave the Kudgiwa Pension for my usual walk as far as the harbor. I go past the meteorological observatory, and I think of the end of the world which is approaching, or, rather, which has been in progress for a long while. If the end of the world could be localized in a precise spot, it would be the meteorological observatory of Pëtkwo: a corrugated-iron roof that rests on four somewhat shaky poles and houses, lined up on a shelf, some recording barometers, hygrometers, and thermographs, with their rolls of lined paper, which turn with a slow clockwork ticking against an oscillating nib. The vane of an anemometer at the top of a tall antenna and the squat funnel of a pluviometer complete the fragile equipment of the observatory, which, isolated on the edge of an escarpment in the municipal garden, against the pearl-gray sky, uniform and motionless, seems a trap for cyclones, a lure set there to attract waterspouts from the remote tropical oceans, offering itself already as the ideal relict of the fury of the hurricanes.

There are days when everything I see seems to me charged with meaning: messages it would be difficult for me to communicate to others, define, translate into words, but which for this very reason appear to me decisive. They are announcements or presages that concern me and the world at once: for my part, not only the external events of my existence but also what happens inside, in the depths of me; and for the world, not some particular event but the general way of being of all things. You will understand therefore my difficulty in speaking about it, except by allusion.

Monday. Today I saw a hand thrust out of a window of the prison, toward the sea. I was walking on the seawall of the port, as is my habit, until I was just below the old fortress. The fortress is entirely enclosed by its oblique walls; the windows, protected by double or triple grilles, seem blind. Even knowing that prisoners are confined in there, I have always looked on the fortress as an element of inert nature, of the mineral kingdom. Therefore the appearance of the hand amazed me, as if it had emerged from the cliff. The hand was in an unnatural position; I suppose the windows are set high in the cells and cut out of the wall; the prisoner must have performed an acrobat's feat—or, rather, a contortionist's—to get his arm through grille after grille, to wave his hand in the free air. It was not a prisoner's signal to me, or to anyone else; at any rate I did not take it as such; indeed, then and there I did not think of the prisoners at all; I must say that the hand seemed white and slender to me, a hand not unlike my own, in which nothing suggested the roughness one would expect in a convict. For me it was like a sign coming from the stone: the stone wanted to inform me that our substance was common, and therefore something of what constitutes my person would remain, would not be lost with the end of the world; a communication will still be possible in the desert bereft of life, bereft of my life and all memory of me. I am telling the first impressions I noted, which are the ones that count.

Today I reached the belvedere from which you can glimpse, down below, a little stretch of beach, deserted, facing the gray sea. The wicker chairs with their high curved backs, like baskets, against the wind, arranged in a semicircle, seemed to suggest a world in which the human race has disappeared and things can do nothing but bespeak its absence. I felt a kind of vertigo, as if I were merely plunging from one world to another, and in each I arrived shortly after the end of the world had taken place.

I passed the belvedere again half an hour later. From one chair, its back to me, a little ribbon was flapping. I went down the steep promontory path, as far as a shelf from which the angle of vision changed. As I expected, seated in the chair, completely hidden by the wicker shields, there was Miss Zwida, in her white straw hat, her drawing pad open on her lap; she was copying a seashell. I was not pleased to see her; this morning's negative signs dissuaded me from striking up a conversation; for about three weeks now I have been encountering her alone in my walks on the cliffs and the dunes, and I want nothing more than to address her—indeed, it is with this intention that I come down from my pension every day, but every day something deters me.

Miss Zwida is staying at the Hotel of the Sea Lily; I went there to ask the desk clerk her name. Perhaps she found out; holiday people at this season in Pëtkwo are very few; the young ones could be counted on your fingers. Encountering me so often, she is perhaps expecting me to address her one day.

The motives that constitute an obstacle to a possible meeting between the two of us are several. In the first place, Miss Zwida collects and draws seashells; I had a beautiful collection of shells, years ago, when I was a boy, but then I gave it up and have forgotten everything: classifications, morphology, geographical distribution of the various species. A conversation with Miss Zwida would lead me inevitably to talk about seashells, and I cannot decide what attitude to take, whether to pretend absolute ignorance or to call on a remote experience now vague; it is my relationship with my life, consisting of things never concluded and half erased, that the subject of seashells forces me to contemplate; hence the uneasiness that finally puts me to flight.

In addition there is the fact that this girl's application in drawing seashells denotes in her a search for formal perfection which the world can and therefore must attain; I, on the contrary, have been convinced for some time that perfection is not produced except marginally and by chance; therefore it deserves no interest at all, the true nature of things being revealed only in disintegration. If I were to approach Miss Zwida, I would have to express some appreciation of her drawings—which are of highly refined quality, for that matter, as far as I have been able to see—and therefore, at least at first, I would have to pretend to agree with an aesthetic and moral ideal that I reject, or else declare my feelings at the very start, with the risk of wounding her.

Third obstacle: the condition of my health, which, though much improved thanks to this stay by the sea on doctors' orders, affects my opportunities to go out and meet strangers; I am still subject to intermittent attacks, and especially to periodic worsening of a tiresome eczema, which discourages me from any notion of sociability.

Every now and then I exchange a few words with the meteorologist, Mr. Kauderer, when I meet him at the observatory. Mr. Kauderer always goes by at noon, to check the readings. He is a tall, thin man, with a gloomy face, a bit like an American Indian. He rides along on his bicycle, staring straight ahead, as if maintaining his balance on the seat demanded all his concentration. He props his bicycle against the shed, slips a bag from the handlebars, and takes from it a ledger with broad, short pages. He climbs the steps to the platform and marks down the figures recorded by the instruments, some in pencil, others with a thick fountain pen, never relaxing his concentration for a second. He wears knickerbockers under a long topcoat; all his clothing is gray, or black-and-white check, including his visored cap. It is only when he has concluded these operations that he notices me observing him and greets me cordially.

I have come to realize that Mr. Kauderer's presence is important for me: that someone still evinces so much scrupulousness and methodical attention, though I know perfectly well it is all futile, has a reassuring effect on me, perhaps because it makes up for my vague way of living, about which—despite the conclusions I have reached—I continue to feel guilty. Therefore I stop and watch the meteorologist, and even converse with him, though it is not the conversation in itself that interests me. He talks to me about the weather, naturally, in detailed technical terms, and of the effects of the swings of pressure on the health, but also of the unsettled times in which we live, citing as example some episodes of local life or even news items he has read in the papers. At these moments he reveals a less reserved character than appears at first sight; indeed, he tends to warm to his subject and become verbose, especially in disapproving of the majority's way of acting and thinking, because he is a man who tends to be dissatisfied.

Today Mr. Kauderer told me that, because he is planning to go away for a few days, he will have to find someone to take his place in recording the data, but he does not know anyone he can trust. In the course of the conversation he asked me if I would be interested in learning to read the meteorological instruments, in which case he would teach me. I did not answer yes or no, or at least I did not mean to give a precise answer, but I found myself beside him on the platform while he was explaining how to establish the maximum and the minimum, the progress of the pressure, the amount of precipitation, the velocity of the winds. In short, almost without my realizing it, he entrusted me with the job of replacing him for the next few days, starting tomorrow at noon. Though my acceptance was a bit forced, since I was given no time to reflect or to suggest that I could not make up my mind on the spot, this assignment does not displease me.

Tuesday. This morning I spoke for the first time with Miss Zwida. The job of recording the meteorological readings certainly had a part in helping me overcome my hesitation, in the sense that, for the first time during my days at Pëtkwo, there was something previously established that I could not avoid; so that, however our conversation might go, at a quarter to twelve I would say, "Ah, I almost forgot: I must rush along to the observatory, because it is time to record the readings." And I would take my leave, perhaps reluctantly, perhaps with relief, but in any event with the certainty that I could not do otherwise. I believe I already understood vaguely yesterday, when Mr. Kauderer made me the offer, that this assignment would encourage me to speak with Miss Zwida, but only now has the matter become clear to me—assuming that it is clear.

Miss Zwida was drawing a sea urchin. She was seated on a folding stool, on the pier. The sea urchin was lying on a rock, open; it contracted its prickles trying in vain to right itself. The girl's drawing was a study of the mollusk's soft pulp, as it dilated and contracted, rendered in chiaroscuro, and with thick, bristling cross-hatching all around. The speech I had in mind, on the form of seashells as a deceptive harmony, a container concealing the true substance of nature, was no longer apposite. The sight of both the sea urchin and the drawing transmitted unpleasant and cruel sensations, like viscera exposed to the gaze. I struck up a conversation by saying that there was nothing harder to draw than a sea urchin: whether the container of prickles was seen from above, or whether the mollusk was overturned, despite the radial symmetry of its structure, it offered few pretexts for a linear rendering. She answered that she was interested in drawing it because it was an image that recurred in her dreams, and she wanted to rid herself of it. Taking my leave, I asked if we could see each other tomorrow morning at the same place. She said that tomorrow she had other engagements, but that the day after tomorrow she would be going out again with her drawing pad and I might easily meet her.

As I was checking the barometers, two men approached the shed. I had never seen them: bundled in heavy coats, dressed all in black, their collars turned up. They asked me whether Mr. Kauderer was there, then where had he gone, did I know his address, when he would be back. I answered that I didn't know and asked who they were and why they asked.

"It's not important," they said, going away.

Wednesday. I went to the hotel to leave a bunch of violets for Miss Zwida. The desk clerk told me she had gone out early. I wandered around for a long time, hoping to run into her. In the yard before the fortress was the line of the prisoners' relatives: this is visiting day at the prison. In the midst of the humble women with kerchiefs on their heads and the crying children I saw Miss Zwida. Her face was covered by a black veil under the brim of her hat, but her demeanor was unmistakable: she stood with her head high, her neck straight and somehow haughty.

In a corner of the yard, as if observing the line at the

door of the prison, were the two men in black who had questioned me yesterday at the observatory.

The sea urchin, the little veil, the two strangers: the color black continues to appear to me in circumstances bound to attract my attention, messages that I interpret as a summons from the night. I realize that for a long time I have tended to reduce the presence of darkness in my life. The doctors' prohibition of going out after sunset has confined me for months within the boundaries of the daytime world. But this is not all: the fact is that I find in the day's light, in this diffused, pale, almost shadowless luminosity, a darkness deeper than the night's.

Wednesday evening. Every evening I spend the first hours of darkness penning these pages, which I do not know if anyone will ever read. The *pâte de verre* globe in my room at the Kudgiwa Pension illuminates the flow of my writing, perhaps too nervous for a future reader to decipher. Perhaps this diary will come to light many, many years after my death, when our language will have undergone who knows what transformations, and some of the words and expressions I use normally will seem outdated and of ambiguous meaning. In any case, the person who finds this diary will have one certain advantage over me: with a written language it is always possible to reconstruct a dictionary and a grammar, isolate sentences, transcribe them or paraphrase them in another language, whereas I am trying to read in the succession of things presented to me every day the world's intentions toward me, and I grope my way, knowing that there can exist no dictionary that will translate into words the burden of obscure allusions that lurks in these things. I would like this hovering of presentiments and suspicions to reach the person who reads me not as an accidental obstacle to understanding what I write, but as its very substance; and if the process of my thoughts seems elusive to him who, setting out from radically changed mental habits, will seek to follow it, the important thing is that I convey to him the effort I am making to read between the lines of things the evasive meaning of what is in store for me.

Thursday. Thanks to a special permit from the director's office—Miss Zwida explained to me—she can enter the prison on visitors' day and sit at the table in the parlor with her drawing pad and her charcoal. The simple humanity of the prisoners' relatives offers some interesting subjects for studies from life.

I had asked her no question, but since she had realized that I saw her yesterday in the yard, she felt it her duty to explain her presence in that place. I would have preferred her to tell me nothing, because I feel no attraction toward drawings of human figures and I would not have known how to comment on them if she had shown them to me, an eventuality that, however, did not occur. I thought those drawings were perhaps kept in a special album, which she left in the prison office between times, since yesterday—I recalled clearly—she did not have with her the inseparable bound album or her pencil box.

"If I knew how to draw, I would apply myself only to studying the form of inanimate objects," I said somewhat imperiously, because I wanted to change the subject and also because a natural inclination does truly lead me to recognize my moods in the motionless suffering of things.

Miss Zwida proved at once to be in agreement: the object she would have drawn most willingly, she said, was one of those little anchors with four flukes, known as "grapnels," which the fishing boats use. She pointed some out to me as we passed the boats tied up at the dock, and she explained to me the difficulty that the four barbs represented for anyone wanting to draw them in their various angles and perspectives. I understood that the object contained a message for me, and I should decipher it: the anchor, an exhortation to attach myself, to cling, to delve, to end my fluctuating condition, my remaining on the surface. But such an interpretation left room for doubts: this could also be an invitation to cast off, to set forth toward the open sea. Something in the grapnel's form, the four hooked teeth, the four iron arms worn by the scraping against the rock of the seabed, warned me that no decision would preclude laceration and suffering. Still, I could be relieved that it was not a heavy, ocean-going anchor, but a light little anchor: I was not therefore being asked to renounce the open-mindedness of youth, but only to linger for a moment, to reflect, to sound out the darkness of myself. "To be able to draw this object at my leisure from every point of view," Zwida said, "I should have one that I could keep with me and become familiar with. Do you think I could buy one from a fisherman?"

"We can ask," I said.

"Why do you not try to purchase one? I dare not do it myself, because a young lady from the city who shows interest in a crude fishermen's implement would arouse some wonder."

I saw myself in the act of presenting her with the iron grapnel as if it were a bunch of flowers: the image in its incongruity had a strident, fierce quality. Certainly a meaning was hidden there that eluded me; and, vowing to meditate on it calmly, I answered yes.

"I would like the grapnel with its hawser attached," Zwida specified. "I can spend hours drawing a heap of coiled rope. So ask for a very long rope: ten—no, twelve—meters."

Thursday evening. The doctors have given me permission to consume alcoholic beverages in moderation. To celebrate the news, at sunset I entered the tavern, The Star of Sweden, to have a cup of hot rum. At the bar there were fishermen, customs agents, day laborers. Over all their voices rang out the voice of one elderly man in the uniform of a prison guard, who was boasting drunkenly through the sea of chatter. "And every Wednesday the perfumed young lady slips me a hundred-crown note to leave her alone with the convict. And by Thursday the hundred crowns are already gone in so much beer. And when the visiting hour is over, the young lady comes out with the stink of jail in her elegant clothes; and the prisoner goes back to his cell with the lady's perfume in his jailbird's suit. And I'm left with the smell of beer. Life is nothing but trading smells."

"Life and also death, you might say," interjected another drunk, whose profession, as I learned at once, was gravedigger. "With the smell of beer I try to get the smell of death off me. And only the smell of death will get the smell of beer off you, like all the drinkers whose graves I have to dig."

I took this dialogue as a warning to be on guard: the world is falling apart and tries to lure me into its disintegration.

Friday. The fisherman had become suspicious all of a sudden: "What do you need it for? What use do you have for a grapnel?"

These were indiscreet questions; I should have answered, "To draw it," but I knew Miss Zwida's shyness about revealing her artistic activity in an environment incapable of appreciating it; besides, the right answer, on my part, would have been, "To think about it," so just imagine whether I would have been understood.

"That is my business," I answered. We had started out conversing amiably, since we had met the night before at the tavern, but all of a sudden our dialogue had turned curt.

"Go to a ship's chandler," the fisherman said, brusquely. "I do not sell my belongings."

With the shopkeeper the same thing happened: as soon

as I asked my question, his face turned grim. "We can't sell such things to foreigners," he said. "We want no trouble with the police. And with a rope twelve meters long into the bargain . . . Not that I suspect you, but it would not be the first time somebody threw a grapnel up to the bars of the prison, to help a prisoner escape. . . ."

"Escape" is one of those words I cannot hear without abandoning myself to endless ruminations. The search for the anchor in which I am engaged seems to indicate to me an avenue of escape, perhaps of a metamorphosis, a resurrection. With a shudder I dismiss the thought that the prison is my mortal body and the escape that awaits me the separation of the soul, the beginning of a life beyond this earth.

Saturday. It was my first outing at night after many months, and this caused me no little apprehension, especially because of the head colds to which I am subject; so before going out, I put on a balaclava helmet and over it a wool cap and, over that, a felt hat. Bundled up like this, and moreover with a scarf around my neck and another around my waist, a woolen jacket, a fur jacket, a leather coat, and lined boots, I could recover a certain security. The night, as I was then able to ascertain, was mild and serene. But I still failed to understand why Mr. Kauderer felt impelled to make an appointment with me at the cemetery, in the heart of the night, through a mysterious note delivered to me in great secrecy. If he had come back, why could we not meet as we had every day? And if he had not come back, whom was I on my way to meet at the cemetery?

To open the gate for me there was the gravedigger I had already met at The Star of Sweden. "I am looking for Mr. Kauderer," I said to him.

He answered, "Mr. Kauderer is not here. But since the cemetery is the home of those who are not here, come in."

Leaning from the steep slope

I was proceeding among the gravestones when a swift, rustling shadow grazed me; it braked and got down from the seat. "Mr. Kauderer!" I exclaimed, amazed at seeing him ride around on his bicycle among the graves, his headlight turned off.

"Ssssh," he silenced me. "You are committing serious imprudences. When I entrusted the observatory to you, I did not suppose you would compromise yourself in an escape attempt. I must tell you we are opposed to individual escapes. You have to know how to wait. We have a more general plan to carry forward, a long-term plan."

Hearing him say "we" as he made a broad, sweeping gesture, I thought he was speaking in the name of the dead. It was the dead, whose spokesman Mr. Kauderer obviously was, who had declared they did not yet want to accept me among them. I felt an undeniable relief.

"It is also your fault that I shall have to prolong my absence," he added. "Tomorrow or the next day you will be summoned by the police chief, who will question you about the grapnel. Be very careful not to involve me in this business; bear in mind that the chief's questions will all be aimed at making you confess something involving me. You know nothing about me, except that I am traveling and I have not told you when I will be back. You can say that I asked you to take my place in recording the readings for a few days only. For that matter, starting tomorrow, you are relieved of the duty of going to the observatory."

"No! Not that!" I cried, gripped by a sudden desperation, as if at that moment I had realized that only the checking of the meteorological instruments enabled me to master the forces of the universe and recognize an order in it.

Sunday. Early in the morning, I went to the meteorological observatory, I climbed on the platform, and I stood there listening to the tick of the recording instruments, like the music of the celestial spheres. The wind sped through the morning sky, transporting soft clouds; the clouds arrayed themselves in cirrus festoons, then in cumuli; toward nine-thirty there was a rain shower, and the pluviometer collected a few centiliters; there followed a partial rainbow, of brief duration; the sky darkened again, the nib of the barograph descended, tracing an almost vertical line; the thunder rumbled and the hail rattled. From my position up there I felt as if I had the storms and the clear skies in my hand, the thunderbolts and the mists: not like a god, no, do not believe me mad, I did not feel I was Zeus the Thunderer, but a bit like a conductor who has before him a score already written and who knows that the sounds rising from the instruments correspond to a pattern of which he is the principal curator and possessor. The corrugated-iron roof resounded like a drum beneath the downpour; the anemometer spun; that universe all crashes and leaps was translatable into figures to be lined up in my ledger; a supreme calm presided over the texture of the cataclysms.

In that moment of harmony and fullness, a creak made me look down. Huddled between the steps of the platform and the supporting poles of the shed was a bearded man, dressed in a rough, striped tunic, soaked with rain. He was looking at me with pale, steady eyes.

"I have escaped," he said. "Do not betray me. You must go and inform someone. Will you? This person is at the Hotel of the Sea Lily."

I sensed at once that in the perfect order of the universe a breach had opened, an irreparable rent.

[4]

Listening to someone read aloud is very different from reading in silence. When you read, you can stop or skip sentences: you are the one who sets the pace. When someone else is reading, it is difficult to make your attention coincide with the tempo of his reading: the voice goes either too fast or too slow.

And then, listening to someone who is translating from another language involves a fluctuation, a hesitation over the words, a margin of indecision, something vague, tentative. The text, when you are the reader, is something that is there, against which you are forced to clash; when someone translates it aloud to you, it is something that is and is not there, that you cannot manage to touch.

Furthermore, Professor Uzzi-Tuzii had begun his oral translation as if he were not quite sure he could make the words hang together, going back over every sentence to iron out the syntactical creases, manipulating the phrases until they were not completely rumpled, smoothing them, clipping them, stopping at every word to illustrate its idiomatic uses and its connotations, accompanying himself with inclusive gestures as if inviting you to be content with approximate equivalents, breaking off to state grammatical rules, etymological derivations, quoting the classics. But just when you are convinced that for the professor philology and erudition mean more than what the story is telling, you realize the opposite is true: that academic envelope serves only to protect everything the story says and does not say, an inner afflatus always on the verge of being dispersed at contact with the air, the echo of a vanished knowledge revealed in the penumbra and in tacit allusions.

Torn between the necessity to interject glosses on mul-

tiple meanings of the text and the awareness that all interpretation is a use of violence and caprice against a text,
the professor, when faced by the most complicated passages, could find no better way of aiding comprehension
than to read them in the original. The pronunciation of
that unknown language, deduced from theoretical rules,
not transmitted by the hearing of voices with their individual accents, not marked by the traces of use that
shapes and transforms, acquired the absoluteness of
sounds that expect no reply, like the song of the last bird
of an extinct species or the strident roar of a just-invented
jet plane that shatters in the sky on its first test flight.

Then, little by little, something started moving and
flowing between the sentences of this distraught recitation. The prose of the novel had got the better of the
uncertainties of the voice; it had become fluent, transparent, continuous; Uzzi-Tuzii swam in it like a fish, accompanying himself with gestures (he held his hands open
like flippers), with the movement of his lips (which allowed the words to emerge like little air bubbles), with
his gaze (his eyes scoured the page like a fish's eyes scour-
ing the seabed, but also like the eyes of an aquarium visitor as he follows a fish's movements in an illuminated
tank).

Now, around you, there is no longer the room of the
department, the shelves, the professor: you have entered
the novel, you see that Nordic beach, you follow the footsteps of the delicate gentleman. You are so absorbed that
it takes you a while to become aware of a presence at your
side. Out of the corner of your eye you glimpse Ludmilla.
She is there, seated on a pile of folio volumes, also completely caught up in listening to the continuation of the
novel.

Has she just arrived at this moment, or did she hear the
beginning? Did she enter silently, without knocking? Was
she already here, hidden among these shelves? (She came

Chapter four

here to hide, Irnerio said. They come here to do unspeakable things, Uzzi-Tuzii said). Or is she an apparition summoned by the spell released through the words of the professor-sorcerer?

He continues his recitation, Uzzi-Tuzii, and shows no sign of surprise at the presence of the new listener, as if she had always been there. Nor does he react with a start wnen she, hearing him pause longer than the other times, asks him, "And then?"

The professor snaps the book shut. "Then nothing. *Leaning from the steep slope* breaks off here. Having written these first pages of his novel, Ukko Ahti sank into a deep depression which, in the space of a few years, led him to three unsuccessful suicide attempts and one that succeeded. The fragment was published in the collection of his posthumous writings, along with scattered verses, an intimate diary, and his notes for an essay on the incarnation of Buddha. Unfortunately, it was impossible to find any plan or sketch explaining how Ahti intended to develop the plot. Though incomplete, or perhaps for this very reason, *Leaning from the steep slope* is the most representative work of Cimmerian prose, for what it reveals and even more for what it hides, for its reticence, withdrawal, its disappearing...."

The professor's voice seems about to die away. You crane your neck, to make sure he is still there, beyond the bookcase-partition that separates him from your vision, but you are no longer able to glimpse him; perhaps he has ducked into the hedge of academic publications and bound collections of reviews, growing thinner and thinner until he can slip into the interstices greedy for dust, perhaps overwhelmed by the erasing destiny that looms over the object of his studies, perhaps engulfed by the empty chasm of the brusque interruption of the novel. On the edge of this chasm you would like to take your stand, supporting Ludmilla or clinging to her; your hands try to grasp her hands....

Chapter four

"Don't ask where the rest of this book is!" It is a shrill cry that comes from an undefined spot among the shelves. "All books continue in the beyond. . . ." The professor's voice goes up and down; where has he got to? Perhaps he is rolling around beneath the desk, perhaps he is hanging himself from the lamp in the ceiling.

"Continue where?" you ask, perched on the edge of the precipice. "Beyond what?"

"Books are the steps of the threshold. . . . All Cimmerian authors have passed it. . . . Then the wordless language of the dead begins, which says the things that only the language of the dead can say. Cimmerian is the last language of the living, the language of the threshold! You come here to try to listen there, beyond. . . . Listen. . . ."

But you are no longer listening to anything, the two of you. You have also disappeared, flattened in a corner, one clinging to the other. Is this your answer? Do you want to demonstrate that the living also have a wordless language, with which books cannot be written but which can only be lived, second by second, which cannot be recorded or remembered? First comes this wordless language of living bodies—is this the premise you wish Uzzi-Tuzii would take into account?—then the words books are written with, and attempts to translate that first language are vain; then . . .

"Cimmerian books are all unfinished," Uzzi-Tuzii sighs, "because they continue beyond . . . in the other language, in the silent language to which all the words we believe we read refer. . . ."

"Believe . . . Why believe? I like to read, really to read." It is Ludmilla who is speaking like this, with conviction and warmth. She is seated opposite the professor, dressed in a simple, elegant fashion, in light colors. Her way of living in the world, filled with interest in what the world can give her, dismisses the egocentric abyss of the suicide's novel that ends by sinking into itself. In her voice you seek the confirmation of your need to cling to the things that exist, to read what is written and nothing else, dispelling the ghosts that escape your grasp. (Even if your embrace—confess it—occurred only in your imagination, it is still an embrace that can happen at any moment. . . .)

But Ludmilla is always at least one step ahead of you. "I like to know that books exist that I will still be able to read . . ." she says, sure that existent objects, concrete albeit unknown, must correspond to the strength of her desire. How can you keep up with her, this woman who is always reading another book besides the one before her eyes, a book that does not yet exist, but which, since she wants it, cannot fail to exist?

The professor is there at his desk; in the cone of light from a desk lamp his hands surface, suspended, or barely resting on the closed volume, as if in a sad caress.

"Reading," he says, "is always this: there is a thing that is there, a thing made of writing, a solid, material object, which cannot be changed, and through this thing we measure ourselves against something else that is not present, something else that belongs to the immaterial, invisible world, because it can only be thought, imagined, or because it was once and is no longer, past, lost, unattainable, in the land of the dead. . . ."

"Or that is not present because it does not yet exist, something desired, feared, possible or impossible," Ludmilla says. "Reading is going toward something that is about to be, and no one yet knows what it will be. . . ." (There, now you see the Other Reader leaning forward to peer beyond the edge of the printed page at the ships of the rescuers or the invaders appearing on the horizon, the storms. . . .) "The book I would like to read now is a novel in which you sense the story arriving like still-vague thunder, the historical story along with the individual's story, a novel that gives the sense of living through an upheaval that still has no name, has not yet taken shape. . . ."

Chapter four

"Well said, sister dear, I see you're making progress!" Among the shelves a girl has appeared, with a long neck and a bird's face, a steady, bespectacled gaze, a great clump of curly hair; she is dressed in a loose tunic and tight pants. "I was coming to tell you I had found the novel you were looking for, and it is the very one our seminar on the feminist revolution needs. You're invited, if you want to hear us analyze it and debate it!"

"Lotaria, you don't mean to tell me," Ludmilla exclaims, "that you, too, have come upon *Leaning from the steep slope*, the unfinished novel of Ukko Ahti, the Cimmerian writer!"

"You are misinformed, Ludmilla. That is the novel, but it isn't unfinished, and it isn't written in Cimmerian but in Cimbrian; the title was later changed to *Without fear of wind or vertigo*, and the author signed it with a different pseudonym, Vorts Viljandi."

"It's a fake!" Professor Uzzi-Tuzii cries. "It's a well-known case of forgery! The material is apocryphal, disseminated by the Cimbrian nationalists during the anti-Cimmerian propaganda campaign at the end of the First World War!"

Crowding behind Lotaria is the vanguard of a phalanx of young girls with limpid, serene eyes, slightly alarming eyes, perhaps because they are too limpid and serene. Among them a pale man forces his way, bearded, with a sarcastic gaze and a systematically disillusioned curl to his lips.

"I'm terribly sorry to contradict an illustrious colleague," he says, "but the authenticity of this text has been proved by the discovery of the manuscripts that the Cimmerians had hidden!"

"I am amazed, Galligani," Uzzi-Tuzii groans, "that you lend the authority of your chair in Erulo-Altaic languages and literatures to such a vulgar fraud! And, moreover, one connected with territorial claims that have nothing to do with literature!"

"Uzzi-Tuzii, please," Professor Galligani retorts, "don't lower the debate to this level. You know very well that Cimbrian nationalism is quite remote from my interests, as I hope Cimmerian chauvinism is from yours. Comparing the spirit of the two literatures, I ask myself this question: who goes further in the negation of values?"

The Cimbro-Cimmerian debate does not seem to affect Ludmilla, now occupied with a single thought: the possibility that the interrupted novel might continue. "Can what Lotaria says be true?" she asks you in a whisper. "For once I wish she were right, that the beginning the professor read had a sequel, no matter in what language...."

"Ludmilla," Lotaria says, "we're going to our study group. If you want to follow the discussion of Viljandi's novel, come along. You can invite your friend, too, if he's interested."

Here you are, enrolled behind Lotaria's banner. The group takes its place in a classroom, around a table. You and Ludmilla would like to sit as close as possible to the bundle of manuscript Lotaria is holding before her, which seems to contain the novel in question.

"We have to thank Professor Galligani, of Cimbric literature," Lotaria begins, "for having kindly put at our disposal a rare copy of *Without fear of wind or vertigo* and for personally taking part in our seminar. I would like to underline this open attitude, which is all the more admirable when you compare it with the lack of understanding in other teachers of related disciplines. . . ." And Lotaria gives her sister a look, to make sure she doesn't miss the hostile reference to Uzzi-Tuzii.

To put the novel in context, Galligani is asked to supply some historical notes. "I will confine myself to recalling," he says, "how the provinces that made up the Cimmerian state became, after the Second World War, part of the Cimbric People's Republic. Putting in order the documents of the Cimmerian archives, which had been scattered at the time of the fighting, the Cimbrians were able to re-evaluate the complex personality of a writer like Vorts Viljandi, who wrote both in Cimmerian and in Cimbric, but of whose works the Cimmerians published only those in their language—a scant number, for that matter. Far more important in quantity and in quality were the works in Cimbric, concealed by the Cimmerians, notably the vast novel *Without fear of wind or vertigo,* whose opening chapter apparently also exists in a first draft in Cimmerian, signed with the pseudonym Ukko Ahti. It is beyond dispute, in any case, that it was only after his definitive choice of the Cimbric language that the author found his genuine inspiration for this novel. . . .

"I won't give you the whole history," the professor continues, "of the variable fortunes of this book in the Cimbric People's Republic. First published as a classic, translated also into German so that it could be disseminated abroad (this is the translation we are using now), it later suffered during the campaigns for ideological rectification, and was withdrawn from circulation and even from the libraries. We now believe, on the other hand, that its revolutionary content was far ahead of its time. . . ."

You are impatient, you and Ludmilla, to see this lost book rise from its ashes, but you must wait until the girls and the young men of the study group have been handed out their assignments: during the reading there must be some who underline the reflections of production methods, others the processes of reification, others the sublimation of repression, others the sexual semantic codes, others the metalanguages of the body, others the transgression of roles, in politics and in private life.

And now Lotaria opens her folder, begins to read. The

barbed-wire fences dissolve like cobwebs. All follow in silence, you two and the others.

You immediately realize that you are listening to something that has no possible connection with *Leaning from the steep slope* or with *Outside the town of Malbork* or even with *If on a winter's night a traveler*. You exchange a quick glance, you and Ludmilla, or, rather, two glances: first questioning, then agreeing. Whatever it may be, this is a novel where, once you have got into it, you want to go forward, without stopping.

Without
fear
of wind
or vertigo

At five in the morning, military vehicles crossed the city; outside the food stores lines began to form, housewives with tallow lanterns; on the walls the propaganda slogans, painted during the night by the teams of the various factions of the Provisional Council, were not yet dry.

When the band's musicians had put their instruments back in their cases and came out of the basement, the air was green. For part of the way the patrons of the New Titania walked in a group behind the musicians, as if reluctant to sever the bond that had formed in the club during the night among the people gathered there, by chance or habit, and they went forward in a single party, the men inside the turned-up collars of their overcoats, assuming a cadaverous look, like mummies brought into the open air from the sarcophagi, which, preserved for four thousand years, in a moment crumble to dust; but a wave of excitement, on the contrary, infected the women, who sang, each to herself, leaving their cloaks open over their low-cut evening dresses, swishing their long skirts through the puddles in unsteady dance movements, thanks to that process peculiar to intoxication which makes a new euphoria bloom from the collapse and dulling of the previous euphoria, and in all of them there seemed to remain the hope that the party was not yet over, that the players at a certain point would stop in the middle of the street, reopen their cases, and again take out their saxophones and double basses.

Opposite the former Levinson Bank, guarded by squads of People's Guards with bayonets fixed and cockades on their caps, the party of night owls, as if the word had been given, broke up, and each went off his own way, not saying good-bye to anyone. The three of us were left together: Valerian and I took Irina by the arm, one on each side. I was always at Irina's right, to leave room for the holster of the heavy pistol I was wearing, hanging from my belt; as for Valerian, who was in civilian clothes since he was a member of the Heavy Industry Commission, if he was wearing a pistol—and I believe he had one—it was surely one of those flat ones you can carry in your pocket. Irina at that hour became silent, almost gloomy, and a kind of fear crept into us—I speak for myself, but I'm sure Valerian shared my mood, even if we never exchanged any confidences on the subject—because we felt this was when she truly took possession of the two of us, and however mad the things she would drive us to do once her magic circle had closed and imprisoned us, they would be nothing compared to what she was concocting now in her imagination, never pausing in the face of any excess, in the exploration of the senses, in mental elation, in cruelty. The truth is that we were all very young, too young for everything we were experiencing; I mean us men, because Irina had the precocity of women of her sort, even though in years she was the youngest of the three; and she made us do what she wanted.

She began whistling silently, Irina, with a smile in her eyes, as if savoring in advance an idea that had come to her; then her whistle became audible, a comic march from an operetta then in fashion, and we, always a bit afraid of what she was preparing for us, began to follow her, also whistling, and we marched in step as if to an irresistible fanfare, feeling ourselves at once victims and victors.

This was as we passed the Church of Saint Apollonia, then transformed into a lazaretto for cholera patients, with the coffins displayed outside on sawhorses surrounded by great circles of lime so that people wouldn't approach, waiting for the cemetery wagons. An old woman was praying, kneeling outside the church, and as we proceeded to the sound of our irresistible march, we almost trampled on her. She raised against us a little fist, withered and yellow, wrinkled as a chestnut, propping herself up with the other fist on the cobblestones, as she shouted, "Down with the gentry!" or, rather, "Down with! Gentry!" as if they were two curses, in crescendo, and as if in calling us gentry she considered us doubly cursed, and then a word in the local dialect that means "brothel people," and also something like "It will end"; but at that moment she noticed my uniform and was silent, hanging her head.

I am narrating this incident in all its details because— not immediately, but afterward—it was considered a premonition of everything that was to happen, and also because all these images of the period must cross the page like the army vehicles crossing the city (even if the words "army vehicles" evoke somewhat indefinite images; it's not bad for a certain indefiniteness to remain in the air, appropriate to the confusion of the period), like the canvas streamers hung between one building and the next to urge the citizenry to subscribe to the national loan, like the processions of workers whose routes must not coincide because they are organized by rival trade unions, one demonstrating in favor of the unlimited continuation of the strike in the Kauderer munitions factories, the other for the end of the strike in order to assist arming the people against the counterrevolutionary armies about to surround the city. All these oblique lines, intersecting, should define the space where we moved, I and Valerian and Irina, where our story can emerge from nothingness, find a point of departure, a direction, a plot.

I had met Irina the day the front collapsed, less than twelve kilometers from the Eastern Gate. While the citizens' militia—boys under eighteen and old men from the reserves—was taking up a position around the low buildings of the Slaughterhouse—a place whose very name had a ring of ill omen, but we didn't yet know for whom—a flood of people was withdrawing into the city over the Iron Bridge. Peasant women balancing on their heads baskets with geese peeping out, hysterical pigs running off among the legs of the crowd, followed by yelling children (the hope of saving something from the army's requisitions drove the rural families to scatter their children and their hogs as much as possible, sending them off at random), soldiers on foot or on horseback who were deserting their units or trying to regain the body of the dispersed forces, elderly noblewomen at the head of caravans of maidservants and bundles, stretchers with the wounded, patients discharged from the hospitals, wandering peddlers, officials, monks, gypsies, pupils from the former College of Officers' Daughters in their traveling uniform—all were channeled through the grilles of the bridge as if swept along by the cold, damp wind that seemed to blow from the rents in the map, from the breaches that ripped fronts and frontiers. There were many that day seeking refuge in the city: those who feared the spreading of riots and looting and those instead who had their own good reasons for not being found in the path of the reactionary armies; those who sought protection under the fragile legality of the Provisional Council and those who wanted only to hide in the confusion in order to act undisturbed against the law, whether new or old. Each felt his personal survival was at stake, and precisely where any talk of solidarity would have seemed out of place, because what counted was clawing and biting to clear a path for yourself, there was nevertheless a kind of common ground and understanding established, so that in the face of obstacles, efforts were united and all understood one another without too many words.

It may have been this, or it may have been that in general confusion youth recognizes itself and rejoices: whatever it was, crossing the Iron Bridge in the midst of the crowd that morning, I felt satisfied and lighthearted, in harmony with the others, with myself, and with the world, as I had not felt for a long time. (I would not like to use the wrong word; I will say, rather: I felt in harmony with the disharmony of others, myself, and the world.) I was already at the end of the bridge, where a flight of steps led to the shore and the river of people slowing down and jamming, forcing some to shove backward to avoid being pushed against those who were going down the steps more slowly—legless veterans who rested first on one crutch then on the other, horses led by the bit in a diagonal line so the iron of their hoofs would not slip on the edges of the iron steps, motorcycles with sidecars that had to be lifted and carried (they would have done better to take the Wagon Bridge, as the pedestrians did not fail to shout at them, inveighing, but this would have meant adding a good mile to the trip)—when I became aware of the girl who was coming down beside me.

She wore a cloak with fur at hem and cuffs, a broad-brimmed hat with a veil and a rose: not only young and attractive but also elegant, as I noticed immediately afterward. While I was looking at her obliquely, I saw her open her eyes wide, raise her gloved hand to her mouth which was gaping in a cry of terror, and then sink backward. She would surely have fallen and been trampled by that crowd advancing like a herd of elephants if I had not been quick to grab her by the arm.

"Are you ill?" I said to her. "Lean on me. It's nothing, don't worry."

She was rigid, unable to take another step.

"The void, the void down below," she was saying. "Help . . . vertigo . . ."

There was nothing visible that could explain any vertigo, but the girl was truly panic-stricken.

"Don't look down, and hold on to my arm. Follow the others; we're already at the end of the bridge," I say to her, hoping that these are the right notions to reassure her.

And then she says, "I feel all these footsteps come loose from the stairs and move forward in the void, then plunge . . . a crowd falling . . ." And she digs in her heels.

I look through the spaces between the iron steps at the colorless flow of the river down below, transporting chunks of ice like white clouds. In a distress that lasts an instant, I seem to be feeling what she feels: that every void continues in the void, every gap, even a short one, opens onto another gap, every chasm empties into the infinite abyss. I put my arm around her shoulders; I try to resist the shoves of those who want to proceed down, who curse at us: "Hey, let us past! Go do your hugging somewhere else! Shameless!" But the only way to elude the human landslide that is striking us would be to walk faster into the air, to fly. . . . There: I, too, feel suspended as if over a precipice. . . .

Perhaps it is this story that is a bridge over the void, and as it advances it flings forward news and sensations and emotions to create a ground of upsets both collective and individual in the midst of which a path can be opened while we remain in the dark about many circumstances both historical and geographical. I clear my path through the wealth of details that cover the void I do not want to notice and I advance impetuously, while instead the female character freezes on the edge of a step amid the shoving crowd, until I manage to carry her down, almost a dead weight, step by step, to set her feet on the cobbles of the street along the river.

She collects herself; she raises before her a haughty gaze; she resumes walking and does not stop; her stride does not hesitate; she sets off toward Mill Street; I can hardly keep up with her.

The story must also work hard to keep up with us, to report a dialogue constructed on the void, speech by speech. For the story, the bridge is not finished: beneath every word there is nothingness.

"Feeling better?" I ask her.

"It's nothing. I have dizzy spells when I least expect them, even if there is no danger in sight. . . . Altitude or depth makes no difference. . . . If I gaze at the sky at night, and I think of the distance of the stars . . . Or even in the daytime . . . If I were to lie down here, for example, with my eyes facing up, my head would swim. . . ." And she points to the clouds that are passing swiftly, driven by the wind. She speaks of her head swimming as of a temptation that somehow attracts her.

I am a bit disappointed that she hasn't said a word of thanks. I remark, "This isn't a good place to lie down and look at the sky, by day or by night. You can take it from me: I know about it."

As between the iron steps of the bridge, in the dialogue, intervals of emptiness open between one speech and the next.

"You know about looking at the sky? Why? Are you an astronomer?"

"No, another kind of observer." And I point out to her on the collar of my uniform the insignia of the artillery. "Days under bombardments, watching the shrapnel fly."

Her gaze passes from the insignia to the epaulets that I

Without fear of wind or vertigo

don't have, then to the not very obvious chevrons of rank
sewn on my sleeves. "You come from the front, Lieutenant?"

"Alex Zinnober," I introduce myself. "I don't know if I
can be called a lieutenant. In our regiment, ranks have
been abolished, but orders change all the time. For the
moment, I'm a soldier with two stripes on his sleeves,
that's all."

"I'm Irina Piperin, as I was also before the revolution.
For the future, I don't know. I used to design fabrics,
and as long as there's a shortage of cloth, I'll make designs
for the air."

"With the revolution, there are people who change so
much they become unrecognizable, and other people who
feel they are the same selves as before. It must be a sign
that they were prepared in advance for the new times. Is
that the case?"

She makes no reply. I add, "Unless it's their total rejec-
tion that preserves them from changes. Is that your situation?"

"I . . . You tell me first: how much do you think you
have changed?"

"Not much. I realize I have retained certain points of
honor from before: catch a woman about to fall, for example, even if nowadays nobody says thank you."

"We all have moments of weakness, women and men,
and it isn't impossible, Lieutenant, that I may have an
opportunity to return your kindness of a moment ago." In
her voice there is a hint of harshness, or perhaps of pique.

At this point the dialogue—which has concentrated all
attention on itself, almost making one forget the visual
upheaval of the city—could break off; the usual military
vehicles cross the square and the page, separating us, or
else the usual lines of women outside the shops or the
usual processions of workers carrying signs. Irina is far
away now, the hat with the rose is sailing over a sea of

84

gray caps, of helmets, kerchiefs; I try to follow her, but she doesn't turn around.

Several paragraphs ensue, bristling with names of generals and deputies, concerned with the shelling and retreats from the front, about schisms and unifications in the parties represented in the Council, punctuated by climatic annotations: downpours, frosts, racing clouds, windstorms. All this, in any case, solely as a frame for my moods: a festive abandonment to the wave of events, or of withdrawal into myself as if concentrating myself into an obsessive pattern, as if everything around me served only to disguise me, to hide me, like the sandbag defenses that are being raised more or less on all sides (the city seems to be preparing to fight street by street), the fences that every night billposters of various factions cover with manifestos that are immediately soaked by the rain and become illegible because of the absorbent paper and the cheap ink.

Every time I pass the building that houses the Heavy Industry Commission I say to myself: Now I'll go and call on my friend Valerian. I have been repeating this to myself since the day of my arrival. Valerian is the closest friend I have here in the city. But, every time, I postpone the visit because of some important assignments I have to take care of. And yet you would say I apparently enjoy a freedom unusual for a soldier in service: the nature of my duties is not quite clear; I come and go among the offices of various headquarters; I am rarely seen in the barracks, as if I were not on strength in any unit; nor, for that matter, am I obviously glued to a desk.

Unlike Valerian, who doesn't budge from his desk. The day I go up to look for him I find him there, but he doesn't seem intent on government duties: he is cleaning a revolver. He chuckles into his ill-shaven beard, seeing me. He says: "So, you've come to fall into this trap, too, along with us."

"Or to trap others," I answer.

"The traps are one inside the other, and they all snap shut at the same time." He seems to want to warn me of something.

The building where the commission offices are installed was the residence of a war profiteer and his family; it was confiscated by the revolution. Some of the furnishings are gaudy and luxurious and have remained to mingle with the grim bureaucratic equipment; Valerian's office is cluttered with boudoir chinoiserie: vases with dragons, lacquered coffers, a silk screen.

"Who do you want to trap in this pagoda? An Oriental queen?"

From behind the screen a woman comes: short hair, a gray silk dress, milk-colored stockings.

"Male dreams don't change, not even with the revolution," she says, and in the aggressive sarcasm in her voice I recognize my passing acquaintance from the Iron Bridge.

"You see? There are ears that listen to our every word . . ." Valerian says to me, laughing.

"The revolution does not put dreams on trial, Irina Piperin," I answer her.

"Nor does it save us from nightmares," she retorts.

Valerian intervenes: "I didn't know you two were acquainted."

"We met in a dream," I say. "We were falling off a bridge."

And she says: "No. Each has a different dream."

"And there are even some who happen to wake up in a safe place like this, guaranteed against any vertigo . . ." I insist.

"Vertigo is everywhere." And she takes the revolver that Valerian has finished reassembling, breaks it, puts her eye to the barrel as if to see whether it's properly cleaned, spins the chamber, slips a bullet into one of the holes, raises the hammer, holds the weapon aimed at her eye, again spinning the chamber. "It seems a bottomless pit. You feel the summons of the void, the temptation to fall, to join the darkness that is beckoning. . . ."

"Hey, weapons aren't things to joke around with," I say, and hold out a hand, but she trains the revolver on me.

"Why not?" she says. "Women can't, but you men can? The real revolution will be when women carry arms."

"And men are disarmed? Does that seem fair to you, comrade? Women armed to do what?"

"To take your place. We on top, and you underneath. So you men can feel a bit of what it's like to be a woman. Go on, move, go over there, go over beside your friend," she commands, still aiming the weapon at me.

"Irina has a certain constancy in her ideas," Valerian warns me. "It's no good contradicting her."

"And now?" I ask, and I look at Valerian, expecting him to intervene and put an end to the joke.

Valerian's eyes are on Irina, but his gaze is lost, as if he is in a trance, as if in absolute surrender, as if he expects pleasure only from submission to her whim.

An outrider from Military High Command enters with a bundle of files. When it is opened, the door hides Irina, who disappears. Valerian, as if nothing had happened, deals with his tasks.

"Tell me . . ." I ask him, as soon as we can speak. "Do those jokes seem right to you?"

"Irina doesn't joke," he says, without raising his eyes from the papers. "You'll see."

Now, from that moment, time changes shape, the night expands, the nights become a single night in the city crossed by our now inseparable trio, a single night that reaches its climax in Irina's room, in a scene that is meant to be private but is also one of exhibition and challenge, the ceremony of that secret and sacrificial cult of which Irina is at once priestess and divinity, profaner and victim.

The story resumes its interrupted progress; now the space that it must cover is overloaded, thick, it leaves no crevice open to the horror of the void among the geometric-patterned draperies, the pillows, the atmosphere impregnated with the odor of our naked bodies, Irina's breasts barely protruding from her skinny chest, the dark areolas that would be more in proportion on a more swollen bosom, the narrow, pointed pubes in the form of an isosceles triangle (the word "isosceles," once I had associated it with Irina's pubes, is charged for me with such sensuality that I cannot say it without making my teeth chatter). Near the center of the scene, the lines tend to twist, to become sinuous like the smoke from the brazier where she is burning the poor surviving aromas from an Armenian spice shop whose borrowed fame as an opium den had sparked the looting by the mob avenging morality, to twist—the lines again—like the invisible rope that binds us, the three of us, and the more we writhe to free ourselves the more our knots tighten, dig into our flesh. In the center of this tangle, in the heart of the drama of this secret association of ours, there is the secret I bear within me and cannot reveal to anyone, least of all to Irina and Valerian, the secret mission that has been entrusted to me: to discover the identity of the spy who has infiltrated the Revolutionary Committee and who is about to deliver the city into the hands of the Whites.

In the midst of the revolutions which that windy winter swept the streets of the capital like gusts of the north wind, a secret revolution was being born, which would transform the powers of bodies and sexes: this Irina believed, and she had succeeded in imposing this belief not only on Valerian, who, a district judge's son with a degree in political economy, follower of Indian sages and Swiss theosophists, was the preordained adept of every doctrine within the confines of the conceivable, but also on me, who came from such a harder school, on me, who knew

that in a short time the future was going to be decided
between the Revolutionary Tribunal and the Whites'
Court-Martial, and that two firing squads, one on one side
and one on the other, were waiting with their weapons at
order arms.

I tried to escape, insinuating myself with crawling
movements toward the center of the spirals, where the
lines slithered like serpents following the writhing of
Irina's limbs, supple and restless, in a slow dance where it
is not the rhythm that counts but the knotting and loosen-
ing of serpentine lines. There are two serpents whose
heads Irina grasps with her hands, and they react to her
grasp, intensifying their own aptitude for rectilinear pene-
tration, while she was insisting, on the contrary, that the
maximum of controlled power should correspond to a rep-
tile pliability bending to overtake her in impossible contortions.

Because this was the first article of faith of the cult
Irina had established: that we abandon the standard idea
of verticality, of the straight line, the surviving ill-
concealed male pride that had remained with us even
when we accepted our condition as slaves of a woman
who allowed no jealousies between us, no supremacies of
any kind. "Down," Irina said, and her hand pressed the
back of Valerian's head, her fingers sinking into the young
economist's woolly hair, a straw-red color, not allowing
him to raise his face to the level of her womb, "farther
down!" And meanwhile she looked at me with diamond
eyes and wanted me to watch, wanted our two gazes also
to proceed along serpentine and continuous paths. I felt
her gaze which did not abandon me for an instant, and
meanwhile I felt on me another gaze which followed me
at every moment and in every place, the gaze of an invisible power that was expecting of me only one thing:
death, no matter whether it was the death I was to bring
to others, or my own.

Without fear of wind or vertigo

I was awaiting the moment when the thong of Irina's gaze would be loosened. There: she half-closes her eyes; there: I am slithering in the shadow, behind the pillows, the sofas, the brazier; there: where Valerian has left his clothes folded in perfect order, as is his habit, I crawl in the shadow of Irina's lowered eyelids, I search Valerian's pockets, his wallet, I hide in the darkness of her clenched eyelids, in the darkness of the cry that comes from her throat, I find the paper, folded double, with my name written by a steel nib, under the formula of the death sentence for treason, signed and countersigned below the regimental rubber stamps.

[5]

At this point they throw open the discussion. Events, characters, settings, impressions are thrust aside, to make room for the general concepts.

"The polymorphic-perverse sexuality . . ."

"The laws of a market economy . . ."

"The homologies of the signifying structures . . ."

"Deviation and institutions . . ."

"Castration . . ."

Only you have remained suspended there, you and Ludmilla, while nobody else thinks of continuing the reading.

You move closer to Lotaria, reach out one hand toward the loose sheets in front of her, and ask, "May I?"; you try to gain possession of the novel. But it is not a book: it is one signature that has been torn out. Where is the rest?

"Excuse me, I was looking for the other pages, the rest," you say.

"The rest? . . . Oh, there's enough material here to discuss for a month. Aren't you satisfied?"

"I didn't mean to discuss; I wanted to read . . ." you say.

"Listen, there are so many study groups, and the Erulo-Altaic Department had only one copy, so we've divided it up; the division caused some argument, the book came to pieces, but I really believe I captured the best part."

Seated at a café table, you sum up the situation, you and Ludmilla. "To recapitulate: *Without fear of wind or vertigo* is not *Leaning from the steep slope*, which, in turn, is not *Outside the town of Malbork*, which is quite different from *If on a winter's night a traveler*. The only thing we can do is go to the source of all this confusion."

"Yes. It's the publishing house that subjected us to

these frustrations, so it's the publishing house that owes us satisfaction. We must go and ask them."

"If Ahti and Viljandi are the same person?"

"First of all, ask about *If on a winter's night a traveler*, make them give us a complete copy, and also a complete copy of *Outside the town of Malbork*. I mean copies of the novels we began to read, thinking they had that title; and then, if their real titles and authors are different, the publishers must tell us and explain the mystery behind these pages that move from one volume to another."

"And in this way," you add, "perhaps we will find a trail that will lead us to *Leaning from the steep slope*, unfinished or completed, whichever it may be . . ."

"I must admit," Ludmilla says, "that when I heard the rest had been found, I allowed my hopes to rise."

". . . and also to *Without fear of wind or vertigo*, which is the one I'd be impatient to go on with now. . . ."

"Yes, me, too, though I have to say it isn't my ideal novel. . . ."

Here we go again. The minute you think you're on the right track, you promptly find yourself blocked by a switch: in your reading, in the search for the lost book, in the identification of Ludmilla's tastes.

"The novel I would most like to read at this moment," Ludmilla explains, "should have as its driving force only the desire to narrate, to pile stories upon stories, without trying to impose a philosophy of life on you, simply allowing you to observe its own growth, like a tree, an entangling, as if of branches and leaves. . . ."

On this point you are in immediate agreement with her; putting behind you pages lacerated by intellectual analyses, you dream of rediscovering a condition of natural reading, innocent, primitive. . . .

"We must find again the thread that has been lost," you say. "Let's go to the publishers' right now."

And she says, "There's no need for both of us to confront them. You go and then report."

Chapter five

You're hurt. This hunt excites you because you're pursuing it with her, because the two of you can experience it together and discuss it as you are experiencing it. Now, just when you thought you had reached an accord with her, an intimacy, not so much because now you also call each other *tu,* but because you feel like a pair of accomplices in an enterprise that perhaps nobody else can understand.

"Why don't you want to come?"

"On principle."

"What do you mean?"

"There's a boundary line: on one side are those who make books, on the other those who read them. I want to remain one of those who read them, so I take care always to remain on my side of the line. Otherwise, the unsullied pleasure of reading ends, or at least is transformed into something else, which is not what I want. This boundary line is tentative, it tends to get erased: the world of those who deal with books professionally is more and more crowded and tends to become one with the world of readers. Of course, readers are also growing more numerous, but it would seem that those who use books to produce other books are increasing more than those who just like to read books and nothing else. I know that if I cross that boundary, even as an exception, by chance, I risk being mixed up in this advancing tide; that's why I refuse to set foot inside a publishing house, even for a few minutes."

"What about me, then?" you reply.

"I don't know about you. Decide for yourself. Everybody reacts in a different way."

There's no making this woman change her mind. You will carry out the expedition by yourself, and you and she will meet here again, in this café, at six.

"You've come about your manuscript? It's with the reader; no, I'm getting that wrong, it's been read, very interesting, of course, now I remember! Remarkable sense of language, heartfelt denunciation, didn't you receive our letter? We're very sorry to have to tell you, in the letter it's all explained, we sent it some time ago, the mail is so slow these days, you'll receive it of course, our list is overloaded, unfavorable economic situation. Ah, you see? You've received it. And what else did it say? Thanking you for having allowed us to read it, we will return it promptly. Ah, you've come to collect the manuscript? No, we haven't found it, do just be patient a bit longer, it'll turn up, nothing is ever lost here, only today we found a manuscript we'd been looking for these past ten years, oh, not another ten years, we'll find yours sooner, at least let's hope so, we have so many manuscripts, piles this high, if you like we'll show them to you, of course you want your own, not somebody else's, that's obvious, I mean we preserve so many manuscripts we don't care a fig about, we'd hardly throw away yours which means so much to us, no, not to publish it, it means so much for us to give it back to you."

The speaker is a little man, shrunken and bent, who seems to shrink and bend more and more every time anyone calls him, tugs at his sleeve, presents a problem to him, empties a pile of proofs into his arms. "Mr. Cavedagna!" "Look, Mr. Cavedagna!" "We'll ask Mr. Cavedagna!" And every time, he concentrates on the query of the latest interlocutor, his eyes staring, his chin quivering, his neck twisting in the effort to keep pending and in plain view all the other unresolved queries, with the mournful patience of overnervous people and the ultrasonic nervousness of overpatient people.

When you came into the main office of the publishing firm and explained to the doormen the problem of the wrongly bound books you would like to exchange, first they told you to go to Administration; then, when you added that it wasn't only the exchange of books that interested you but also an explanation of what had hap-

Chapter five

pened, they sent you to Production; and when you made
it clear that what mattered to you was the continuation of
the story of the interrupted novels, "Then you'd better
speak with our Mr. Cavedagna," they concluded. "Have a
seat in the waiting room; some others are already in there;
your turn will come."

And so, making your way among the other visitors, you
heard Mr. Cavedagna begin several times the story of the
manuscript that couldn't be found, each time addressing
different people, yourself included, and each time being
interrupted before realizing his mistake, by visitors or by
other editors and employees. You realize at once that Mr.
Cavedagna is that person indispensable to every firm's
staff, on whose shoulders his colleagues tend instinctively
to unload all the most complex and tricky jobs. Just as you
are about to speak to him, someone arrives bearing a production schedule for the next five years to be brought up
to date, or an index of names in which all the page numbers must be changed, or an edition of Dostoyevsky that
has to be reset from beginning to end because every time
it reads Maria now it should read Mar'ja and every time
it says Pyotr it has to be corrected to Pëtr. He listens to
everybody, though always tormented by the thought of
having broken off the conversation with a previous postu-
lant, and as soon as he can he tries to appease the more
impatient, assuring them he hasn't forgotten them, he is
keeping their problem in mind. "We much admired the
atmosphere of fantasy. . . ." ("What?" says a historian of
Trotskyite splinter groups in New Zealand, with a jolt.)
"Perhaps you should tone down some of the scatological
images. . . ." ("What are you talking about?" protests a
specialist in the macroeconomy of the oligopolises.)

Suddenly Mr. Cavedagna disappears. The corridors of
the publishing house are full of snares: drama coopera-
tives from psychiatric hospitals roam through them,
groups devoted to group analysis, feminist commandos.

Chapter five

Mr. Cavedagna, at every step, risks being captured, besieged, swamped.

You have turned up here at a time when those hanging around publishing houses are no longer aspiring poets or novelists, as in the past, would-be poetesses or lady writers; this is the moment (in the history of Western culture) when self-realization on paper is sought not so much by isolated individuals as by collectives: study seminars, working parties, research teams, as if intellectual labor were too dismaying to be faced alone. The figure of the author has become plural and moves always in a group, because nobody can be delegated to represent anybody: four ex-convicts of whom one is an escapee, three former patients with their male nurse and the male nurse's manuscript. Or else there are pairs, not necessarily but tendentially husband and wife, as if the shared life of a couple had no greater consolation than the production of manuscripts.

Each of these characters has asked to speak with the person in charge of a certain department or the expert in a certain area, but they all end up being shown in to Mr. Cavedagna. Waves of talk from which surface the vocabularies of the most specialized and most exclusive disciplines and schools are poured over this elderly editor, whom at first glance you defined as "a little man, shrunken and bent," not because he is more of a little man, more shrunken, more bent than so many others, or because the words "little man, shrunken and bent" are part of his way of expressing himself, but because he seems to have come from a world where they still—no: he seems to have emerged from a book where you still encounter—you've got it: he seems to have come from a world in which they still read books where you encounter "little men, shrunken and bent."

Without allowing himself to be distracted, he lets the arrays of problems flow over his bald pate, he shakes his

Chapter five

head, and he tries to confine the question to its more practical aspects: "But couldn't you, forgive me for asking, include the footnotes in the body of the text, and perhaps condense the text a bit, and even—the decision is yours— turn it into a footnote?"

"I'm a reader, only a reader, not an author," you hasten to declare, like a man rushing to the aid of somebody about to make a misstep.

"Oh, really? Good, good! I'm delighted!" And the glance he gives you really is a look of friendliness and gratitude. "I'm so pleased. I come across fewer and fewer readers. . . ."

He is overcome by a confidential urge: he lets himself be carried away; he forgets his other tasks; he takes you aside. "I've been working for years and years for this publisher . . . so many books pass through my hands . . . but can I say that I read? This isn't what I call reading. . . . In my village there were few books, but I used to read, yes, in those days I did read. . . . I keep thinking that when I retire I'll go back to my village and take up reading again, as before. Every now and then I set a book aside, I'll read this when I retire, I tell myself, but then I think that it won't be the same thing any more. . . . Last night I had a dream, I was in my village, in the chicken coop of our house, I was looking, looking for something in the chicken coop, in the basket where the hens lay their eggs, and what did I find? A book, one of the books I read when I was a boy, a cheap edition, the pages tattered, the black-and-white engravings all colored, by me, with crayons . . . You know? As a boy, in order to read, I would hide in the chicken coop. . . ."

You start to explain to him the reason for your visit. He understands at once, and doesn't even let you continue: "You, too! The mixed-up signatures, we know all about it, the books that begin and don't continue, the entire recent

97

production of the firm is in turmoil, you've no idea. We can't make head or tail of it any more, my dear sir."

In his arms he has a pile of galleys; he sets them down gently, as if the slightest jolt could upset the order of the printed letters. "A publishing house is a fragile organism, dear sir," he says. "If at any point something goes askew, then the disorder spreads, chaos opens beneath our feet. Forgive me, won't you? When I think about it I have an attack of vertigo." And he covers his eyes, as if pursued by the sight of billions of pages, lines, words, whirling in a dust storm.

"Come, come, Mr. Cavedagna, don't take it like this." Now it's your job to console him. "It was just a reader's simple curiosity, my question. . . . But if there's nothing you can tell me . . ."

"What I know, I'll tell you gladly," the editor says. "Listen. It all began when a young man turned up in the office, claiming to be a translator from the whatsitsname, from the youknowwhat. . . ."

"Polish?"

"No, no, Polish indeed! A difficult language, one not many people know . . ."

"Cimmerian?"

"Not Cimmerian. Farther on. What do you call it? This person passed himself off as an extraordinary polyglot, there was no language he didn't know, even whatchamacallit, Cimbrian, yes, Cimbrian. He brings us a book written in that language, a great big novel, very thick, whatsitsname, the *Traveler*, no, the *Traveler* is by the other one, *Outside the town* . . ."

"By Tazio Bazakbal?"

"No, not Bazakbal, this was the *Steep slope*, by whosit. . . ."

"Ahti?"

"Bravo, the very one. Ukko Ahti."

"But . . . I beg your pardon: isn't Ukko Ahti a Cimmerian author?"

Chapter five

"Well, to be sure, he was Cimmerian before, Ahti was; but you know what happened, during the war, after the war, the boundary adjustments, the Iron Curtain, the fact is that now there is Cimbria where Cimmeria used to be, and Cimmeria has shifted farther on. And so Cimmerian literature was also taken over by the Cimbrians, as part of their war reparations. . . ."

"This is the thesis of Professor Galligani, which Professor Uzzi-Tuzii rejects. . . ."

"Oh, you can imagine the rivalry at the university between departments, two competing chairs, two professors who can't stand the sight of each other, imagine Uzzi-Tuzii admitting that the masterpiece of his language has to be read in the language of his colleague. . . ."

"The fact remains," you insist, "that *Leaning from the steep slope* is an unfinished novel, or, rather, barely begun. . . . I saw the original. . . ."

"*Leaning* . . . Now, don't get me mixed up, it's a title that sounds similar but isn't the same, it's something with *Vertigo*, yes, it's the *Vertigo* of Viljandi."

"*Without fear of wind or vertigo*? Tell me: has it been translated? Have you published it?"

"Wait. The translator, a certain Ermes Marana, seemed a young man with all the proper credentials: he hands in a sample of the translation, we schedule the title, he is punctual in delivering the pages of the translation, a hundred at a time, he pockets the payments, we begin to pass the translation on to the printer, to have it set, in order to save time. . . . And then, in correcting the proofs, we notice some misconstructions, some oddities. . . . We send for Marana, we ask him some questions, he becomes confused, contradicts himself. . . . We press him, we open the original text in front of him and request him to translate a bit orally. . . . He confesses he doesn't know a single word of Cimbrian!"

"And what about the translation he turned in to you?"

"He had put the proper names in Cimbrian, no, in

Cimmerian, I can't remember, but the text he had translated was from another novel. . . ."

"What novel?"

"What novel? we ask him. And he says: A Polish novel
(there's your Polish!) by Tazio Bazakbal . . ."

"Outside the town of Malbork . . ."

"Exactly. But wait a minute. That's what he said, and
for the moment we believed him; the book was already on
the presses. We stop everything, change the title page, the
cover. It was a big setback for us, but in any case, with
one title or another, by one author or the other, the novel
was there, translated, set, printed. . . . We calculated that
all this to-ing and fro-ing with the print shop, the bindery,
the replacement of all the first signatures with the wrong
title page—in other words, it created a confusion that
spread to all the new books we had in stock, whole runs
had to be scrapped, volumes already distributed had to be
recalled from the booksellers. . . ."

"There's one thing I don't understand: what novel are
you talking about now? The one with the station or the
one with the boy leaving the farm? Or—?"

"Bear with me. What I've told you is only the beginning. Because by now, as is only natural, we no longer
trust this gentleman, and we want to see the picture
clearly, compare the translation with the original. And
what do we discover next? It wasn't the Bazakbal, either,
it was a novel translated from the French, a book by an
almost unknown Belgian author, Bertrand Vandervelde,
entitled . . . Wait: I'll show you."

Cavedagna goes out, and when he reappears he hands
you a little bundle of photocopies. "Here, it's called *Looks
down in the gathering shadow*. We have here the French
text of the first pages. You can see with your own eyes,
judge for yourself what a swindle! Ermes Marana translated this trashy novel, word by word, and passed it off to
us as Cimmerian, Cimbrian, Polish. . . ."

Chapter five

You leaf through the photocopies and from the first glance you realize that this *Regarde en bas dans l'épaisseur des ombres* by Bertrand Vandervelde has nothing in common with any of the four novels you have had to give up reading. You would like to inform Cavedagna at once, but he is producing a paper attached to the file, which he insists on showing you: "You want to see what Marana had the nerve to reply when we charged him with this fraud? This is his letter. . . ." And he points out a paragraph for you to read.

"What does the name of an author on the jacket matter? Let us move forward in thought to three thousand years from now. Who knows which books from our period will be saved, and who knows which authors' names will be remembered? Some books will remain famous but will be considered anonymous works, as for us the epic of Gilgamesh; other authors' names will still be well known, but none of their works will survive, as was the case with Socrates; or perhaps all the surviving books will be attributed to a single, mysterious author, like Homer."

"Did you ever hear such reasoning?" Cavedagna exclaims; then he adds, "And he might even be right, that's the rub. . . ."

He shakes his head, as if seized by a private thought; he chuckles slightly, and sighs slightly. This thought of his, you, Reader, can perhaps read on his brow. For many years Cavedagna has followed books as they are made, bit by bit, he sees books be born and die every day, and yet the true books for him remain others, those of the time when for him they were like messages from other worlds. And so it is with authors: he deals with them every day, he knows their fixations, indecisions, susceptibilities, egocentricities, and yet the true authors remain those who for him were only a name on a jacket, a word that was part of the title, authors who had the same reality as their characters, as the places mentioned in the books, who existed and didn't exist at the same time, like those characters and those countries. The author was an invisible point from which the books came, a void traveled by ghosts, an underground tunnel that put other worlds in communication with the chicken coop of his boyhood. . . .

Somebody calls him. He hesitates a moment, undecided whether to take back the photocopies or to leave them with you. "Mind you, this is an important document; it can't leave these offices, it's the corpus delicti, there could be a trial for plagiarism. If you want to examine it, sit down here at this desk, and remember to give it back to me, even if I forget it, it would be a disaster if it were lost. . . ."

You could tell him it didn't matter, this isn't the novel you were looking for, but partly because you rather like its opening, and partly because Mr. Cavedagna, more and more worried, has been swept away by the whirlwind of his publishing activities, there is nothing for you to do but start reading *Looks down in the gathering shadow.*

Looks down in the gathering shadow

It was all very well for me to pull up the mouth of the plastic bag: it barely reached Jojo's neck, and his head stuck out. Another way would be to put him into the sack head first, but that still didn't solve the problem, because then his feet emerged. The solution would have been to make him bend his knees, but much as I tried to help him with some kicks, his legs, which had become stiff, resisted, and in the end when I did succeed, legs and sack bent together: he was still harder to move and the head stuck out worse than before.

"When will I manage really to get rid of you, Jojo?" I said to him, and every time I turned him around I found that silly face of his in front of me, the heart-throb mustache, the hair soldered with brilliantine, the knot of his tie sticking out of the sack as if from a sweater, I mean a sweater dating from the years when he still followed the fashion. Maybe Jojo had arrived at the fashion of those years a bit late, when it was no longer the fashion anywhere, but having envied as a young man those characters dressed like that, with their hair like that, from their brilliantine to their black patent-leather shoes with velvet saddles, he had identified that look with good fortune, and once he had made it he was too taken up with his own success to look around and notice that the men he wanted to resemble had a completely different appearance.

The brilliantine held well; even when I pressed his skull, to push him down into the sack, his crown of hair remained spherical and split only into compact strips that stood up in an arc. The knot of his tie had gone a bit crooked; instinctively I started to straighten it, as if a corpse with a crooked tie might attract more attention than a corpse that was neat.

"You need another sack to stick over his head," Bernadette said, and once again I had to admit that girl's intelligence was superior to what you would expect from one of her background.

The trouble was that we couldn't manage to find another large-size plastic bag. There was only one, for a kitchen garbage can, a small orange sack that could serve very well to conceal his head, but not to conceal the fact that this was a human body contained in one sack, with the head contained in a smaller one.

But the way things were, we couldn't stay in that basement any longer, we had to get rid of Jojo before daylight, we had already been carrying him around for a couple of hours as if he were alive, a third passenger in my convertible, and we had already attracted the attention of too many people. For instance, those two cops on their bicycles who came over quietly and stopped to look at us as we were about to tip him into the river (the Pont de Bercy had seemed deserted a moment before), and immediately Bernadette and I start slapping him on the back, Jojo slumped there, his head and hands swaying over the rail, and I cry, "Go ahead, vomit it all up, *mon vieux*, it'll clear your head!" And, both of us supporting him, his arms around our necks, we carry him to the car.

At that moment the gas that accumulates in the belly of corpses is expelled noisily; the two cops burst out laughing. I thought that Jojo dead had quite a different character from the living Jojo, with his finicky manners; and, alive, he wouldn't have been so generous, coming to the aid of two friends who were risking the guillotine for his murder.

Then we started looking for the plastic bag and the can of gas, and now all we had to find was the place. It seems impossible, in a big city like Paris, but you can waste hours looking for the right place to burn up a corpse. "Isn't there a forest at Fontainebleau?" I say, starting the motor, to Bernadette, who has sat down beside me again. "Tell me the way; you know the road." And I thought that perhaps when the sun had tinged the sky gray we would be coming back into the city in the line of trucks carrying vegetables, and in a clearing among the hornbeams nothing would be left of Jojo but a charred and fetid residue, and my past as well. And as well, I say, this might be the time when I can convince myself that all my pasts are burned and forgotten, as if they had never existed.

How many times had I realized that my past was beginning to weigh on me, that there were too many people who thought I was in their debt, materially and morally—for example, at Macao, the parents of the girls of the "Jade Garden" (I mention them because there's nothing worse than Chinese relations when it comes to not being able to get rid of them) and yet when I hired the girls I made a straightforward deal, with them and their families, and I paid cash, so as not to see them constantly turning up there, the skinny mothers and fathers in white socks, with a bamboo basket smelling of fish, with that lost expression as if they had come from the country, whereas they all lived in the port quarter. As I was saying, how many times, when the past weighed too heavily on me, had I been seized by that hope of a clean break: to change jobs, wife, city, continent—one continent after the other, until I had made the whole circle—habits, friends, business, customers. It was a mistake, but when I realized that, it was too late.

Because in this way all I did was to accumulate past after past behind me, multiplying the pasts, and if one life was too dense and ramified and embroiled for me to bear it always with me, imagine so many lives, each with its own past and the pasts of the other lives that continue to become entangled one with the others. It was all very well for me to say each time: What a relief, I'll turn the mileage back to zero, I'll erase the blackboard. The morning after the day I arrived in a new country, this zero had already become a number with so many ciphers that the meter was too small, it filled the blackboard from one side to the other, people, places, likes, dislikes, missteps. Like that night when we were looking for the right place to burn up Jojo, our headlights searching among the tree trunks and the rocks, and Bernadette pointing to the dashboard: "Look. Don't tell me we're out of gas." She was right. With all the things on my mind, I had forgotten to fill the tank, and now we risked ending up miles from nowhere with a broken-down car, at a time when all the service stations were closed. Fortunately, we hadn't set fire to Jojo yet: if we had come to a halt only a short distance from the pyre, we couldn't have run off on foot, leaving behind a car that could be identified as mine. In other words, all we could do was pour into our tank the can of gas meant to soak Jojo's blue suit, his monogrammed silk shirt, and then beat it back to the city as fast as possible, trying to dream up another plan for getting rid of him.

It was all very well for me to say that every time I had landed in a jam I had always extricated myself, from every lucky situation as well as from every disaster. The past is like a tapeworm, constantly growing, which I carry curled up inside me, and it never loses its rings no matter how hard I try to empty my guts in every WC, English-style or Turkish, or in the slop jars of prisons or the bed-pans of hospitals or the latrines of camps, or simply in the bushes, taking a good look first to make sure no snake will pop out, like that time in Venezuela. You can't change your past any more than you can change your name; in spite of all the passports I've had, with names I can't even remember, everybody has always called me Ruedi the Swiss. Wherever I went and however I introduced myself, there has always been somebody who knew who I was and what I had done, even though my appearance has changed a lot with the passing years, especially since my head has become hairless and yellow as a grapefruit, which happened during the typhoid epidemic aboard the *Stjärna*, because, considering the cargo we were carrying, we couldn't approach shore or even radio for help.

Anyway, the conclusion to which all stories come is that the life a person has led is one and one alone, uniform and compact as a shrunken blanket where you can't distin-guish the fibers of the weave. And so if by chance I hap-pen to dwell on some ordinary detail of an ordinary day, the visit of a Singhalese who wants to sell me a litter of newborn crocodiles in a zinc tub, I can be sure that even in this tiny, insignificant episode there is implicit every-thing I have experienced, all the past, the multiple pasts I have tried in vain to leave behind me, the lives that in the end are soldered into an overall life, my life, which con-tinues even in this place from which I have decided I must not move any more, this little house with a court-yard garden in the Parisian *banlieu* where I have set up my tropical-fish aquarium, a quiet business, which forces me more than any other would to lead a stable life, be-cause you can't neglect the fish, not even for one day, and as for women, at my age you have earned the right not to feel like getting involved in new troubles.

Looks down in the gathering shadow

Bernadette is a different story. With her I could say I had proceeded without a single error: as soon as I had learned Jojo was back in Paris and was on my trail, I didn't delay a moment before setting out on his trail, and so I discovered Bernadette, and I was able to get her on my side, and we worked out the job together, without his suspecting a thing. At the right moment I drew the curtain aside and the first thing I saw of him—after all the years in which we had lost sight of each other—was the piston movement of his big hairy behind between her white knees; then the neatly combed hair on the back of his head on the pillow, beside her face, a bit wan, moving ninety degrees to leave me free to strike. Everything happened in the quickest and cleanest way, giving him no time to turn and recognize me, to know who had arrived to spoil his party, maybe not even to become aware of crossing the border between the hell of the living and the hell of the dead.

It was better like that, for me to look him in the face only as a dead man. "The game's over, you old bastard," I couldn't help saying to him, in an almost affectionate voice, while Bernadette was dressing him neatly, including the patent-leather-and-velvet shoes, because we had to carry him outside pretending he was so drunk he couldn't stand on his own feet. And I happened to think of our first meeting all those years ago in Chicago, in the back of old Mrs. Mikonikos's shop, full of busts of Socrates, when I realized that I had invested the insurance money from the faked fire in his rusty slot machines and that he and the old paralytic nymphomaniac had me in their power. The day before, looking from the dunes at the frozen lake, I had tasted such freedom as I had never felt for years, and in the course of twenty-four hours the space around me had closed again, and everything was being decided in a block of stinking houses between the Greek neighborhood and the Polish neighborhood. My

108

life had known turning points of this sort by the dozen, in one direction or the other, but after that I never stopped trying to get even with him, and since then the list of my losses had only grown longer. Even now that the smell of corpse began to rise through his cheap cologne, I realized that the game with him wasn't yet over, that Jojo dead could ruin me yet again as he had ruined me so often when alive.

I'm producing too many stories at once because what I want is for you to feel, around the story, a saturation of other stories that I could tell and maybe will tell or who knows may already have told on some other occasion, a space full of stories that perhaps is simply my lifetime, where you can move in all directions, as in space, always finding stories that cannot be told until other stories are told first, and so, setting out from any moment or place, you encounter always the same density of material to be told. In fact, looking in perspective at everything I am leaving out of the main narration, I see something like a forest that extends in all directions and is so thick that it doesn't allow light to pass: a material, in other words, much richer than what I have chosen to put in the foreground this time, so it is not impossible that the person who follows my story may feel himself a bit cheated, seeing that the stream is dispersed into so many trickles, and that of the essential events only the last echoes and reverberations arrive at him; but it is not impossible that this is the very effect I aimed at when I started narrating, or let's say it's a trick of the narrative art that I am trying to employ, a rule of discretion that consists in maintaining my position slightly below the narrative possibilities at my disposal.

Which, if you look closer, is the sign of real wealth, solid and vast, in the sense that if, we'll assume, I had only one story to tell, I would make a huge fuss over this story and would end up botching it in my rage to show it in its

true light, but, actually having in reserve a virtually unlimited supply of narratable material, I am in a position to
handle it with detachment and without haste, even allowing a certain irritation to be perceptible and granting myself the luxury of expatiating on secondary episodes and
insignificant details.

Every time the little gate creaks—I'm in the shed with
the tanks at the end of the garden—I wonder from which
of my pasts the person is arriving, seeking me out even
here: maybe it is only the past of yesterday and of this
same suburb, the squat Arab garbage collector who in
October begins his rounds for tips, house by house, with a
Happy New Year card, because he says that his colleagues
keep all the December tips for themselves and he never
gets a penny; but it could also be the more distant pasts
pursuing old Ruedi, finding the little gate in the Impasse:
smugglers from Valais, mercenaries from Katanga, croup-
iers from the Varadero casino and the days of Fulgencio
Batista.

Bernadette had no part in any of my pasts; she knew
nothing of the old business between Jojo and me that had
forced me to eliminate him like that, maybe she believed I
had done it for her, for what she had told me of the life he
has forced her into. And for the money, naturally, which
was no pittance, even if I couldn't yet say that I felt it in
my pocket. It was our common interest that kept us together: Bernadette is a girl who catches on right away; in
that mess, either we managed to get out of it together or
we were both done for. But certainly Bernadette had something else in the back of her mind: a girl like her, if she's
going to get by, has to be able to count on somebody who
knows his way around; if she had got me to rid her of Jojo,
it was in order to put me in his place. There had been all
too many stories of this sort in my past, and they had all
been total losses for me; this was why I had retired from
business and didn't want to go back into it.

And so, when we were about to begin our nighttime wanderings, with him all snappily dressed and sitting properly in the back of the convertible, and her sitting beside me up front, forced to stretch one arm back to hold him steady, as I was about to start the engine, suddenly she flings her left leg over the gearshift and puts it on top of my right leg. "Bernadette!" I cry. "What are you doing?" And she explains to me that when I burst into the room I interrupted her at a moment when she can't be interrupted; never mind whether with one of us or the other, she had to pick up at that same point and keep on till the end. Meanwhile with one hand she was holding the dead man and with the other she was unbuttoning me, all three of us crammed into that tiny car, in a public parking lot of the Faubourg Saint-Antoine. Wriggling her legs in contortions—harmonious ones, I must say—she sat astride my knees and almost smothered me in her bosom as in a landslide. Jojo meanwhile was falling on top of us, but she was careful to push him aside, her face only inches from the face of the dead man, who looked at her with the whites of his widened eyes. As for me, caught by surprise like this, with my physical reactions following their own course, obviously preferring to obey her than to follow my own terrified spirit, without even having to move, since she thought of everything—well, I realized then that what we were doing was a ceremony to which she attached a special meaning, there before the dead man's eyes, and I felt the soft, very tenacious grip closing and I couldn't escape her.

"You've got it wrong, girl," I would have liked to say to her. "That dead man died because of another story, not yours, a story that hasn't ended yet." I would have liked to tell her that there was another woman between me and Jojo, in that story not yet ended, and if I keep skipping from one story to another it's because I keep circling around that story and escaping, as if it were the first day of my escape, the minute I learned that she and Jojo had joined forces to ruin me. It's a story that sooner or later I'll also end up telling, but in the midst of all the others, not giving more importance to one than to another, not putting any special passion into it beyond the pleasure of narrating and remembering, because even remembering evil can be a pleasure when the evil is mixed I won't say with good, but with variety, the volatile, the changeable, in other words with what I can also call good, which is the pleasure of seeing things from a distance and narrating them as what is past.

"This will also be fun to tell when we're out of it," I said to Bernadette, getting into that elevator with Jojo in the plastic sack. Our plan was to drop him off the terrace of the top floor into a very narrow courtyard, where the next morning whoever found him would think of suicide or else a misstep during a robbery. And what if someone got into the elevator at one of the other floors and saw us with the sack? I would say the elevator had been called upstairs just as we were taking out the garbage. In fact it would soon be dawn.

"You can foresee all possible situations," Bernadette says. And how could I have managed otherwise, I would like to say to her, having to watch out for Jojo's mob for so many years, when he had his men in all the key cities of the big traffic? But I would have to explain to her the whole background of Jojo and that other woman, who never stopped demanding that I get him back the stuff that they said they lost through my fault, demanding I put around my neck again that chain of blackmail that still forces me to spend the night looking for a resting place for an old friend in a plastic sack.

With the Singhalese, too, I thought there was something behind the visit. "I don't handle crocodiles, *jeune homme*," I said to him. "Try the zoo, I deal in other articles, I supply the shops downtown, private aquariums in people's apartments, exotic fish, at the most turtles. They ask for iguanas now and then, but I don't stock them. Too delicate."

The boy—he must have been eighteen—stayed put; his mustache and eyelashes seemed like black feathers on his orange cheeks.

"Who sent you to me? Satisfy my curiosity," I asked him, because when Southeast Asia is involved, I am always distrustful, and I have my own good reasons.

"Mademoiselle Sibylle," he says.

"What does my daughter have to do with crocodiles?" I cry. It's true, she's been living on her own for some time now, but whenever I hear news of her I become uneasy. I don't know why, the thought of children has always inspired me with a kind of remorse.

And so I learn that in a boîte on Place Clichy, Sibylle does a number with alligators; at first the news made such a nasty impression on me that I didn't ask for further details. I knew she was working in nightclubs, but the idea that she exhibits herself in public with a crocodile seems to me the last thing a father could wish as the future of his only daughter; at least for a man like me, who had a Protestant upbringing.

"What's it called, this great nightclub?" I say, livid. "I'd like to go and have a look for myself."

He hands me a little cardboard advertisement, and I immediately feel cold sweat down my back, because that name, the Nouvelle Titania, looks familiar to me, all too familiar, even if these are memories from another part of the globe.

"And who runs it?" I ask. "Yes, the manager, the boss!"

"Ah, Madame Tatarescu, you mean. . . ." And he lifts the zinc tub again, to take the litter away.

I was staring at that tangle of green scales, claws, tails, gaping mouths, and it was as if I had been clubbed on the skull, my ears transmitted nothing now but a grim buzz, a roar, the trumpet of the beyond, as soon as I had heard the name of that woman from whose destroying influence I had managed to tear Sibylle, covering our traces across two oceans, constructing for the girl and me a calm, silent life. All in vain. Vlada had caught up with her daughter, and through Sibylle she again had me in her power, with the capacity only she possessed for rousing in me the fiercest aversion and the darkest attraction. Already she was sending me a message in which I could recognize her: that roiling of reptiles, to remind me that evil was the only vital element for her, that the world was a pit of crocodiles which I could not escape.

In the same way I looked, leaning from the terrace, down at the bottom of that leprous courtyard. The sky was already brightening, but down there the darkness was still thick, and I could barely make out the irregular stain that Jojo had become after hurtling through the void with the flaps of his jacket spread out like wings and after shattering all his bones with a boom like a firearm's.

The plastic sack had remained in my hand. We could leave it there, but Bernadette was afraid that if they found it, they would be able to reconstruct the way things had gone, so it was best to take it away and get rid of it.

On the ground floor, as we opened the elevator, there were three men with their hands in their pockets.

"Hello, Bernadette."

And she said, "Hello."

I didn't like the idea of her knowing them, especially since the way they dressed, though more up to date than Jojo's, betrayed, to my eyes, a certain family likeness.

"What are you carrying in that sack? Let's have a look," the biggest of the three says.

"See for yourself. It's empty," I say, calmly.

He sticks one hand into it. "What's this, then?" He takes out a black patent-leather shoe with a velvet saddle.

[6]

The pages of photocopying stop at this point, but for you the only thing that matters now is to continue your reading. Somewhere the complete volume must exist; you look around, seeking it with your gaze, but promptly lose heart; in this office books are considered raw material, spare parts, gears to be dismantled and reassembled. Now you understand Ludmilla's refusal to come with you; you are gripped by the fear of having also passed over to "the other side" and of having lost that privileged relationship with books which is peculiar to the reader: the ability to consider what is written as something finished and definitive, to which there is nothing to be added, from which there is nothing to be removed. But you are consoled by the faith Cavedagna continues to cherish in the possibility of innocent reading, even here.

Now the elderly editor reemerges from the glass partitions. Grab him by the sleeve, tell him you want to read the rest of *Looks down in the gathering shadow*.

"Ah, heaven only knows where it's got to. . . . All the papers in the Marana business have vanished. His typescripts, the original texts, Cimbrian, Polish, French. He's vanished, everything's vanished, overnight."

"And you've heard no more from him?"

"No, he wrote. . . . We've received many letters. . . . Tales that don't make any sense . . . I won't try to tell them to you, because I wouldn't know where to begin. I would have to spend hours reading through the entire correspondence."

"Could I have a look at it?"

Realizing you are determined to see the thing through, Cavedagna agrees to have them bring you the "Marana, Ermes" file from the archives.

"Do you have some free time? Good. Sit here and read. Then you can tell me what you think. Who knows? Maybe you'll be able to make some sense out of it."

In writing to Cavedagna, Marana always has some practical reason: to justify his delay in the delivery of the translations, to press for payment of the advances, to point out new foreign publications they shouldn't let slip through their fingers. But among these normal subjects of business correspondence appear hints of intrigues, plots, mysteries, and to explain these hints, or to explain why he is unwilling to say more, Marana in the end becomes embroiled in increasingly frenzied and garbled volubility.

The letters are addressed from places scattered over five continents, although they never seem to have been entrusted to the normal post, but, rather, to random messengers who mail them elsewhere, so the stamps on the envelopes do not correspond to the countries of provenance. The chronology is also uncertain: there are letters that refer to previous communications, which, however, prove to have been written later; there are letters that promise further explanations, which instead are found in pages dated a week earlier.

"Cerro Negro," the name—it would seem—of a remote village in South America, appears in the heading of the last letters; but exactly where it is, whether climbing up the Cordillera of the Andes or enshrouded in the forests of the Orinoco, cannot be comprehended from the contradictory glimpses of the landscape that are suggested. The letter you have before you looks like a normal business letter: but how on earth did a Cimmerian-language publishing firm end up down there? And how, if their editions are aimed at the limited market of Cimmerian emigrants in the two Americas, can they publish Cimmerian translations of *brand-new books* by the most celebrated international authors for which they have the *world rights* also in the authors' original languages? The fact remains that

Chapter six

Ermes Marana, who apparently has become their manager, offers Cavedagna an option on the new and eagerly awaited novel *In a network of lines that enlace* by the famous Irish writer Silas Flannery.

Another letter, again from Cerro Negro, is written, on the contrary, in a tone of inspired evocation: reporting—it seems—a local legend, it tells of an old Indian known as the Father of Stories, a man of immemorial age, blind and illiterate, who uninterruptedly tells stories that take place in countries and in times completely unknown to him. The phenomenon has brought expeditions of anthropologists and parapsychologists; it has been determined that many novels published by famous authors had been recited word for word by the wheezing voice of the Father of Stories several years before their appearance. The old Indian, according to some, is the universal source of narrative material, the primordial magma from which the individual manifestations of each writer develop; according to others, a seer who, thanks to his consumption of hallucinatory mushrooms, manages to establish communication with the inner world of the strongest visionary temperaments and pick up their psychic waves; according to still others he is the reincarnation of Homer, of the storyteller of the *Arabian Nights*, of the author of the Popol Vuh, as well as of Alexandre Dumas and James Joyce; but there are those who reply that Homer has no need of metempsychosis, since he never died and has continued through the millennia living and composing, the author, besides the couple of poems usually attributed to him, also of many of the most famous narratives known to man. Ermes Marana, putting a tape recorder to the mouth of the cave where the old man hides . . .

But from a previous letter, this time headed New York, the origin of the unpublished works offered by Marana would seem to be something quite different:

117

Chapter six

"The headquarters of the OEPHLW, as you see from the letterhead, is in the old Wall Street district. Ever since the business world deserted these austere buildings, their ecclesiastical appearance, inspired by English banks, has become quite sinister. I press a buzzer. 'It's Ermes. I'm bringing you the beginning of the Flannery novel.' They have been waiting for me for some time, since I wired from Switzerland that I had managed to persuade that elderly author of thrillers to entrust to me the beginning of the novel he was unable to continue, assuring him that our computers would be capable of completing it easily, programmed as they are to develop all the elements of a text with perfect fidelity to the stylistic and conceptual models of the author."

The delivery of those pages to New York was not easy, if we are to believe what Marana writes from a capital in black Africa, giving his adventurous streak free rein:

"We went on, immersed, the plane in a curly cream of clouds, I in the reading of the unpublished work of Silas Flannery, *In a network of lines that enlace*, precious manuscript lusted after by the international publishing world, which I had daringly taken from the author. And suddenly the mouth of a sawed-off Tommy gun is placed on the bridge of my eyeglasses.

"A commando of armed young people has taken over the plane; the reek of perspiration is unpleasant; I soon realize that their chief objective is the capture of my manuscript. These kids belong to the OAP, surely; but the latest bunch of militants are totally unknown to me; grave, hairy faces and a superior attitude are not characteristics that allow me to distinguish which of the movement's two wings they belong to.

". . . I won't tell you at length about the puzzled peregrinations of our aircraft, whose route kept bouncing from one control tower to another, inasmuch as no airport was prepared to receive us. Finally President Butamatari, a dictator with humanistic leanings, allowed the exhausted jet to land on the bumpy runway of his airport, which bordered on the brousse, and he assumed the role of mediator between the extremist commando and the terrified chancelleries of the great powers. For us hostages the days stretch out limp and frayed under a zinc lean-to in the dusty desert. Bluish vultures peck at the ground, pulling out earthworms."

It becomes clear, from the way he addresses them as soon as he is face to face with them, that there is a bond between Marana and the OAP pirates:

" 'Go home, babies, and tell your boss next time to send more bright-eyed scouts, if he wants to bring his bibliography up to date.' They look at me with that adenoidal, sleepy expression of agents caught off guard. This sect consecrated to the worship and the unearthing of secret books has ended up in the hands of kids who have only a vague idea of their mission. 'Who are you?' they ask me. The moment they hear my name they stiffen. New to the organization, they couldn't have known me personally, and all they knew about me was the slander circulated after my expulsion: double or triple or quadruple agent, in the service of God knows who and what. Nobody knows that the Organization of Apocryphal Power, which I founded, had a meaning only as long as my control kept it from falling under the sway of unreliable gurus. 'You took us for those Wing of Light characters, didn't you?' they say to me. 'For your information, we are the Wing of Shadow, and we won't fall into your traps!' This was what I wanted to know. I merely shrugged my shoulders and smiled. Wing of Shadow or Wing of Light, for both sides I'm the traitor to be eliminated, but here they can do nothing to me any more, since President Butamatari, who has guaranteed them the right of asylum, has taken me under his protection. . . ."

Chapter six

But why should the OAP hijackers want to get possession of that manuscript? You glance through the papers, seeking an explanation, but you find mostly the bragging of Marana, who gives himself credit for diplomatically arranging the agreement by which Butamatari, having disarmed the commando and got hold of the Flannery manuscript, assures its restitution to the author, asking in exchange that the author commit himself to writing a dynastic novel that will justify the leader's imperial coronation and his aims of annexing the bordering territories.

"I was the one who proposed the formula of the agreement and conducted the negotiations. Once I introduced myself as the representative of the 'Mercury and the Muses' agency, specializing in the advertising and exploitation of literary and philosophical works, the situation took its proper course. Having gained the African dictator's trust, having regained that of the Celtic writer (by purloining his manuscript, I have saved it from the capture plots devised by various secret organizations), I then found it easy to persuade the parties to accept a contract advantageous for both. . . ."

An earlier letter, headed from Liechtenstein, permits a reconstruction of the preliminary relations between Flannery and Marana: "You must not believe the rumors in circulation, according to which this Alpine principality houses only the administrative and fiscal headquarters of the limited company that holds the copyright and signs the contracts of the fertile, best-selling author, whose personal whereabouts are unknown and whose actual existence is in doubt. . . . I must say that my first encounters, with secretaries who shunted me to attorneys, who shunted me to agents, seemed to confirm your information. . . . The company that exploits this elderly author's endless verbal production of thrills, crimes, and embraces is structured like an efficient private bank. But the atmosphere reigning there was one of uneasiness and anxiety, as if on the eve of a crash. . . .

"It didn't take me long to discover the reasons: for several months Flannery has been suffering a crisis. He can't write a line; the numerous novels he has begun and for which he has been paid advances by publishers all over the world, involving banks and financing on an international level, these novels in which the brands of liquor to be drunk by the characters, the tourist spots to be visited, the haute-couture creations, furnishings, gadgets, have already been determined by contract through specialized advertising agencies, all remain unfinished, at the mercy of this spiritual crisis, unexplained and unforeseen. A team of ghost writers, experts in imitating the master's style in all its nuances and mannerisms, is ready and waiting to step in and plug the gaps, polish and complete the half-written texts so that no reader could distinguish the parts written by one hand from those by another. . . . (It seems that their contribution has already played a considerable role in our man's most recent production.) But now Flannery is telling everybody to wait; he postpones deadlines, announces changes of plan, promises to get back to work as soon as possible, rejects offers of help. According to the more pessimistic rumors, he has started writing a diary, a notebook of reflections, in which nothing ever happens, only moods and the description of the landscape he contemplates for hours from his balcony, through a spyglass. . . ."

In a more euphoric vein the message that, some days later, Marana sends from Switzerland goes: "Make a note of this: where all fail, Ermes Marana succeeds! I have succeeded in speaking with Flannery in person. He was on the terrace of his chalet, watering the potted zinnias. He is a trim, calm old man, pleasant-mannered, as long as he isn't seized by one of his nervous fits. . . . I could give you a great deal of news about him, valuable for your publishing activities, and I will do so the moment I receive some token of your interest, via telex to the bank where I have an account whose number I will now give you. . . ."

The reasons that Marana was impelled to visit the old novelist are not clear from the correspondence: to some extent it seems that he introduced himself as representative of the OEPHLW of New York (Organization for the Electronic Production of Homogenized Literary Works), offering him technical assistance to finish his novel ("Flannery turned pale, trembled, clutched the manuscript to his bosom. 'No, not that,' he said, 'I would never allow it'"); and partly he seems to have gone there to defend the interests of a Belgian writer who had been shamelessly plagiarized by Flannery, Bertrand Vandervelde. . . . But when Marana wrote Cavedagna asking to be put in contact with the writer-recluse, the original idea was apparently to propose, as background for the climactic episodes of his next novel, *In a network of lines that enlace*, an island in the Indian Ocean "that stands out with its ocher-colored beaches against the cobalt deep." The proposition was made in the name of a Milanese real-estate investment firm, with a view toward developing the island, creating a village of bungalows purchasable on the installment plan and by correspondence.

Marana's duties in this firm seem to be connected with "public relations for the development of Developing Countries, with special reference to revolutionary movements, before and after their coming to power, with the aim of procuring and guaranteeing construction permits under the various changes of regime." In this guise, his first mission was carried out in a sultanate of the Persian Gulf where he was to negotiate the subcontract for the construction of a skyscraper. A fortuitous occasion, connected with his work as a translator, had opened to him doors normally closed to any European. . . . "The latest wife of the Sultan comes from our country, a woman of sensitive and restless temperament who suffers from the isolation in which she is confined by the geographical position, the local customs, and by court etiquette, though she is sustained by her insatiable passion for reading. . . ."

Forced to abandon the novel *Looks down in the gathering shadow* because of a production defect in her copy, the young Sultana wrote to the translator, protesting. Marana rushed to Arabia. "An old woman, veiled and bleary, motioned me to follow her. In a roofed garden, among the bergamots and the lyrebirds and the jets of fountains, she came toward me, cloaked in indigo, a mask on her face, green silk dotted with white gold, a strand of aquamarines on her brow. . . ."

You would like to know more about this Sultana; your eyes nervously scour the pages of thin airmail paper as if you expected to see her appear at any moment. . . . But it seems that Marana, too, in filling page after page, is moved by the same desire, is pursuing her as she conceals herself. . . . With each letter the story proves more complicated: writing to Cavedagna from "a sumptuous residence at the edge of the desert," Marana tries to explain his sudden disappearance, telling how the Sultan's emissaries obliged him by force (or persuaded him with an appetizing contract?) to move down there, to continue his work, exactly as before. . . . The Sultan's wife must never remain without books that please her: a clause in the marriage contract is involved, a condition the bride imposed on her august suitor before agreeing to the wedding. . . . After a serene honeymoon in which the young sovereign received the latest works of the major Western literatures in the original languages, which she reads fluently, the situation became tricky. . . . The Sultan fears, apparently with reason, a revolutionary plot. His secret service dis-

Chapter six

covered that the conspirators receive coded messages hidden in pages printed in our alphabet. He decreed an embargo, in effect ever since, and ordered the confiscation of all Western books in his lands. Also, the supplying of his consort's personal library has been stopped. An innate mistrust—supported, it seems, by specific evidence—leads the Sultan to suspect his wife of conniving with the revolutionaries. But failure to fulfill the famous clause in the marriage contract would bring about a rupture very onerous for the reigning dynasty, as the lady did not hesitate to threaten in the storm of wrath that overwhelmed her when the guards tore from her hands a novel she had barely begun—the one by Bertrand Vandervelde, to be precise.

It was then that the secret service of the sultanate, learning that Ermes Marana was translating that novel into the lady's native language, persuaded him, with convincing arguments of diverse nature, to move to Arabia. The Sultana receives regularly each evening the stipulated quantity of fictional prose, no longer in the original editions, but in typescript fresh from the translator's hands. If a coded message were hidden in the succession of words or letters of the original, it would now be irretrievable. . . .

"The Sultan sent for me to ask me how many pages I still have to translate in order to finish the book. I realized that in his suspicions of political-conjugal infidelity, the moment he most fears is the drop in tension that will follow the end of the novel, when, before beginning another, his wife will again be attacked by impatience with her condition. He knows the conspirators are waiting for a sign from the Sultana to light the fuse, but she has given orders never to disturb her while she is reading, not even if the palace were about to blow up. . . . I have my own reasons for fearing that moment, which could mean the loss of my privileges at court. . . ."

Chapter six

And so Marana proposes to the Sultan a stratagem prompted by the literary tradition of the Orient: he will break off this translation at the moment of greatest suspense and will start translating another novel, inserting it into the first through some rudimentary expedient; for example, a character in the first novel opens a book and starts reading. The second novel will also break off to yield to a third, which will not proceed very far before opening into a fourth, and so on. . . .

Many feelings distress you as you leaf through these letters. The book whose continuation you were already enjoying in anticipation, vicariously through a third party, breaks off again. . . . Ermes Marana appears to you as a serpent who injects his malice into the paradise of reading. . . . In the place of the Indian seer who tells all the novels of the world, here is a trap-novel designed by the treacherous translator with beginnings of novels that remain suspended . . . just as the revolt remains suspended, while the conspirators wait in vain to begin it with their illustrious accomplice, and time weighs motionless on the flat shores of Arabia. . . . Are you reading or daydreaming? Do the effusions of a graphomane have such power over you? Are you also dreaming of the petroliferous Sultana? Do you envy the lot of the man decanting novels in the seraglios of Arabia? Would you like to be in his place, to establish that exclusive bond, that communion of inner rhythm, that is achieved through a book's being read at the same time by two people, as you thought possible with Ludmilla? You cannot help giving the faceless lady reader evoked by Marana the features of the Other Reader whom you know; you already see Ludmilla among the mosquito nets, lying on her side, the wave of her hair flowing on the page, in the enervating season of the monsoons, while the palace conspiracy sharpens its blades in silence, and she abandons herself to the flow of reading as if to the sole possible action of life in a world where only arid sand remains over strata of oily bitumen and the risk of death for reasons of state and the division of sources of energy. . . .

You look through the correspondence again seeking more recent news of the Sultana. . . . You see other female figures appear and disappear:

in the island in the Indian Ocean, a woman on a beach "dressed in a pair of big dark glasses and a smearing of walnut oil, placing between her person and the beams of the dog days' sun the brief shield of a popular New York magazine." The issue she is reading publishes in advance the beginning of the new thriller by Silas Flannery. Marana explains to her that magazine publication of the first chapter is the sign that the Irish writer is ready to conclude contracts with firms interested in having brands of whisky appear in the novel, or of champagne, automobile models, tourist spots. "It seems his imagination is stimulated, the more advertising commissions he receives." The woman is disappointed: she is a devoted reader of Silas Flannery. "The novels I prefer," she says, "are those that make you feel uneasy from the very first page. . . ."

from the terrace of the Swiss chalet, Silas Flannery is looking through a spyglass mounted on a tripod at a young woman in a deck chair, intently reading a book on another terrace, two hundred meters below in the valley. "She's there every day," the writer says. "Every time I'm about to sit down at my desk I feel the need to look at her. Who knows what she's reading? I know it isn't a book of mine, and instinctively I suffer at the thought, I feel the jealousy of my books, which would like to be read the way she reads. I never tire of watching her: she seems to live in a sphere suspended in another time and another space. I sit down at the desk, but no story I invent corresponds to what I would like to convey." Marana asks

126

him if this is why he is no longer able to work. "Oh, no, I write," he answered; "it's now, only now that I write, since I have been watching her. I do nothing but follow the reading of that woman, seen from here, day by day, hour by hour. I read in her face what she desires to read, and I write it faithfully." "Too faithfully," Marana interrupts him, icily. "As translator and representative of the interests of Bertrand Vandervelde, author of the novel that woman is reading, *Looks down in the gathering shadow*, I warn you to stop plagiarizing it!" Flannery turns pale; a single concern seems to occupy his mind: "Then, according to you, that reader . . . the books she is devouring with such passion are novels by Vandervelde? I can't bear it. . . ."

in the African airport, among the hostages of the hijacking who are waiting sprawled on the ground, fanning themselves or huddled into the blankets distributed by the hostesses at nightfall, when the temperature dropped suddenly, Marana admires the imperturbability of a young woman who is crouching off to one side, her arms grasping her knees, raised beneath her long skirt to act as lectern; her hair, falling on the book, hiding her face; her hand limply turning the pages as if all that mattered were decided there, in the next chapter. "In the degradation that prolonged and promiscuous captivity imposes on the appearance and the behavior of all of us, this woman seems to me protected, isolated, enveloped as if in a distant moon. . . ." It is then that Marana thinks: I must convince the OAP pirates that the book that made setting up their whole risky operation worthwhile is not the one they have confiscated from me, but this one that she is reading. . . .

in New York, in the control room, the reader is soldered to the chair at the wrists, with pressure manometers and a stethoscopic belt, her temples beneath their crown of hair

127

held fast by the serpentine wires of the encephalogram that mark the intensity of her concentration and the frequency of stimuli. "All our work depends on the sensitivity of the subject at our disposal for the control tests: and it must, moreover, be a person of strong eyesight and nerves, to be subjected to the uninterrupted reading of novels and variants of novels as they are turned out by the computer. If reading attention reaches certain highs with a certain continuity, the product is viable and can be launched on the market; if attention, on the contrary, relaxes and shifts, the combination is rejected and its elements are broken up and used again in other contexts." The man in the white smock rips off one encephalogram after another, as if they were pages from a calendar. "Worse and worse," he says. "Not one novel being produced holds up. Either the programming has to be revised or the reader is not functioning." I look at the slim face between the blinders and the visor, impassive also because of the earplugs and the chin strap that keeps the jaw from moving. What will her fate be?

You find no answer to this question that Marana lets fall almost with indifference. Holding your breath, you have followed from letter to letter the transformations of the woman reader, as if it were always the same person. But even if they were many persons, to all of them you attribute the appearance of Ludmilla. . . . Isn't it like her to insist that now one can ask of the novel only to stir a depth of buried anguish, as the final condition of truth which will save it from being an assembly-line product, a destiny it can no longer escape? The image of her naked under the equatorial sun already seems more credible to you than that of her behind the Sultana's veil, but it could still be a single Mata Hari who moves, pensively, through extra-European revolutions to open the way for the bulldozers of a cement firm. . . . Dispel this image, and receive that of the deck chair as it comes toward you through the limpid Alpine air. Here you are ready to drop everything: leave, track down Flannery's hideaway, simply to watch with a spyglass the woman reading or to seek her traces in the diary of the blocked writer. . . . (Or is what tempts you the idea of being able to resume your own reading of *Looks down in the gathering shadow,* even under another title and signed by another name?) But now Marana transmits more and more distressing news: there she is hostage of hijackers, then prisoner in a Manhattan slum. How did she end up over there, chained to an instrument of torture? Why is she being forced to undergo as a torment what is her natural condition, reading? And what hidden plan makes the paths of these characters cross constantly: she, Marana, the mysterious sect that steals manuscripts?

As far as you are able to gather from hints scattered through these letters, Apocryphal Power, riven by internecine battles and eluding the control of its founder, Ermes Marana, has broken into two groups: a sect of enlightened followers of the Archangel of Light and a sect of nihilist followers of the Archon of Shadow. The former are convinced that among the false books flooding the world they can track down the few that bear a truth perhaps extrahuman or extraterrestrial. The latter believe that only counterfeiting, mystification, intentional falsehood can represent absolute value in a book, a truth not contaminated by the dominant pseudo truths.

"I thought I was alone in the elevator," Marana writes, again from New York. "Instead a form rises at my side: a youth with hair of arboreal extent had been crouched in a corner, wrapped in clothes of rough canvas. This is not a proper elevator so much as a freight elevator, a cage closed by a folding gate. At every floor a perspective of deserted rooms appears, faded walls with the mark of vanished furniture and uprooted pipes, a desert of moldy floors and ceilings. Using his red hands with their long wrists, the young man stops the elevator between two floors.

" 'Give me the manuscript. We're the ones you have brought it to, not the others. Even if you were thinking the opposite. This is a *true* book, even if its author has written so many false ones. So it comes to us.'

"With a judo movement he knocks me to the floor and seizes the manuscript. I realize at this moment that the young fanatic is convinced he is holding the diary of Silas Flannery's spiritual crisis and not the outline of one of his usual thrillers. It's amazing how prompt these secret sects are to pick up any piece of news, whether true or false, that coincides with their expectations. Flannery's crisis had aroused the two rival factions of Apocryphal Power and, with opposing hopes, they had unleashed their informers in the valleys around the novelist's chalet. The Wing of Shadow people, knowing that the great fabricator of assembly-line novels was no longer able to believe in his tricks, had convinced themselves that his next novel would mark the switch from cheap and relative bad faith to essential and absolute bad faith, the masterpiece of falsity as knowledge, and would therefore be the book they had been seeking for such a long time. The Wing of Light followers, on the other hand, thought that from the crisis of such a professional in falsehood only a cataclysm of truth could be born, and this is what they believed the writer's diary of which there was so much talk would be. . . . At the rumor, circulated by Flannery, that I had stolen an important manuscript from him, each side identified the manuscript with the object of its search, and both set out to find me, the Wing of Shadow causing the hijacking of the plane, the Wing of Light that of the elevator. . . .

"The arboreal young man, having hidden the manuscript in his jacket, slipped out of the elevator, slammed the gate in my face, and is now pressing the button to make me disappear downward, after hurling a final threat at me: 'The score with you isn't settled, Agent of Mystification! We still have to liberate our Sister chained to the machine of the Counterfeiters!' I laugh as I slowly sink. 'There is no machine, kiddo. It's the Father of Stories who dictates our books!'

"He brings the elevator back up. 'Did you say the Father of Stories?' He has turned pale. For years the followers of the sect have been searching for the old blind man, across all the continents, where his legend is handed down in countless local variants.

" 'Yes, go tell that to the Archangel of Light! Tell him I've found the Father of Stories! I have him in my hands, and he's working for me! Electronic machine, my foot!' And now I'm the one who presses the DOWN button."

At this point three simultaneous desires are competing in your soul. You would be ready to leave immediately, cross the ocean, explore the continent beneath the Southern Cross until you can find the latest hiding place of Ermes Marana and wrest the truth from him, or at least get from him the continuations of the interrupted novels. At the same time you want to ask Cavedagna if he can immediately let you read *In a network of lines that enlace* by the pseudo (or genuine?) Flannery, which might also be the same thing as *Looks down in the gathering shadow* by the genuine (or pseudo?) Vandervelde. And you can't wait to run to the café where you are to meet Ludmilla, to tell her the confused results of your investigation and to convince yourself, by seeing her, that there can be nothing in common between her and the women readers encountered around the world by the mythomane translator.

The last two desires are easily satisfied, and are not mutually exclusive. In the café, waiting for Ludmilla, you begin to read the book sent by Marana.

In a network of lines that enlace

The first sensation this book should convey is what I feel when I hear the telephone ring; I say "should" because I doubt that written words can give even a partial idea of it: it is not enough to declare that my reaction is one of refusal, of flight from this aggressive and threatening summons, as it is also a feeling of urgency, intolerableness, coercion that impels me to obey the injunction of that sound, rushing to answer even though I am certain that nothing will come of it save suffering and discomfort. Nor do I believe that instead of an attempted description of this state of the spirit, a metaphor would serve better— for example, the piercing sting of an arrow that penetrates a hip's naked flesh. This is not because one cannot employ an imaginary sensation to portray a known sensation— though nobody these days knows the feeling of being struck by an arrow, we all believe we can easily imagine it, the sense of being helpless, without protection in the presence of something that reaches us from alien and unknown spaces, and this also applies very well to the ring of the telephone—but, rather, because the arrow's per-

emptory inexorability, without modulations, excludes all
the intentions, implications, hesitations possible in the
voice of someone I do not see, though even before he says
anything I can already predict, if not what he will say, at
least what my reaction to what he is about to say will be.
Ideally, the book would begin by giving the sense of a
space occupied by my presence, because all around me
there are only inert objects, including the telephone, a
space that apparently cannot contain anything but me,
isolated in my interior time, and then there is the interruption of the continuity of time, the space is no longer
what it was before because it is occupied by the ring, and
my presence is no longer what it was before because it is
conditioned by the will of this object that is calling. The
book would have to begin by conveying all this not
merely immediately, but as a diffusion through space and
time of these rings that lacerate the continuity of space
and time and will.

Perhaps the mistake lies in establishing that at the beginning I and a telephone are in a finite space such as my
house would be, whereas what I must communicate is my
situation with regard to numerous telephones that ring;
these telephones are perhaps not calling me, have no relation to me, but the mere fact that I can be called to a
telephone suffices to make it possible or at least conceivable that I may be called by all telephones. For example,
when the telephone rings in a house near mine, for a moment I wonder if it is ringing in my house—a suspicion
that immediately proves unfounded but which still leaves
a wake, since it is possible that the call might really be for
me and through a wrong number or crossed wires it has
gone to my neighbor, and this is all the more possible
since in that house there is nobody to answer and the
telephone keeps ringing, and then in the irrational logic
that ringing never fails to provoke in me, I think: Perhaps
it is indeed for me, perhaps my neighbor is at home but

does not answer because he knows, perhaps also the person calling knows he is calling a wrong number but does so deliberately to keep me in this state, knowing I cannot answer but know that I should answer.

Or else the anxiety when I have just left the house and I hear a telephone ringing that could be in my house or in another apartment and I rush back, I arrive breathless, having run up the stairs, and the telephone falls silent and I will never know if the call was for me.

Or else also when I am out in the streets, and I hear telephones ring in strange houses; even when I am in strange cities, in cities where my presence is unknown to anyone, even then, hearing a ring, my first thought every time for a fraction of a second is that the telephone is calling me, and in the following fraction of a second there is the relief of knowing myself excluded for the moment from every call, unattainable, safe, but this relief also lasts a mere fraction of a second, because immediately afterward I think that it is not only that strange telephone that is ringing; many kilometers away, hundreds, thousands of kilometers, there is also the telephone in my house, which certainly at that same moment is ringing repeatedly in the deserted rooms, and again I am torn between the necessity and the impossibility of answering.

Every morning before my classes begin I do an hour of jogging; that is, I put on my Olympic sweatsuit and I go out to run, because I feel the need to move, because the doctors have ordered it to combat the excess weight that oppresses me, and also to relieve my nerves a little. During the day in this place, if you do not go to the campus, to the library, to audit colleagues' courses, or to the university coffee shop, you do not know where to go; therefore the only thing is to start running this way or that on the hill, among the maples and the willows, as many students do and also many of my colleagues. We cross on the rustling paths of leaves and sometimes we say "Hi!" to each other, sometimes nothing, because we have to save our breath. This, too, is an advantage running has over other sports: everybody is on his own and is not required to answer to others.

The hill is entirely built up, and as I run I pass two-story wooden houses with yards, all different and all similar, and every so often I hear a telephone ring. This makes me nervous; instinctively I slow down; I prick up my ears to hear whether somebody is answering and I become impatient when the ringing continues. Continuing my run, I pass another house in which a telephone is ringing, and I think: There is a telephone chasing me, there is somebody looking up all the numbers on Chestnut Lane in the directory, and he is calling one house after the other to see if he can overtake me.

Sometimes the houses are all silent and deserted, squirrels run up the tree trunks, magpies swoop down to peck at the feed set out for them in wooden bowls. As I run, I feel a vague sensation of alarm, and even before I can pick up the sound with my ear, my mind records the possibility of the ring, almost summons it up, sucks it from its own absence, and at that moment from a house comes, first muffled then gradually more distinct, the trill of the bell, whose vibrations perhaps for some time had already been caught by an antenna inside me before my hearing perceived them, and there I go rushing in an absurd frenzy, I am the prisoner of a circle in whose center is the telephone ringing inside that house, I run without moving away, I hover without shortening my stride.

"If nobody has answered by now, it means nobody is home. . . . But why do they keep calling, then? What are they hoping? Does a deaf man perhaps live there, and do they hope that by insisting they will make themselves heard? Perhaps a paralytic lives there, and you have to allow a great deal of time so that he can crawl to the phone. . . . Perhaps a suicide lives there, and as long as you keep calling him, some hope remains of preventing his extreme act. . . ." I think perhaps I should try to make myself useful, lend a hand, help the deaf man, the paralytic, the suicide. . . . And at the same time I think—in the absurd logic at work inside me—that in doing so, I could make sure the call is not by chance for me. . . .

Still running, I push open the gate, enter the yard, circle the house, explore the ground behind it, dash behind the garage, to the tool shed, the doghouse. Everything seems deserted, empty. Through an open window in the rear a room can be seen, in disorder, the telephone on the table continuing to ring. The shutter slams; the window frame is caught in the tattered curtain.

I have circled the house three times; I continue to perform the movements of jogging, raising elbows and heels, breathing with the rhythm of my run so that it is clear my intrusion is not that of a thief; if they caught me at this moment I would have a hard time explaining that I came in because I heard the telephone ring. A dog barks; not here—it is the dog of another house that cannot be seen—but for a moment the signal "barking dog" is stronger in me than the "ringing telephone," and this is enough to open a passage in the circle that was holding me prisoner there; now I resume running among the trees along the street, leaving behind me the increasingly muffled ringing.

I run until there are no more houses. In a field I stop to catch my breath. I do some knee bends, some push-ups, I massage the muscles of my legs so they will not get cold. I look at the time. I am late, I must go back if I do not want to keep my students waiting. All I need is for the rumor to spread that I go running through the woods when I should be teaching. . . . I fling myself onto the return road, paying no attention to anything; I will not even recognize that house, I will pass it without noticing. For that matter, the house is exactly like the others in every respect, and the only way it could stand out would be if the telephone were to ring again, which is impossible. . . .

In a network of lines that enlace

The more I turn these thoughts over in my head, as I run downhill, the more I seem to hear that ring again; it grows more and more clear and distinct, there, I am again in sight of the house and the telephone is still ringing. I enter the garden, I go around behind the house, I run to the window. I have only to reach out to pick up the receiver. Breathless, I say, "He's not here . . ." and from the receiver a voice—a bit vexed, but only a bit, for what is most striking about this voice is its coldness, its calm—says: "Now, you listen to me. Marjorie is here, she'll be waking in a little while, but she's tied up and can't get away. Write down this address carefully: one-fifteen Hillside Drive. If you come to get her, OK; otherwise, there's a can of kerosene in the basement and a charge of plastic attached to a timer. In half an hour this house will go up in flames. . . ."

"But I'm not—" I begin to answer.

They have already hung up.

Now what do I do? Of course I could call the police, the fire department, on this same telephone, but how can I explain, how can I justify the fact that I, in other words how can I who have nothing to do with it have anything to do with it? I start running again, I circle the house once more, then I resume my way.

I am sorry for this Marjorie, but if she has got herself into such a jam she must be mixed up in God knows what things, and if I stepped forward to save her, nobody would believe that I do not know her, there would be a great scandal, I am a professor at another university invited here as visiting professor, the prestige of both universities would suffer. . . .

To be sure, when a life is in the balance these considerations should take a back seat. . . . I slow down. I could enter any one of these houses, ask them if they will let me call the police, say first of all quite clearly that I do not know this Marjorie, I do not know any Marjorie. . . .

137

In a network of lines that enlace

To tell the truth, here at the university there is a student named Marjorie, Marjorie Stubbs: I noticed her immediately among the girls attending my classes. She is a girl who you might say appealed to me a lot, too bad that the time I invited her to my house to lend her some books an embarrassing situation may have been created. It was a mistake to invite her: this was during my first days of teaching, they did not yet know the sort I am here, she could misunderstand my intentions, that misunderstanding in fact took place, an unpleasant misunderstanding, even now very hard to clarify because she has that ironic way of looking at me, and I am unable to address a word to her without stammering, the other girls also look at me with an ironic smile. . . .

Yes, I would not want this uneasiness now reawakened in me by the name Marjorie to keep me from intervening to help another Marjorie, whose life is in danger. . . . Unless it is the same Marjorie . . . Unless that telephone call was aimed personally at me . . . A very powerful band of gangsters is keeping an eye on me, they know that every morning I go jogging along that road, maybe they have a lookout on the hill with a telescope to follow my steps, when I approach that deserted house they call on the telephone, it is me they are calling, because they know the unfortunate impression I made on Marjorie that day at my house and they are blackmailing me. . . .

Almost without realizing it, I find myself at the entrance to the campus, still running, in jogging garb and running shoes, I did not stop by my house to change and pick up my books, now what do I do? I continue running across the campus, I meet some girls drifting over the lawn in little groups, they are my students already on their way to my class, they look at me with that ironic smile I cannot bear.

Still making running movements, I stop Lorna Clifford and I ask her, "Is Stubbs here?"

In a network of lines that enlace

The Clifford girl blinks. "Marjorie? She hasn't shown up for two days. . . . Why?"

I have already run off. I leave the campus. I take Grosvenor Avenue, then Cedar Street, then Maple Road. I am completely out of breath, I am running only because I cannot feel the ground beneath my feet, or my lungs in my chest. Here is Hillside Drive. Eleven, fifteen, twenty-seven, fifty-one; thank God the numbers go fast, skipping from one decade to the next. Here is 115. The door is open, I climb the stairs, I enter a room in semidarkness. There is Marjorie, tied on a sofa, gagged. I release her. She vomits. She looks at me with contempt.

"You're a bastard," she says to me.

[7]

You are seated at a café table, reading the Silas Flannery novel Mr. Cavedagna has lent you and waiting for Ludmilla. Your mind is occupied by two simultaneous concerns: the interior one, with your reading, and the other, with Ludmilla, who is late for your appointment. You concentrate on your reading, trying to shift your concern for her to the book, as if hoping to see her come toward you from the pages. But you're no longer able to read, the novel has stalled on the page before your eyes, as if only Ludmilla's arrival could set the chain of events in motion again.

They page you. It is your name the waiter is repeating among the tables. Get up, you're wanted on the telephone. Is it Ludmilla? It is. "I'll explain later. I can't come now."

"Look: I have the book! No, not that one, none of those: a new one. Listen. . . ." Surely you don't mean to tell her the story of the book over the telephone? Wait and hear her out, hear what she wants to say to you.

"You join me," Ludmilla says. "Yes, come to my house. I'm not at home now, but I won't be long. If you get there first, you can go on in and wait for me. The key is under the mat."

A nonchalant simplicity in her way of living, the key under the mat, trust in her fellow man—also very little to be stolen, of course. You run to the address she has given you. You ring, in vain. As she told you, she isn't home. You find the key. You enter the penumbra of the lowered blinds.

A single girl's house, Ludmilla's house: she lives alone. Is this the first thing you want to verify? Whether there are signs of a man's presence? Or do you prefer to avoid knowing it as long as possible, to live in ignorance, in suspicion? Certainly something restrains you from snooping around (you have raised the blinds slightly, but only slightly). Perhaps it is the consideration that if you take advantage of her trust to carry out a detective investigation, then you are unworthy of it. Or perhaps it's because you think you already know by heart what a single girl's little apartment is like; even before looking at it, you could list the inventory of its contents. We live in a uniform civilization, within well-defined cultural models: furnishings, decorative elements, blankets, record player have been chosen among a certain number of given possibilities. What can they reveal to you about what she is really like?

What are you like, Other Reader? It is time for this book in the second person to address itself no longer to a general male you, perhaps brother and double of a hypocrite I, but directly to you who appeared already in the second chapter as the Third Person necessary for the novel to be a novel, for something to happen between that male Second Person and the female Third, for something to take form, develop, or deteriorate according to the phases of human events. Or, rather, to follow the mental models through which we live our human events. Or, rather, to follow the mental models through which we attribute to human events the meanings that allow them to be lived.

This book so far has been careful to leave open to the Reader who is reading the possibility of identifying himself with the Reader who is read: this is why he was not given a name, which would automatically have made him the equivalent of a Third Person, of a character (whereas to you, as Third Person, a name had to be given, Ludmilla), and so he has been kept a pronoun, in the abstract condition of pronouns, suitable for any attribute and any action. Let us see, Other Reader, if the book can succeed in drawing a true portrait of you, beginning with the frame and enclosing you from every side, establishing the outlines of your form.

You appeared for the first time to the Reader in a bookshop; you took shape, detaching yourself from a wall of shelves, as if the quantity of books made the presence of a young lady Reader necessary. Your house, being the place in which you read, can tell us the position books occupy in your life, if they are a defense you set up to keep the outside world at a distance, if they are a dream into which you sink as if into a drug, or bridges you cast toward the outside, toward the world that interests you so much that you want to multiply and extend its dimensions through books. To understand this, our Reader knows that the first step is to visit the kitchen.

The kitchen is the part of the house that can tell the most things about you: whether you cook or not (one would say yes, if not every day, at least fairly regularly), whether only for yourself or also for others (often only for yourself, but with care, as if you were cooking also for others; and sometimes also for others, but nonchalantly, as if you were cooking only for yourself), whether you tend toward the bare minimum or toward gastronomy (your purchases and gadgets suggest elaborate and fanciful recipes, at least in your intentions; you may not necessarily be greedy, but the idea of a couple of fried eggs for supper would probably depress you), whether standing over the stove represents for you a painful necessity or also a pleasure (the tiny kitchen is equipped and arranged in such a way that you can move practically and without too much effort, trying not to linger there too long but also being able to stay there without reluctance). The appliances are in their place, useful animals whose merits must be remembered, though without devoting special worship to them. Among the utensils a certain aesthetic tendency is noticeable (a panoply of half-moon choppers, in decreasing sizes, when one would be enough), but in general the decorative elements are also serviceable objects, with few concessions to prettiness. The provisions can tell us something about you: an assortment of herbs, some naturally in regular use, others that seem to be there to complete a collection; the same can be said of the mustards; but it is especially the ropes of garlic hung within reach that suggest a relationship with food not careless or generic. A glance into the refrigerator allows other valuable data to be gathered: in the egg slots only one egg remains; of lemons there is only a half and that half-dried; in other words, in basic supplies a certain neglect is noted. On the other hand, there is chestnut purée, black olives, a little jar of salsify or horseradish: it is clear that when shopping you succumb to the lure of the goods on display and don't bear in mind what is lacking at home.

Observing your kitchen, therefore, can create a picture of you as an extroverted, clearsighted woman, sensual and methodical; you make your practical sense serve your imagination. Could a man fall in love with you, just seeing your kitchen? Who knows? Perhaps the Reader, who was already favorably disposed.

He is continuing his inspection of the house to which you let him have the keys. There are countless things that you accumulate around you: fans, postcards, perfume bottles, necklaces hung on the walls. But on closer examination every object proves special, somehow unexpected. Your relationship with objects is selective, personal; only the things you feel yours become yours: it is a relationship with the physicality of things, not with an intellectual or affective idea that takes the place of seeing them and touching them. And once they are attached to you, marked by your possession, the objects no longer seem to be there by chance, they assume meaning as elements of a discourse, like a memory composed of signals and emblems. Are you possessive? Perhaps there is not yet enough evidence to tell: for the present it can be said that you are possessive toward yourself, that you are attached to the signs in which you identify something of yourself, fearing to be lost with them.

In one corner of the wall there are a number of framed photographs, all hung close together. Photographs of whom? Of you at various ages, and of many other people, men and women, and also very old photographs as if taken from a family album; but together they seem to have the function, not so much of recalling specific people, as of forming a montage of the stratifications of existence. The frames are all different, nineteenth-century Art Nouveau floral forms, frames in silver, copper, enamel, tortoiseshell, leather, carved wood: they may reflect the notion of enhancing those fragments of real life, but they may also be a collection of frames, and the photographs may be there only to occupy them; in fact some frames are occupied by pictures clipped from newspapers, one encloses an illegible page of an old letter, another is empty.

Nothing is hung on the rest of the wall, nor does any furniture stand against it. And the whole house is somewhat similar: bare walls here, crammed ones there, as if resulting from a need to concentrate signs into a kind of dense script, surrounded by the void in which to find repose and refreshment again.

The arrangement of the furniture and the objects on it is never symmetrical, either. The order you seek to attain (the space at your disposal is limited, but you show a certain care in exploiting it, to make it seem more extensive) is not the superimposition of a scheme, but the achievement of a harmony among the things that are there.

In short: are you tidy or untidy? Your house does not answer peremptory questions with a yes or a no. You have an idea of order, to be sure, even a demanding one, but in practice no methodical application corresponds to it. Obviously your interest in the home is intermittent; it follows the difficulty of your days, the ups and downs of your moods.

Are you depressive or euphoric? The house, in its wisdom, seems to have taken advantage of your moments of euphoria to prepare itself to shelter you in your moments of depression.

Are you really hospitable, or is the way you allow acquaintances to come into the house a sign of indifference? The Reader is looking for a comfortable place to sit and read without invading those spaces clearly reserved for you; he is forming the idea that a guest can be very comfortable in your house provided he can adjust to your rules.

What else? The potted plants don't seem to have been watered for several days, but perhaps you deliberately chose the kind that don't require much attention. For the rest, in these rooms there is no trace of dogs or cats or birds: you are a woman who tends not to increase responsibilities, and this can be a sign either of egoism or of concentration on other, less extrinsic, concerns, as also a sign that you do not need symbolic substitutes for the natural drives that lead you to be concerned with others, to take part in their stories, in life, in books. . . .

Let's have a look at the books. The first thing noticed, at least on looking at those you have most prominent, is that the function of books for you is immediate reading; they are not instruments of study or reference or components of a library arranged according to some order. Perhaps on occasion you have tried to give a semblance of order to your shelves, but every attempt at classification was rapidly foiled by heterogeneous acquisitions. The chief reason for the juxtaposition of volumes, besides the dimensions of the tallest or the shortest, remains chronological, as they arrived here, one after the other; anyway, you can always put your hand on any one, also because they are not very numerous (you must have left other bookshelves in other houses, in other phases of your existence), and perhaps you don't often find yourself hunting for a book you have already read.

In short, you don't seem to be a Reader Who Rereads. You remember very well everything you have read (this is one of the first things you communicated about yourself); perhaps for you each book becomes identified with your reading of it at a given moment, once and for all. And as you preserve them in your memory, so you like to preserve the books as objects, keeping them near you.

Among your books, in this assortment that does not make up a library, a dead or dormant part can still be distinguished, which is the store of volumes put aside, books read and rarely reread, or books you have not and will not read but have still retained (and dusted), and then a living part, which is the books you are reading or plan to read or from which you have not yet detached yourself or books you enjoy handling, seeing around you. Unlike the provisions in the kitchen, here it is the living part, for immediate consumption, that tells most about you. Numerous volumes are scattered, some left open, others with makeshift bookmarks or corners of the pages folded down. Obviously you have the habit of reading several books at the same time, you choose different things to read for the different hours of the day, the various corners of your home, cramped as it is: there are books meant for the bedside table, those that find their place by the armchair, in the kitchen, in the bathroom.

It could be an important feature to be added to your portrait: your mind has interior walls that allow you to partition different times in which to stop or flow, to concentrate alternately on parallel channels. Is this enough to say you would like to live several lives simultaneously? Or that you actually do live them? That you separate your life with one person or in one environment from your life with others, elsewhere? That in every experience you take for granted a dissatisfaction that can be redeemed only in the sum of all dissatisfactions?

Reader, prick up your ears. This suspicion is being insinuated into your mind, to feed your anxiety as a jealous man who still doesn't recognize himself as such. Ludmilla, herself reader of several books at once, to avoid being caught by the disappointment that any story might cause her, tends to carry forward, at the same time, other stories also. . . .

(Don't believe that the book is losing sight of you, Reader. The you that was shifted to the Other Reader can, at any sentence, be addressed to you again. You are always a possible you. Who would dare sentence you to loss of the you, a catastrophe as terrible as the loss of the I. For a second-person discourse to become a novel, at least two you's are required, distinct and concomitant, which stand out from the crowd of he's, she's, and they's.)

And yet the sight of the books in Ludmilla's house proves reassuring for you. Reading is solitude. To you Ludmilla appears protected by the valves of the open book like an oyster in its shell. The shadow of another man, probable, indeed certain, is if not erased, thrust off to one side. One reads alone, even in another's presence. But what, then, are you looking for here? Would you like to penetrate her shell, insinuating yourself among the pages of the books she is reading? Or does the relationship between one Reader and the Other Reader remain that of two separate shells, which can communicate only through partial confrontations of two exclusive experiences?

You have with you the book you were reading in the

café, which you are eager to continue, so that you can then hand it on to her, to communicate again with her through the channel dug by others' words, which, as they are uttered by an alien voice, by the voice of that silent nobody made of ink and typographical spacing, can become yours and hers, a language, a code between the two of you, a means to exchange signals and recognize each other.

A key turns in the lock. You fall silent, as if you wanted to surprise her, as if to confirm to yourself and to her that your being here is something natural. But the footstep is not hers. Slowly a man materializes in the hall, you see his shadow through the curtains, a leather windbreaker, a step indicating familiarity with the place but hesitant, as of someone looking for something. You recognize him. It is Irnerio.

You must decide immediately what attitude to take. The dismay at seeing him enter her house as if it were his is stronger than the uneasiness at being here yourself, half hidden. For that matter, you knew perfectly well that Ludmilla's house is open to her friends: the key is under the mat. Ever since you entered you have felt somehow brushed by faceless shadows. Irnerio is at least a known ghost. As you are for him.

"Ah, you're here." He takes note of you first but isn't surprised. This naturalness, which a moment ago you wanted to impose, doesn't cheer you now.

"Ludmilla isn't home," you say, at least to establish your precedence in the information, or actually in the occupation of the territory.

"I know," he says, indifferent. He searches around, handles the books.

"Can I be of help?" you proceed, as though you wanted to provoke him.

"I was looking for a book," Irnerio says.

"I thought you never read," you reply.

"It's not for reading. It's for making. I make things with books. I make objects. Yes, artworks: statues, pictures, whatever you want to call them. I even had a show. I fix the books with mastic, and they stay as they were. Shut, or open, or else I give them forms, I carve them, I make holes in them. A book is a good material to work with; you can make all sorts of things with it."

"And Ludmilla agrees?"

"She likes my things. She gives me advice. The critics say what I do is important. Now they're putting all my works in a book. They took me to talk with Mr. Cavedagna. A book with photographs of all my works. When this book is printed, I'll use it for another work, lots of works. Then they'll put them in another book, and so on."

"I meant, does Ludmilla agree with your taking away her books. . . ."

"She has lots. . . . Sometimes she gives me books herself, specifically for me to work on them, books she has no use for. But just any book won't do for me. There are some books that immediately give me the idea of what I can make from them, but others don't. Sometimes I have an idea, but I can't make it until I find the right book." He is disarranging the volumes on a shelf; he weighs one in his hand, observes its spine and its edge, puts it down. "There are books I find likable, and books I can't bear, and I keep coming across them."

And now the Great Wall of books you hoped would keep this barbarian invader far from Ludmilla is revealed as a toy that he takes apart with complete confidence. You laugh bitterly. "Apparently you know Ludmilla's library by heart. . . ."

"Oh, it's always the same stuff, mostly. . . . But it's nice to see the books all together. I love books. . . ."

"I don't follow you."

"Yes, I like to see books around. That's why it's nice here, at Ludmilla's. Don't you think so?"

The massing of written pages binds the room like the

thickness of the foliage in a dense wood, no, like stratifications of rock, slabs of slate, slivers of schist; so you try to see through Irnerio's eyes the background against which the living form of Ludmilla must stand out. If you are able to win his trust, Irnerio will reveal to you the secret that intrigues you, the relationship between the Non-reader and the Other Reader, Ludmilla. Quickly, ask him something on this subject, anything. "But you"—this is the only question that comes to your mind—"while she's reading, what do you do?"

"I don't mind watching her read," Irnerio says. "And besides, somebody has to read books, right? At least I can rest easy: I won't have to read them myself."

You have little cause to rejoice, Reader. The secret that is revealed to you, the intimacy between the two of them, consists in the complementary relationship of two vital rhythms. For Irnerio all that counts is the life lived instant by instant; art for him counts as expenditure of vital energy, not as a work that remains, not as that accumulation of life that Ludmilla seeks in books. But he also recognizes, without need of reading, that energy somehow accumulated, and he feels obliged to bring it back into circulation, using Ludmilla's books as the material base for works in which he can invest his own energy, at least for an instant.

"This one suits me," Irnerio says and is about to stick a volume in the pocket of his windbreaker.

"No, leave that one alone. It's the book I'm reading. And besides, it's not mine, I have to return it to Cavedagna. Pick another. Here, take this one. . . . It's almost the same. . . ."

You have picked up a volume with a red band—LATEST BEST SELLER BY SILAS FLANNERY—and this already explains the resemblance, since all of Flannery's novels are brought out in a specially designed series. But that isn't the only thing: the title that stands out on the dust jacket is *In a network of lines that* . . . These are two copies of the same book! You weren't expecting this. "Why, this really is odd! I would never have thought that Ludmilla already had it. . . ."

Irnerio holds up his hands. "This isn't Ludmilla's. I don't want to have anything to do with that stuff. I thought there weren't any more of them around."

"Why? Whose is it? What do you mean?"

Irnerio picks up the volume with two fingers, goes toward a little door, opens it, throws the book inside. You have followed him; you stick your head into a dark little storeroom; you see a table with a typewriter, a tape recorder, dictionaries, a voluminous file. From the file you take the sheet that acts as title page, you carry it to the light, you read: "Translation by Ermes Marana."

You are thunderstruck. Reading Marana's letters, you felt you were encountering Ludmilla at every turn. . . . Because you can't stop thinking of her: this is how you explained it, a proof of your being in love. Now, moving around Ludmilla's house, you come upon traces of Marana. Is it an obsession persecuting you? No, from the very beginning what you felt was a premonition that a relationship existed between them. . . . Jealousy, which has been a kind of game you played with yourself, now grips you relentlessly. And it isn't only jealousy: it is suspicion, distrust, the feeling that you cannot be sure of anything or anyone. . . . The pursuit of the interrupted book, which instilled in you a special excitement since you were conducting it together with the Other Reader, turns out to be the same thing as pursuing her, who eludes you in a proliferation of mysteries, deceits, disguises. . . .

"But . . . what's Marana got to do with it?" you ask. "Does he live here?"

Irnerio shakes his head. "He was here. Now time has passed. He shouldn't come back here again. But by now all his stories are so saturated with falsehood that anything said about him is false. He's succeeded in this, at least. The books he brought here look the same as the others on the outside, but I recognize them at once, at a distance. And when I think that there shouldn't be any more here, any more of his papers, except in that storeroom . . . But every now and then some trace of him pops up again. Sometimes I suspect he puts them here, he comes when nobody's around and keeps making his usual deals, secretly. . . ."

"What deals?"

"I don't know. . . . Ludmilla says that whatever he touches, if it isn't false already, becomes false. All I know is that if I tried to make my works out of books that were his, they would turn out false: even if they looked the same as the ones I'm always making. . . ."

"But why does Ludmilla keep his things in that storeroom? Is she waiting for him to come back?"

"When he was here, Ludmilla was unhappy. . . . She didn't read any more. . . . Then she ran away. . . . She was the first to go off. . . . Then he went. . . ."

The shadow is going away. You can breathe again. The past is closed. "What if he showed up again?"

"She'd leave once more. . . ."

"For where?"

"Hmm . . . Switzerland . . . I don't know. . . ."

"Is there another man in Switzerland?" Instinctively you have thought of the writer with the spyglass.

"You can call him another man, but it's an entirely different sort of story. The old thriller guy . . ."

"Silas Flannery?"

"She said that when Marana convinces her that the difference between the true and the false is only a prejudice of ours, she feels the need to see someone who makes books the way a pumpkin vine makes pumpkins—that's how she put it. . . ."

Chapter seven

The door opens suddenly. Ludmilla enters, flings her coat onto a chair, her packages. "Ah, how marvelous! So many friends! Sorry I'm late!"

You are having tea, sitting with her. Irnerio should also be there, but his armchair is empty.

"He was there. Where has he gone?"

"Oh, he must have left. He comes and goes without saying anything."

"People come and go like that, in your house?"

"Why not? How did you get in?"

"I, and all the others!"

"What is this? A jealous scene?"

"What right would I have?"

"Do you think that the time will come when you could have the right? If so, it's best not even to begin."

"Begin what?"

You set the cup on the coffee table. You move from the armchair to the sofa, where she is sitting.

(To begin. You're one who said it, Ludmilla. But how to establish the exact moment in which a story begins? Everything has already begun before, the first line of the first page of every novel refers to something that has already happened outside the book. Or else the real story is the one that begins ten or a hundred pages further on, and everything that precedes it is only a prologue. The lives of individuals of the human race form a constant plot, in which every attempt to isolate one piece of living that has a meaning separate from the rest—for example, the meeting of two people, which will become decisive for both— must bear in mind that each of the two brings with himself a texture of events, environments, other people, and that from the meeting, in turn, other stories will be derived which will break off from their common story.)

* * *

Chapter seven

You are in bed together, you two Readers. So the moment has come to address you in the second person plural, a very serious operation, because it is tantamount to considering the two of you a single subject. I'm speaking to you two, a fairly unrecognizable tangle under the rumpled sheet. Maybe afterward you will go your separate ways and the story will again have to shift gears painfully, to alternate between the feminine *tu* and the masculine; but now, since your bodies are trying to find, skin to skin, the adhesion most generous in sensations, to transmit and receive vibrations and waves, to compenetrate the fullnesses and the voids, since in mental activity you have also agreed on the maximum agreement, you can be addressed with an articulated speech that includes you both in a sole, two-headed person. First of all the field of action, or of existence, must be established for this double entity you form. Where is the reciprocal identification leading? What is the central theme that recurs in your variations and modulations? A tension concentrated on not losing anything of its own potential, on prolonging a state of reactivity, on exploiting the accumulation of the other's desire in order to multiply one's own charge? Or is it the most submissive abandonment, the exploration of the immensity of strokable and reciprocally stroking spaces, the dissolving of one's being in a lake whose surface is infinitely tactile? In both situations you certainly do not exist except in relation to each other, but, to make those situations possible, your respective egos have not so much to erase themselves as to occupy, without reserve, all the void of the mental space, invest in itself at the maximum interest or spend itself to the last penny. In short, what you are doing is very beautiful but grammatically it doesn't change a thing. At the moment when you most appear to be a united *voi*, a second person plural, you are two *tu*'s, more separate and circumscribed than before.

(This is already true now, when you are still occupied,

154

each with the other's presence, in an exclusive fashion. Imagine how it will be in a little while, when ghosts that do not meet will frequent your minds, accompanying the encounters of your bodies tested by habit.)

Ludmilla, now you are being read. Your body is being subjected to a systematic reading, through channels of tactile information, visual, olfactory, and not without some intervention of the taste buds. Hearing also has its role, alert to your gasps and your trills. It is not only the body that is, in you, the object of reading: the body matters insofar as it is part of a complex of elaborate elements, not all visible and not all present, but manifested in visible and present events: the clouding of your eyes, your laughing, the words you speak, your way of gathering and spreading your hair, your initiatives and your reticences, and all the signs that are on the frontier between you and usage and habits and memory and prehistory and fashion, all codes, all the poor alphabets by which one human being believes at certain moments that he is reading another human being.

And you, too, O Reader, are meanwhile an object of reading: the Other Reader now is reviewing your body as if skimming the index, and at some moments she consults it as if gripped by sudden and specific curiosities, then she lingers, questioning it and waiting till a silent answer reaches her, as if every partial inspection interested her only in the light of a wider spatial reconnaissance. Now she dwells on negligible details, perhaps tiny stylistic faults, for example the prominent Adam's apple or your way of burying your head in the hollow of her shoulder, and she exploits them to establish a margin of detachment, critical reserve, or joking intimacy; now instead the accidentally discovered detail is excessively cherished— for example, the shape of your chin or a special nip you take at her shoulder—and from this start she gains impetus, covers (you cover together) pages and pages from top to bottom without skipping a comma. Meanwhile, in the satisfaction you receive from her way of reading you, from the textual quotations of your physical objectivity, you begin to harbor a doubt: that she is not reading you, single and whole as you are, but using you, using fragments of you detached from the context to construct for herself a ghostly partner, known to her alone, in the penumbra of her semiconsciousness, and what she is deciphering is this apocryphal visitor, not you.

Lovers' reading of each other's bodies (of that concentrate of mind and body which lovers use to go to bed together) differs from the reading of written pages in that it is not linear. It starts at any point, skips, repeats itself, goes backward, insists, ramifies in simultaneous and divergent messages, converges again, has moments of irritation, turns the page, finds its place, gets lost. A direction can be recognized in it, a route to an end, since it tends toward a climax, and with this end in view it arranges rhythmic phases, metrical scansions, recurrence of motives. But is the climax really the end? Or is the race toward that end opposed by another drive which works in the opposite direction, swimming against the moments, recovering time?

If one wanted to depict the whole thing graphically, every episode, with its climax, would require a three-dimensional model, perhaps four-dimensional, or, rather, no model: every experience is unrepeatable. What makes lovemaking and reading resemble each other most is that within both of them times and spaces open, different from measurable time and space.

Already, in the confused improvisation of the first encounter, the possible future of a cohabitation is read. Today each of you is the object of the other's reading, each reads in the other the unwritten story. Tomorrow, Reader and Other Reader, if you are together, if you lie down in the same bed like a settled couple, each will turn on the lamp at the side of the bed and sink into his or her book; two parallel readings will accompany the approach of sleep; first you, then you will turn out the light; returning from separated universes, you will find each other fleetingly in the darkness, where all separations are erased, before divergent dreams draw you again, one to one side, and one to the other. But do not wax ironic on this prospect of conjugal harmony: what happier image of a couple could you set against it?

You speak to Ludmilla of the novel you were reading while you waited for her. "It's a book of the sort you like: it conveys a sense of uneasiness from the very first page. . . ."

An interrogative flash passes in her gaze. A doubt seizes you; perhaps this phrase about uneasiness isn't something you heard her say, you read it somewhere. . . . Or perhaps Ludmilla has already stopped believing in anguish as a condition of truth. . . . Perhaps someone has demonstrated to her that anguish, too, is a mechanism, that there is nothing more easily falsified than the unconscious. . . .

"I like books," she says, "where all the mysteries and the anguish pass through a precise and cold mind, without shadows, like the mind of a chessplayer."

"In any case, this is the story of a character who becomes nervous when he hears a telephone ring. One day he's out jogging. . . ."

"Don't tell me any more. Let me read it."

"I didn't get much further myself. I'll bring it to you."

You get out of bed, you go hunt for it in the other room, where the precipitous turn in your relationship with Ludmilla interrupted the normal course of events.

You can't find it.

(You will find it again at an art show: the latest work of the sculptor Irnerio. The page whose corner you had folded down to mark your place is spread out on one of the bases of a compact parallelepiped, glued, varnished with a transparent resin. A charred shadow, as of a flame that is released from inside the book, corrugates the surface of the page and opens there a succession of levels like a gnarled rind.)

"I can't find it, but no matter," you say to her. "I noticed you have another copy anyway. In fact, I thought you had already read it. . . ."

Unknown to her, you've gone into the storeroom to find the Flannery book with the red band. "Here it is."

Ludmilla opens it. There's an inscription: "To Ludmilla . . . Silas Flannery." "Yes, it's my copy. . . ."

"Ah, you've met Flannery?" you exclaim, as if you knew nothing.

"Yes . . . he gave me this book. . . . But I was sure it had been stolen from me, before I could read it. . . ."

"Stolen by Irnerio?"

"Hmm . . ."

It's time for you to show your hand.

"It wasn't Irnerio, and you know it. Irnerio, when he saw it, threw it into that dark room, where you keep . . ."

"Who gave you permission to go rummaging around?"

"Irnerio says that somebody who used to steal your books comes back secretly now to replace them with false books. . . ."

"Irenerio doesn't know anything."

"I do: Cavedagna gave me Marana's letters to read."

"Everything Ermes says is always a trick."

"There's one thing that's true: that man continues to think of you, to see you in all his ravings, he's obsessed by the image of you reading."

"It's what he was never able to bear."

Little by little you will manage to understand something more about the origins of the translator's machinations: the secret spring that set them in motion was his jealousy of the invisible rival who came constantly between him and Ludmilla, the silent voice that speaks to her through books, this ghost with a thousand faces and faceless, all the more elusive since for Ludmilla authors are never incarnated in individuals of flesh and blood, they exist for her only in published pages, the living and the dead both are there always ready to communicate with her, to amaze her, and Ludmilla is always ready to follow them, in the fickle, carefree relations one can have with incorporeal persons. How is it possible to defeat not the authors but the functions of the author, the idea that behind each book there is someone who guarantees a truth in that world of ghosts and inventions by the mere fact of having invested in it his own truth, of having identified himself with that construction of words? Always, since his taste and talent impelled him in that direction, but more than ever since his relationship with Ludmilla became critical, Ermes Marana dreamed of a literature made entirely of apocrypha, of false attributions, of imitations and counterfeits and pastiches. If this idea had succeeded in imposing itself, if a systematic uncertainty as to the identity of the writer had kept the reader from abandoning himself with trust—trust not so much in what was being told him as in the silent narrating voice—perhaps externally the edifice of literature would not have changed at all, but beneath, in the foundations, where the relationship between reader and text is established, something would have changed forever. Then Ermes Marana would no longer have felt himself abandoned by Ludmilla absorbed in her reading: between the book and her there would always be insinuated the shadow of mystification, and he, identifying himself with every mystification, would have affirmed his presence.

Your eye falls on the beginning of the book. "But this

isn't the book I was reading. . . . Same title, same cover, everything the same . . . But it's another book! One of the two is a fake."

"Of course it's a fake," Ludmilla says, in a low voice.

"Are you saying it's a fake because it passed through Marana's hands? But the book I was reading was also one he had sent to Cavedagna! Can they both be fake?"

"There's only one person who can tell us the truth: the author."

"You can ask him, since you're a friend of his. . . ."

"I was."

"Was it to him that you went, when you ran away from Marana?"

"You know everything!" she says, with an ironic tone that gets on your nerves more than anything else.

Reader, you have made up your mind: you will go to see the writer. Meanwhile, turning your back on Ludmilla, you have begun reading the new book contained inside the same cover.

(Same up to a point. The band LATEST BEST SELLER BY SILAS FLANNERY covers the last word of the title. You would only have to raise it to realize that this novel is not entitled *In a network of lines that enlace* like the other one; it is called *In a network of lines that intersect*.)

In a network of lines that intersect

Speculate, reflect: every thinking activity implies mirrors for me. According to Plotinus, the soul is a mirror that creates material things reflecting the ideas of the higher reason. Maybe this is why I need mirrors to think: I cannot concentrate except in the presence of reflected images, as if my soul needed a model to imitate every time it wanted to employ its speculative capacity. (The adjective here assumes all its meanings: I am at once a man who thinks and a businessman, and a collector of optical instruments as well.)

The moment I put my eye to a kaleidoscope, I feel that my mind, as the heterogeneous fragments of colors and lines assemble to compose regular figures, immediately discovers the procedure to be followed: even if it is only the peremptory and ephemeral revelation of a rigorous construction that comes to pieces at the slightest tap of a fingernail on the side of the tube, to be replaced by another, in which the same elements converge in a dissimilar pattern.

Ever since I realized, when still an adolescent, that the

contemplation of the enameled gardens jumbled at the bottom of a well of mirrors stirred my aptitude for practical decisions and bold prognostications, I have been collecting kaleidoscopes. The history of this relatively recent object (the kaleidoscope was patented in 1817 by the Scottish physicist Sir David Brewster, author of a *Treatise on New Philosophical Instruments,* among other works) confined my collection within narrow chronological boundaries. But it was not long before I extended my investigations to a far more illustrious and inspiring antiquarian field: the catoptric instruments of the seventeenth century, little theaters of various design where a figure is seen multiplied by the variation of the angles between the mirrors. My aim is to reconstruct the museum assembled by the Jesuit Athanasius Kircher, author of *Ars Magna Lucis et Umbrae* (1646) and inventor of the "polydyptic theater," in which about sixty little mirrors lining the inside of a large box transform a bough into a forest, a lead soldier into an army, a booklet into a library.

The businessmen to whom, before meetings, I show the collection glance with superficial curiosity at these bizarre apparatuses. They don't know that I have built my financial empire on the very principle of kaleidoscopes and catoptric instruments, multiplying, as if in a play of mirrors, companies without capital, enlarging credit, making disastrous deficits vanish in the dead corners of illusory perspectives. My secret, the secret of my uninterrupted financial victories in a period that has witnessed so many crises and market crashes and bankruptcies, has always been this: that I never thought directly of money, business, profits, but only of the angles of refraction established among shining surfaces variously inclined.

It is my image that I want to multiply, but not out of narcissism or megalomania, as could all too easily be believed: on the contrary, I want to conceal, in the midst of so many illusory ghosts of myself, the true me, who makes them move. For this reason, if I were not afraid of being misunderstood, I would have nothing against reconstructing, in my house, the room completely lined with mirrors according to Kircher's design, in which I would see myself walking on the ceiling, head down, as if I were flying upward from the depths of the floor.

These pages I am writing should also transmit a cold luminosity, as in a mirrored tube, where a finite number of figures are broken up and turned upside down and multiplied. If my figure sets out in all directions and is doubled at every corner, it is to discourage those who want to pursue me. I am a man with many enemies, whom I must constantly elude. When they think they have overtaken me, they will strike only a glass surface on which one of the many reflections of my ubiquitous presence appears and vanishes. I am also a man who pursues his numerous enemies, looming over them and advancing in invincible phalanxes and blocking their path whichever way they turn. In a catoptric world enemies can equally believe that they are surrounding me from every side, but I alone know the arrangement of the mirrors and can put myself out of their reach, while they end up jostling and seizing one another.

I would like my story to express all this through details of financial operations, sudden dramatic shifts at board meetings, telephone calls from brokers in panic, and then also bits of the map of the city, insurance policies, Lorna's mouth when that sentence escaped her, Elfrida's gaze as if pondering some inexorable calculation of hers, one image superimposed on the other, the grid of the map of the city dotted with x's and arrows, motorcycles zooming off and vanishing into the corners of the mirror, motorcycles converging on my Mercedes.

Ever since it became clear to me that my kidnapping would be the exploit most desired not only by the various

bands of specialist crooks but also by my leading colleagues and rivals in the world of high finance, I have
realized that only by multiplying myself, multiplying my
person, my presence, my exits from the house, and my
returns, in short the opportunities for an ambush, could I
make my falling into enemy hands more improbable. So I
then ordered five Mercedes sedans exactly like mine,
which enter and leave the armored gate of my villa at all
hours, escorted by the motorcyclists of my bodyguard,
and bearing inside a shadow, bundled up, dressed in
black, who could be me or an ordinary stand-in. The
companies of which I am president consist of initials with
nothing behind them and some headquarters in inter-
changeable empty rooms; therefore my business meetings
can be held at constantly varying addresses which for
greater safety I order changed at the last minute each
time. More delicate problems stem from my extramarital
relationship with a twenty-nine-year-old divorcée, Lorna
by name, to whom I devote two and sometimes three
weekly sessions of two and three-quarters hours. To protect Lorna the only thing to do was to make it impossible
to locate her, and the system to which I have resorted is
that of parading a multiplicity of simultaneous amorous
encounters, so that it is impossible to understand which
are my counterfeit mistresses and which is the real one.
Every day both I and my doubles visit, on constantly
changing schedules, pied-à-terres scattered all over the
city and inhabited by attractive women. This network of
false mistresses allows me to conceal my true meetings
with Lorna also from my wife, Elfrida, to whom I have
presented this extravaganza as a security measure. As for
Elfrida, my advice that she give maximum publicity to
her movements in order to foil possible criminal plans has
not found her prepared to listen to me. Elfrida tends to
hide, just as she avoids the mirrors in my collection, as if
she feared her image would be shattered by them and

destroyed: an attitude whose deeper motives escape me and which vexes me not a little.

I would like all the details that I am writing down to concur in creating the impression of a high-precision mechanism, but at the same time of a succession of dazzles that reflect something that remains out of eyeshot. For this reason I must not neglect to insert every so often, at the points where the plot becomes thickest, some quotation from an ancient text: for example, a passage from the *De Magia Naturale* of Giovanni Battista della Porta, where he says that the magician—that is, the "minister of Nature"—must know "the reasons that the sight is deceived, the images that are produced under water, and in mirrors made in various forms, which at times dispel images from the mirrors, suspended in the air, and he must know how things done at a distance may be clearly seen."

I soon realized that the uncertainty created by the coming and going of identical automobiles would not suffice to avert the danger of criminal traps: I then thought to apply the multiplying power of catoptric mechanisms to the bandits themselves, organizing false ambushes and false kidnappings of some counterfeit of myself, followed by fake releases after the payment of fake ransoms. For these I had to assume the task of setting up a parallel criminal organization, making more and more intimate contacts with the underworld. I thus came to have at my disposal considerable information on various kidnappings in the works, being thus able to act in time, both to protect myself and to exploit the misfortunes of my business adversaries.

At this point the story could mention that among the virtues of mirrors that the ancient books discuss there is also that of revealing distant and hidden things. The Arab geographers of the Middle Ages, in their descriptions of the harbor of Alexandria, recall the column that stood on the island of Pharos, surmounted by a steel mirror in which, from an immense distance, the ships proceeding off Cyprus and Constantinople and all the lands of the Romans can be seen. Concentrating the rays, curved mirrors can catch an image of the whole. "God Himself, who cannot be seen either by the body or by the soul," Porphyry writes, "allows himself to be contemplated in a mirror." Together with the centrifugal radiation that projects my image along all the dimensions of space, I would like these pages also to render the opposite movement, through which I receive from the mirrors images that direct sight cannot embrace. From mirror to mirror— this is what I happen to dream of—the totality of things, the whole, the entire universe, divine wisdom could concentrate their luminous rays into a single mirror. Or perhaps the knowledge of everything is buried in the soul, and a system of mirrors that would multiply my image to infinity and reflect its essence in a single image would then reveal to me the soul of the universe, which is hidden in mine.

This and nothing else must have been the power of the magic mirrors that are so often mentioned in treatises of the occult sciences and in anathemas of the Inquisitors: to force the God of Darkness to display himself and to join his image with the one the mirror reflects. I had to extend my collection into another field: dealers and auction houses all over the whole world have been alerted to hold for me the extremely rare examples of those Renaissance mirrors which, through their form or through tradition, can be classified as magic.

It was a difficult game, in which every mistake could cost dearly. My first wrong move was persuading my rivals to join me in founding an insurance company against kidnappings. Sure of my network of information in the underworld, I thought I could retain control over every eventuality. I soon learned that my associates maintained even closer relations with the kidnap bands than I did. For the next kidnapping, the ransom demanded would be all the capital of the insurance company; this would then be divided between the outlaws' organization and their accomplices, the stockholders of the company, all this naturally to the disadvantage of the kidnapped person. As to the identity of this victim, there were no doubts: it was to be me.

The plan to trap me envisaged that between the Honda motorcycles of my escort and the armored car in which I rode, three Yamaha motorcycles would interpose themselves, ridden by three false policemen, who would suddenly slam on their brakes before the curve. According to my counterplan, there would instead be three Suzuki motorcycles which would block my Mercedes five hundred meters before, in a fake kidnapping. When I saw myself blocked by three Kawasaki motorcycles at an intersection before the other two, I realized that my counterplan had been frustrated by a counter-counterplan whose author I did not know.

As in a kaleidoscope, the hypotheses I would like to record in these lines break up and diverge, just as before my eyes the map of the city became segmented when I dismantled it piece by piece to locate the crossroads where, according to my informers, the trap would be set for me, and to establish the point at which I could get ahead of my enemies so as to upset their plan in my own favor. Everything now seemed assured to me; the magic mirror brought together all the malevolent powers, putting them at my service. I had not taken into consideration a third kidnapping plan arranged by persons unknown. By whom?

To my great surprise, instead of taking me to a secret hideaway, my kidnappers accompany me to my house, lock me in the catoptric room I had reconstructed with such care from the designs of Athanasius Kircher. The mirror walls reflect on my image an infinite number of times. Had I been kidnapped by myself? Had one of my images cast into the world taken my place and relegated me to the role of reflected image? Had I summoned the Prince of Darkness and was he appearing to me in my own likeness?

On the mirror floor a woman's body lies, bound. It is Lorna. If she makes the slightest movement, her naked flesh unfolds, repeated on all the mirrors. I fling myself upon her, to free her from her bonds and gag, to embrace her; but she turns on me, infuriated. "You think you have me in your hands? You're mistaken!" And she digs her nails into my face. Is she a prisoner with me? Is she my prisoner? Is she my prison?

Meanwhile a door has opened. Elfrida comes forward. "I knew of the danger threatening you and I managed to save you," she says. "The method may have been a bit brutal, but I had no choice. But now I can't find the door of this cage of mirrors any more. Tell me, quickly, how can I get out?"

One eye and one eyebrow of Elfrida, one leg in its tight boot, the corner of her mouth with its thin lips and too-white teeth, a beringed hand clutching a revolver are repeated, enlarged by the mirrors, and among these lacerated fragments of her figure intrude patches of Lorna's skin, like landscapes of flesh. Already I can distinguish no longer what belongs to one and what belongs to the other, I am lost, I seem to have lost myself, I cannot see my reflection but only theirs. In a fragment of Novalis, an adept who has managed to reach the secret dwelling of Isis lifts the veil of the goddess. . . . Now it seems to me that everything that surrounds me is a part of me, that I have managed to become the whole, finally. . . .

[8]

In a deck chair, on the terrace of a chalet in the valley, there is a young woman reading. Every day, before starting work, I pause a moment to look at her with the spyglass. In this thin, transparent air I feel able to perceive in her unmoving form the signs of that invisible movement that reading is, the flow of gaze and breath, but, even more, the journey of the words through the person, their course or their arrest, their spurts, delays, pauses, the attention concentrating or straying, the returns, that journey that seems uniform and on the contrary is always shifting and uneven.

How many years has it been since I could allow myself some disinterested reading? How many years has it been since I could abandon myself to a book written by another, with no relation to what I must write myself? I turn and see the desk waiting for me, the typewriter with a sheet of paper rolled into it, the chapter to begin. Since I have become a slave laborer of writing, the pleasure of reading has finished for me. What I do has as its aim the spiritual state of this woman in the deck chair framed by the lens of my spyglass, and it is a condition forbidden me.

Every day, before starting work, I look at the woman in the deck chair: I say to myself that the result of the unnatural effort to which I subject myself, writing, must be the respiration of this reader, the operation of reading turned into a natural process, the current that brings the sentences to graze the filter of her attention, to stop for a moment before being absorbed by the circuits of her mind and disappearing, transformed into her interior ghosts, into what in her is most personal and incommunicable.

At times I am gripped by an absurd desire: that the sentence I am about to write be the one the woman is reading at that same moment. The idea mesmerizes me so much that I convince myself it is true: I write the sentence hastily, get up, go to the window, train my spyglass to check the effect of my sentence in her gaze, in the curl of her lips, in the cigarette she lights, in the shifts of her body in the deck chair, in her legs, which she crosses or extends.

At times it seems to me that the distance between my writing and her reading is unbridgeable, that whatever I write bears the stamp of artifice and incongruity; if what I am writing were to appear on the polished surface of the page she is reading, it would rasp like a fingernail on a pane, and she would fling the book away with horror.

At times I convince myself that the woman is reading my *true* book, the one I should have written long ago, but will never succeed in writing, that this book is there, word for word, that I can see it at the end of my spyglass but cannot read what is written in it, cannot know what was written by that me who I have not succeeded and will never succeed in being. It's no use my sitting down again at the desk, straining to guess, to copy that true book of mine she is reading: whatever I may write will be false, a fake, compared to my true book, which no one except her will ever read.

And just as I watch her while she reads, suppose she were to train a spyglass on me while I write? I sit at the desk with my back to the window, and there, behind me, I feel an eye that sucks up the flow of the sentences, leads the story in directions that elude me. Readers are my vampires. I feel a throng of readers looking over my shoulder and seizing the words as they are set down on paper. I am unable to write if there is someone watching me: I feel that what I am writing does not belong to me any more. I would like to vanish, to leave behind for that expectation lurking in their eyes the page stuck in the typewriter, or, at most, my fingers striking the keys.

How well I would write if I were not here! If between the white page and the writing of words and stories that take shape and disappear without anyone's ever writing them there were not interposed that uncomfortable partition which is my person! Style, taste, individual philosophy, subjectivity, cultural background, real experience, psychology, talent, tricks of the trade: all the elements that make what I write recognizable as mine seem to me a cage that restricts my possibilities. If I were only a hand, a severed hand that grasps a pen and writes . . . Who would move this hand? The anonymous throng? The spirit of the times? The collective unconscious? I do not know. It is not in order to be the spokesman for something definable that I would like to erase myself. Only to transmit the writable that waits to be written, the tellable that nobody tells.

Perhaps the woman I observe with the spyglass *knows* what I should write; or, rather, *she does not know it,* because she is in fact waiting for me to write what she *does not know;* but what she knows for certain is her waiting, the void that my words should fill.

At times I think of the subject matter of the book to be written as of something that already exists: thoughts already thought, dialogue already spoken, stories already happened, places and settings seen; the book should be simply the equivalent of the unwritten world translated into writing. At other times, on the contrary, I seem to understand that between the book to be written and things that already exist there can be only a kind of complementary relationship: the book should be the written counterpart of the unwritten world; its subject should be what does not exist and cannot exist except when written, but whose absence is obscurely felt by that which exists, in its own incompleteness.

I see that one way or another I keep circling around the idea of an interdependence between the unwritten world and the book I should write. This is why writing presents itself to me as an operation of such weight that I remain crushed by it. I put my eye to the spyglass and train it on the reader. Between her eyes and the page a white butterfly flutters. Whatever she may have been reading, now it is certainly the butterfly that has captured her attention. The unwritten world has its climax in that butterfly. The result at which I must aim is something specific, intimate, light.

Looking at the woman in the deck chair, I felt the need to write "from life," that is, to write not her but her reading, to write anything at all, but thinking that it must pass through her reading.

Now, looking at the butterfly that lights on my book, I would like to write "from life," bearing the butterfly in mind. To write, for example, a crime that is horrible but which somehow "resembles" the butterfly, which would be light and fine like the butterfly.

I could also describe the butterfly, but bearing in mind the horrible scene of a crime, so that the butterfly would become something frightful.

Idea for a story. Two writers, living in two chalets on opposite slopes of the valley, observe each other alternately. One of them is accustomed to write in the morning, the other in the afternoon. Mornings and afternoons, the writer who is not writing trains his spyglass on the one who is writing.

Chapter eight

One of the two is a productive writer, the other a tormented writer. The tormented writer watches the productive writer filling pages with uniform lines, the manuscript growing in a pile of neat pages. In a little while the book will be finished: certainly a best seller—the tormented writer thinks with a certain contempt but also with envy. He considers the productive writer no more than a clever craftsman, capable of turning out machine-made novels catering to the taste of the public; but he cannot repress a strong feeling of envy for that man who expresses himself with such methodical self-confidence. It is not only envy, it is also admiration, yes, sincere admiration: in the way that man puts all of his energy into writing there is certainly a generosity, a faith in communication, in giving others what others expect of him, without creating introverted problems for himself. The tormented writer would give anything if he could resemble the productive writer; he would like to take him as a model; his greatest ambition now is to become like him.

The productive writer watches the tormented writer as the latter sits down at his desk, chews his fingernails, scratches himself, tears a page to bits, gets up and goes into the kitchen to fix himself some coffee, then some tea, then camomile, then reads a poem by Hölderlin (while it is clear that Hölderlin has absolutely nothing to do with what he is writing), copies a page already written and then crosses it all out line by line, telephones the cleaner's (though it was settled that the blue slacks couldn't be ready before Thursday), then writes some notes that will not be useful now but maybe later, then goes to the encyclopedia and looks up Tasmania (though it is obvious that in what he is writing there is no reference to Tasmania), tears up two pages, puts on a Ravel recording. The productive writer has never liked the works of the tormented writer; reading them, he always feels as if he is on the verge of grasping the decisive point, but then it eludes him and he is left with a sensation of uneasiness. But now that he is watching him write, he feels this man is struggling with something obscure, a tangle, a road to be dug leading no one knows where; at times he seems to see the other man walking on a tightrope stretched over the void, and he is overcome with admiration. Not only admiration, also envy; because he feels how limited his own work is, how superficial compared with what the tormented writer is seeking.

On the terrace of a chalet in the bottom of the valley a young woman is sunning herself, reading a book. The two writers observe her with the spyglass. "How enthralled she is! She's holding her breath! How feverishly she turns the pages!" the tormented writer thinks. "Certainly she is reading a novel of great effect, like those of the productive writer!" "How enthralled she is! As if transfigured in meditation, as if she saw a mysterious truth being disclosed!" the productive writer thinks. "Surely she is reading a book rich in hidden meanings, like those of the tormented writer!"

The greatest desire of the tormented writer is to be read the way that young woman is reading. He starts writing a novel as he thinks the productive writer would write it. Meanwhile the greatest desire of the productive writer is to be read the way that young woman is reading; he starts writing a novel as he thinks the tormented writer would write it.

The young woman is approached first by one writer, then by the other. Both tell her they would like her to read the novel they have just finished writing.

The young woman receives the two manuscripts. After a few days she invites the authors to her house, together, to their great surprise. "What kind of joke is this?" She says. "You've given me two copies of the same novel!"

Or else:

The young woman gets the two manuscripts mixed up.

She returns to the productive writer the tormented writer's novel in the productive writer's manner, and to the tormented writer the productive writer's novel in the tormented writer's manner. Both, seeing themselves counterfeited, have a violent reaction and rediscover their personal vein.

Or else:

A gust of wind shuffles the two manuscripts. The reader tries to reassemble them. A single novel results, stupendous, which the critics are unable to attribute. It is the novel that both the productive writer and the tormented writer have always dreamed of writing.

Or else:

The young woman had always been a passionate reader of the productive writer and has loathed the tormented writer. Reading the productive writer's new novel, she finds it phony and realizes that everything he wrote was phony; on the other hand, recalling the tormented writer's works, she now finds them splendid and can't wait to read his new novel. But she finds something completely different from what she was expecting, and she sends him to the devil, too.

Or else:

The same, replacing "productive" with "tormented" and "tormented" with "productive."

Or else:

The young woman was a passionate admirer, et cetera, et cetera, of the productive writer and loathed the tormented one. Reading the productive writer's new novel she doesn't notice at all that something has changed; she likes it, without being especially enthusiastic. As for the manuscript of the tormented writer, she finds it insipid like all the rest of this author's work. She replies to the two writers with a few polite words. Both are convinced that she can't be a very alert reader and they pay no further attention to her.

Or else:

The same, replacing, et cetera.

I read in a book that the objectivity of thought can be expressed using the verb "to think" in the impersonal third person: saying not "I think" but "it thinks" as we say "it rains." There is thought in the universe—this is the constant from which we must set out every time.

Will I ever be able to say, "Today it writes," just like "Today it rains," "Today it is windy"? Only when it will come natural to me to use the verb "write" in the impersonal form will I be able to hope that through me is expressed something less limited than the personality of an individual.

And for the verb "to read"? Will we be able to say, "Today it reads" as we say "Today it rains"? If you think about it, reading is a necessarily individual act, far more than writing. If we assume that writing manages to go beyond the limitations of the author, it will continue to have a meaning only when it is read by a single person and passes through his mental circuits. Only the ability to be read by a given individual proves that what is written shares in the power of writing, a power based on something that goes beyond the individual. The universe will express itself as long as somebody will be able to say, "I read, therefore *it* writes."

This is the special bliss that I see appear in the reader's face, and which is denied me.

On the wall facing my desk hangs a poster somebody gave me. The dog Snoopy is sitting at a typewriter, and in the cartoon you read the sentence, "It was a dark and stormy night. . . ." Every time I sit down here I read, "It was a dark and stormy night . . ." and the impersonality of that *incipit* seems to open the passage from one world to the other, from the time and space of here and now to the time and space of the written word; I feel the thrill of a beginning that can be followed by multiple developments, inexhaustibly; I am convinced there is nothing better than a conventional opening, an attack from which you can expect everything and nothing; and I realize also that this mythomane dog will never succeed in adding to the first seven words another seven or another twelve without breaking the spell. The facility of the entrance into another world is an illusion: you start writing in a rush, anticipating the happiness of a future reading, and the void yawns on the white page.

Ever since I have had this poster before my eyes, I have no longer been able to end a page. I must take this damned Snoopy down from the wall as quickly as possible, but I can't bring myself to do it; that childish figure has become for me an emblem of my condition, a warning, a challenge.

The romantic fascination produced in the pure state by the first sentences of the first chapter of many novels is soon lost in the continuation of the story: it is the promise of a time of reading that extends before us and can comprise all possible developments. I would like to be able to write a book that is only an *incipit*, that maintains for its whole duration the potentiality of the beginning, the expectation still not focused on an object. But how could such a book be constructed? Would it break off after the first paragraph? Would the preliminaries be prolonged indefinitely? Would it set the beginning of one tale inside another, as in the *Arabian Nights*?

Today I will begin by copying the first sentences of a famous novel, to see if the charge of energy contained in that start is communicated to my hand, which, once it has received the right push, should run on its own.

On an exceptionally hot evening early in July, a young man came out of the garret in which he lodged in S. Place and walked slowly, as though in hesitation, towards K. Bridge.

I will copy out also the second, indispensable paragraph to allow myself to be carried along by the flow of the narration:

He had successfully avoided meeting his landlady on the staircase. His garret was under the roof of a high, five-storied house and it was more like a cupboard than a room. And so on until: *He was hopelessly in debt to his landlady, and was afraid of meeting her.*

At this point the next sentence attracts me so much that I can't refrain from copying it: *This was not because he was cowardly and abject: quite the contrary; but for some time past he had been in an overstrained irritable condition, verging on hypochondria.* While I'm about it, I could continue for the whole paragraph, or, indeed, for several pages, until the protagonist introduces himself to the old moneylender. *"Raskolnikov, a student, I came here a month ago," the young man made haste to mutter, with a half bow, remembering that he ought to be more polite.*

I stop before I succumb to the temptation to copy out all of *Crime and Punishment.* For an instant I seem to understand the meaning and fascination of a now inconceivable vocation: that of the copyist. The copyist lived simultaneously in two temporal dimensions, that of reading and that of writing; he could write without the anguish of having the void open before his pen; read without the anguish of having his own act become concrete in some material object.

A man called on me, saying he is my translator, to warn me about an outrageous practice damaging to him and to me: the publication of unauthorized translations of my books. He showed me a volume, which I leafed through without getting much out of it: it was written in Japanese, and the only words in the Latin alphabet were my given name and surname on the title page.

Chapter eight

"I can't even figure out which of my books it is," I said, handing the volume back to him. "Unfortunately, I don't know Japanese."

"Even if you knew the language you wouldn't recognize the book," my visitor said to me. "It's a book you have never written."

He explained to me that the great skill of the Japanese in manufacturing perfect facsimiles of Western products has spread to literature. A firm in Osaka has managed to get hold of the formula of Silas Flannery's novels, and it manages to produce absolutely new ones, and first-class novels at that, so it can invade the world market. Retranslated into English (or, rather, translated into English, from which they claim to have been translated), they cannot be distinguished, by any critic, from true Flannerys.

The news of this diabolical swindle has profoundly upset me, but it goes beyond my understandable fury at the economic and moral injury: I feel also a timid attraction for these fakes, for this extension of myself that blossoms from the terrain of another civilization. I imagine an old Japanese in his kimono crossing a curved little bridge: he is my Nipponese self imagining one of my stories, and hc succeeds in identifying himself with me through a spiritual itinerary that to me is completely alien. Whereby the false Flannerys turned out by the swindling firm in Osaka would be, of course, vulgar imitations; but at the same time they would contain a refined and arcane wisdom that true Flannerys lack completely.

Naturally, in the presence of a stranger, I had to conceal the ambiguity of my reactions, and I acted as if I were interested only in collecting all the data necessary for bringing a lawsuit.

"I will sue the counterfeiters and anyone who cooperates in the dissemination of the faked books!" I said, looking meaningfully into the translator's eyes, because I suspected this young man was not without a role in the shady business. He said his name is Ermes Marana, a name I had never heard. His head is oblong horizontally, like a dirigible, and seems to hide many things behind the convexity of its brow.

I asked him where he lives. "For the moment, in Japan," he answered me.

He declares himself outraged that anyone would make improper use of my name, and ready to help me put an end to the fraud, but he adds that in the final analysis there is nothing to be shocked about, since, in his view, literature's worth lies in its power of mystification, in mystification it has its truth; therefore a fake, as the mystification of a mystification, is tantamount to a truth squared.

He went on expounding to me his theories, according to which the author of every book is a fictitious character whom the existent author invents to make him the author of his fictions. I feel I can share many of his affirmations, but I was careful not to let him know this. He says he is interested in me chiefly for two reasons: first, because I am an author who can be faked; and second, because he thinks I have the gifts necessary to be a great faker, to create perfect apocrypha. I could therefore incarnate what for him is the ideal author, that is, the author who is dissolved in the cloud of fictions that covers the world with its thick sheath. And since for him artifice is the true substance of everything, the author who devised a perfect system of artifices would succeed in identifying himself with the whole.

I must stop thinking of my conversation yesterday with that Marana. I, too, would like to erase myself and find for each book another I, another voice, another name, to be reborn; but my aim is to capture in the book the illegible world, without center, without ego, without I.

When you think about it, this total writer could be a very humble person, what in America they call a ghost writer, a professional of recognized usefulness even if not of great prestige: the anonymous editor who gives book form to what other people have to tell but are unable or lack the time to write; he is the writing hand that gives words to existences too busy existing. Perhaps that was my true vocation and I missed it. I could have multiplied my I's, assumed other people's selves, enacted the selves most different from me and from one another.

But if an individual truth is the only one that a book can contain, I might as well accept it and write my truth. The book of my memory? No, memory is true as long as you do not set it, as long as it is not enclosed in a form. The book of my desires? Those also are true only when their impulse acts independently of my conscious will. The only truth I can write is that of the instant I am living. Perhaps the true book is this diary, in which I try to note down the image of the woman in the deck chair at the various hours of the day, as I observe her in the changing light.

Why not admit that my dissatisfaction reveals an excessive ambition, perhaps a megalomaniac delirium? For the writer who wants to annul himself in order to give voice to what is outside him, two paths open: either write a book that could be the unique book, that exhausts the whole in its pages; or write all books, to pursue the whole through its partial images. The unique book, which contains the whole, could only be the sacred text, the total word revealed. But I do not believe totality can be contained in language; my problem is what remains outside, the unwritten, the unwritable. The only way left me is that of writing all books, writing the books of all possible authors.

If I think I must write *one* book, all the problems of how this book should be and how it should not be block me and keep me from going forward. If, on the contrary, I think that I am writing a whole library, I feel suddenly lightened: I know that whatever I write will be integrated, contradicted, balanced, amplified, buried by the hundreds of volumes that remain for me to write.

The Koran is the holy book about whose compositional process we know most. There were at least two mediations between the whole and the book: Mohammed listened to the word of Allah and dictated, in his turn, to his scribes. Once—the biographers of the Prophet tell us—while dictating to the scribe Abdullah, Mohammed left a sentence half finished. The scribe, instinctively, suggested the conclusion. Absently, the Prophet accepted as the divine word what Abdullah had said. This scandalized the scribe, who abandoned the Prophet and lost his faith.

He was wrong. The organization of the sentence, finally, was a responsibility that lay with him; he was the one who had to deal with the internal coherence of the written language, with grammar and syntax, to channel into it the fluidity of a thought that expands outside all language before it becomes word, and of a word particularly fluid like that of a prophet. The scribe's collaboration was necessary to Allah, once he had decided to express himself in a written text. Mohammed knew this and allowed the scribe the privilege of concluding sentences; but Abdullah was unaware of the powers vested in him. He lost his faith in Allah because he lacked faith in writing, and in himself as an agent of writing.

If an infidel were allowed to excogitate variants on the legends of the Prophet, I would venture this one: Abdullah loses his faith because in writing under dictation he makes a mistake and Mohammed, though he notices it, decides not to correct it, finding the mistaken form preferable. In this case, too, Abdullah would be wrong to be scandalized. It is on the page, not before, that the word, even that of the prophetic raptus, becomes definitive, that is to say, becomes writing. It is only through the confining act of writing that the immensity of the nonwritten becomes legible, that is, through the uncertainties of spelling, the occasional lapses, oversights, unchecked leaps of the word and the pen. Otherwise what is outside of us should not insist on communicating through the word, spoken or written: let it send its messages by other paths.

There: the white butterfly has crossed the whole valley, and from the reader's book has flown here, to light on the page I am writing.

Strange people circulate in this valley: literary agents awaiting my new novel, for which they have already collected advances from publishers all over the world; advertising agents who want my characters to wear certain articles of clothing and drink certain fruit juices; electronic technicians who insist on finishing my unfinished novels with a computer. I try to go out as little as possible; I avoid the village; if I want to take a walk, I choose the mountain trails.

Today I ran into a party of boys who looked like scouts, excited and yet meticulous, arranging some pieces of canvas on a meadow to form geometric patterns.

"Signals for planes?" I asked.

"For flying saucers," they answered. "We're UFO observers. This is a place of transit, a kind of aerial track that has seen a lot of activity lately. They think it's because a writer is living somewhere around here, and the inhabitants of the other planets want to use him for communication."

"What makes you believe that?" I asked.

"The fact is that for some time this writer has been undergoing a crisis and can't write any more. The newspapers are wondering what the reason can be. According to our calculations, it could be the inhabitants of other worlds keeping him inactive, so that he will be drained of terrestrial conditionings and become receptive."

"But why him, particularly?"

"The extraterrestrials can't say things directly. They have to express themselves in an indirect way, a figurative way—for example, through stories that arouse unusual emotions. This writer apparently has a good technique and a certain elasticity of ideas."

"But have you read his books?"

"What he has written so far is of no interest. The book he will write when he emerges from the crisis is the one that could contain the cosmic communications."

"Transmitted to him how?"

"Mentally. He shouldn't even be aware of it. He would believe he is writing as he likes; instead, the message coming from space on waves picked up by his brain would infiltrate what he is writing."

"And would you succeed in decoding the message?"

They did not answer me.

When I think that the interplanetary expectation of these young people will be disappointed, I feel a certain sorrow. After all, I could easily slip into my next book something that might seem to them the revelation of a cosmic truth. For the present I have no idea of what I might invent, but if I start writing, an idea will come to me.

What if it were as they say? If, while I believe I am writing in fun, what I write were really dictated by the extraterrestrials?

It is no use my awaiting a revelation from the sidereal spaces: my novel is not progressing. If I were suddenly to begin filling page after page once more, it would be a sign that the galaxy is aiming its messages at me.

But the only thing I succeed in writing is this diary, the

contemplation of a young woman reading a book, and I do not know what book it is. Is the extraterrestrial message contained in my diary? Or in her book?

A girl came to see me who is writing a thesis on my novels for a very important university seminar in literary studies. I see that my work serves her perfectly to demonstrate her theories, and this is certainly a positive fact—for the novels or for the theories, I do not know which. From her very detailed talk, I got the idea of a piece of work being seriously pursued, but my books seen through her eyes prove unrecognizable to me. I am sure this Lotaria (that is her name) has read them conscientiously, but I believe she has read them only to find in them what she was already convinced of before reading them.

I tried to say this to her. She retorted, a bit irritated: "Why? Would you want me to read in your books only what you're convinced of?"

I answered her: "That isn't it. I expect readers to read in my books something I didn't know, but I can expect it only from those who expect to read something they didn't know."

(Luckily I can watch with my spyglass that other woman reading and convince myself that not all readers are like this Lotaria.)

"What you want would be a passive way of reading, escapist and regressive," Lotaria said. "That's how my sister reads. It was watching her devour the novels of Silas Flannery one after the other without considering any problems that gave me the idea of using those books as the subject of my thesis. This is why I read your works, Mr. Flannery, if you want to know: to show my sister, Ludmilla, how to read an author. Even Silas Flannery."

"Thank you for that 'even.' But why didn't you bring your sister with you?"

"Ludmilla insists it's better not to know authors personally, because the real person never corresponds to the image you form of him from reading his books."

I would say that she could be my ideal reader, this Ludmilla.

Yesterday evening, on entering my study, I saw the shadow of a stranger escaping through the window. I tried to pursue him, but I found no trace of him. Often I seem to hear people hidden in the bushes around the house, especially at night.

Though I leave the house as little as possible, I have the impression that someone is disturbing my papers. More than once I have discovered that some pages were missing from my manuscripts. A few days afterward I would find the pages in their place again. But often I no longer recognize my manuscripts, as if I had forgotten what I had written, or as if overnight I were so changed that I no longer recognized myself in the self of yesterday.

I asked Lotaria if she has already read some books of mine that I lent her. She said no, because here she doesn't have a computer at her disposal.

She explained to me that a suitably programmed computer can read a novel in a few minutes and record the list of all the words contained in the text, in order of frequency. "That way I can have an already completed reading at hand," Lotaria says, "with an incalculable saving of time. What is the reading of a text, in fact, except the recording of certain thematic recurrences, certain insistences of forms and meanings? An electronic reading supplies me with a list of the frequencies, which I have only to glance at to form an idea of the problems the book suggests to my critical study. Naturally, at the highest frequencies the list records countless articles, pronouns, particles, but I don't pay them any attention. I head straight for the words richest in meaning; they can give me a fairly precise notion of the book."

Chapter eight

Lotaria brought me some novels electronically transcribed, in the form of words listed in the order of their frequency. "In a novel of fifty to a hundred thousand words," she said to me, "I advise you to observe immediately the words that are repeated about twenty times. Look here. Words that appear nineteen times:

> blood, cartridge belt, commander, do, have, immediately, it, life, seen, sentry, shots, spider, teeth, together, your . . .

"Words that appear eighteen times:

> boys, cap, come, dead, eat, enough, evening, French, go, handsome, new, passes, period, potatoes, those, until . . .

"Don't you already have a clear idea what it's about?" Lotaria says. "There's no question: it's a war novel, all action, brisk writing, with a certain underlying violence. The narration is entirely on the surface, I would say; but to make sure, it's always a good idea to take a look at the list of words used only once, though no less important for that. Take this sequence, for example:

> underarm, underbrush, undercover, underdog, underfed, underfoot, undergo, undergraduate, underground, undergrowth, underhand, underprivileged, undershirt, underwear, underweight . . .

"No, the book isn't completely superficial, as it seemed. There must be something hidden; I can direct my research along these lines."

Lotaria shows me another series of lists. "This is an entirely different novel. It's immediately obvious. Look at the words that recur about fifty times:

> had, his, husband, little, Riccardo (51) answered, been, before, has, station, what (48) all, barely, bedroom, Mario, some, times (47) morning, seemed, went, whom (46) should (45) hand, listen, until, were (43) Cecilia, Delia, evening, girl, hands, six, who, years (42) almost, alone,

could, man, returned, window (41) me, wanted (40) life (39)

"What do you think of that? An intimatist narration, subtle feelings, understated, a humble setting, everyday life in the provinces . . . As a confirmation, we'll take a sample of words used a single time:

chilled, deceived, downward, engineer, enlargement, fattening, ingenious, ingenuous, injustice, jealous, kneeling, swallow, swallowed, swallowing . . .

"So we already have an idea of the atmosphere, the moods, the social background. . . . We can go on to a third book:

according, account, body, especially, God, hair, money, times, went (29) evening, flour, food, rain, reason, somebody, stay, Vincenzo, wine (38) death, eggs, green, hers, legs, sweet, therefore (36) black, bosom, children, day, even, ha, head, machine, make, remained, stays, stuffs, white, would (35)

"Here I would say we're dealing with a full-blooded story, violent, everything concrete, a bit brusque, with a direct sensuality, no refinement, popular eroticism. But here again, let's go on to the list of words with a frequency of one. Look, for example:

ashamed, shame, shamed, shameful, shameless, shames, shaming, vegetables, verify, vermouth, virgins . . .

"You see? A guilt complex, pure and simple! A valuable indication: the critical inquiry can start with that, establish some working hypotheses. . . . What did I tell you? Isn't this a quick, effective system?"

The idea that Lotaria reads my books in this way creates some problems for me. Now, every time I write a word, I see it spun around by the electronic brain, ranked according to its frequency, next to other words whose identity I cannot know, and so I wonder how many times I have used it, I feel the whole responsibility of writing weigh on those isolated syllables, I try to imagine what conclusions can be drawn from the fact that I have used this word once or fifty times. Maybe it would be better for me to erase it. . . . But whatever other word I try to use seems unable to withstand the test. . . . Perhaps instead of a book I could write lists of words, in alphabetical order, an avalanche of isolated words which expresses that truth I still do not know, and from which the computer, reversing its program, could construct the book, my book.

I have encountered the sister of that Lotaria who is writing a thesis on me. She came unannounced, as if she were passing the house by chance. She said, "I am Ludmilla. I have read all your novels."

Aware that she didn't want to know authors personally, I was surprised to see her. She said her sister always had a partial view of things; for this reason, too, after Lotaria had spoken to her of our meetings, she wanted to check in person, as if to confirm my existence, since I correspond to her ideal model of writer.

This ideal model—to say it in her words—is the author who produces books "as a pumpkin vine produces pumpkins." She also used other metaphors of natural processes that follow their course unperturbed—the wind that shapes the mountain, the wrack of the tides, the annual circles in the bole of trees—but these were metaphors of literary creation in general, whereas the image of the pumpkin referred directly to me.

"Are you angry with your sister?" I asked her, feeling in her words a polemical tone, as of someone accustomed to sustaining her own opinions in argument with others.

"No, with somebody else whom you also know," she said.

Chapter eight

Without too much effort I was able to elicit the story behind her visit. Ludmilla is the friend, or the ex-friend, of that translator Marana, for whom literature is more worthwhile the more it consists of elaborate devices, a complex of cogs, tricks, traps.

"And, in your opinion, what I do is different?"

"I've always thought that you write the way some animals dig holes or build anthills or make beehives."

"I'm not sure what you say is very flattering for me," I replied. "In any case, here, now that you see me, I hope you haven't been disappointed. Do I correspond to the image you had formed of Silas Flannery?"

"I'm not disappointed. On the contrary. But not because you correspond to an image: because you are an absolutely ordinary person, as I was expecting, in fact."

"My novels give you the idea of an ordinary person?"

"No, you see . . . The novels of Silas Flannery are something so well characterized . . . it seems they were already there before, before you wrote them, in all their details. . . . It's as if they passed through you, using you because you know how to write, since, after all, there has to be somebody to write them. . . . I wish I could watch you while you're writing, to see if it really is like that. . . ."

I feel a stab of pain. For this girl I am nothing but an impersonal graphic energy, ready to shift from the unexpressed into writing an imaginary world that exists independently of me. God help me if she knew that I no longer have anything of what she imagines: neither expressive energy nor something to express.

"What do you think you would be able to see? I can't write if somebody is watching me . . ." I reply.

She explains that she believes she has understood this: the truth of literature consists only in the physicality of the act of writing.

"The physicality of the act . . ." These words start whirling in my mind, become associated with images I try in vain to dispel. "The physicality of existing," I stammer. "There, you see, I am here, I am a man who exists, facing you, your physical presence. . . ." And a keen jealousy invades me, not of other people, but of that me made of ink and periods and commas, who wrote the novels I will write no more, the author who continues to enter the privacy of this young woman, while I, I here and now, with the physical energy I feel surging, much more reliable than the creative impulse, I am separated from her by the immense distance of a keyboard and a white page on the roller.

"Communication can be established at various levels," I start explaining; I approach her with movements surely a bit hasty, but the visual and tactile images whirling in my mind urge me to eliminate all separation and all delay.

Ludmilla struggles, frees herself. "Why, what are you doing, Mr. Flannery? That isn't the point! You're mistaken!"

True, I could have made my passes with a bit more style, but at this point it's too late for amends: it's all or nothing now. I continue chasing her around the desk, uttering sentences whose complete foolishness I recognize, such as, "Perhaps you think I'm too old, but on the contrary . . ."

"It's all a misunderstanding, Mr. Flannery," Ludmilla says, and stops, placing between us the bulk of Webster's International Dictionary. "I could easily make love with you; you're a nice, pleasant-looking gentleman. But this would have no relevance to the problem we were discussing. . . . It would have nothing to do with the author Silas Flannery whose novels I read. . . . As I was explaining to you, you are two separate persons, whose relationships cannot interact. . . . I have no doubt that you are concretely this person and not another, though I do find you very similar to many men I have known, but the one who interested me was the other, the Silas Flannery who exists in the works of Silas Flannery, independently of you, here...."

I wipe the sweat from my forehead. I sit down. Something in me has gone: perhaps the ego, perhaps the content of the ego. But wasn't this what I wanted? Isn't depersonalization what I was trying to achieve?

Perhaps Marana and Ludmilla came to tell me the same thing, but I do not know whether it is a liberation or a condemnation. Why have they come to see me particularly, at the moment when I feel most chained to myself, as in a prison?

The moment Ludmilla left I rushed to the spyglass to find solace in the sight of the woman in the deck chair. But she was not there. I began to wonder: what if she were the same one who came to see me? Perhaps it is always and only she who is at the source of all my problems. Perhaps there is a plot to keep me from writing, in which Ludmilla and her sister and the translator are all involved.

"The novels that attract me most," Ludmilla said, "are those that create an illusion of transparency around a knot of human relationships as obscure, cruel, and perverse as possible."

I do not understand whether she has said this to explain what attracts her in my novels, or whether it is what she would like to find in my novels and does not.

The quality of perennial dissatisfaction seems to me characteristic of Ludmilla: it seems to me that her preferences change overnight and today reflect only her restlessness (but in coming back to see me, she seems to have forgotten everything that happened yesterday).

"With my spyglass I can observe a woman who is reading on a terrace in the valley," I told her. "I wonder if the books she reads are calming or upsetting."

"How does the woman seem to you? Calm or upset?"

Chapter eight

"Calm."

"Then she reads upsetting books."

I told Ludmilla the strange ideas that come to me about my manuscripts: how they disappear, return, are no longer what they were before. She told me to be very careful: there is a plot of the apocryphers which has its ramifications everywhere. I asked her if the leader of the plot was her ex-friend.

"Conspiracies always escape from the hands of their leaders," she answered, evasively.

Apocrypha (from the Greek *apokryphos*, hidden, secret): (1) originally referring to the "secret books" of religious sects; later to texts not recognized as canonical in those religions which have established a canon of revealed writings; (2) referring to texts falsely attributed to a period or to an author.

Thus the dictionaries. Perhaps my true vocation was that of author of apocrypha, in the several meanings of the term: because writing always means hiding something in such a way that it then is discovered; because the truth that can come from my pen is like a shard that has been chipped from a great boulder by a violent impact, then flung far away; because there is no certitude outside falsification.

I would like to find Ermes Marana again to propose we go into partnership and flood the world with apocrypha. But where is Marana now? Has he gone back to Japan? I try to make Ludmilla talk about him, hoping she will say something specific. According to her, for his activity the counterfeiter needs to hide in territories where novelists are numerous and productive, so he can camouflage his falsifications, mixing them with a flourishing production of genuine raw materials.

"So he's gone back to Japan, then?" But Ludmilla seems

unaware of any connection between Japan and that man. She places the secret base of the treacherous translator's machinations in quite a different part of the globe. According to his latest messages, Ermes has covered his tracks somewhere near the Cordillera of the Andes. Ludmilla, in any case, is interested in only one thing: that he remain far away. She had taken refuge in these mountains to elude him; now that she is sure of not encountering him, she can go home.

"You mean you're about to leave?" I ask her.

"Tomorrow morning," she tells me.

The news gives me a great sadness. Suddenly I feel alone.

I have spoken again with the flying-saucer observers. This time it was they who came to see me, to check whether by chance I had written the book dictated by the extraterrestrials.

"No, but I know where this book can be found," I said, approaching the spyglass. For some time I have had the idea that the interplanetary book could be the one the girl in the deck chair is reading.

On the familiar terrace the girl was not to be seen. Disappointed, I was shifting the spyglass around the valley when I saw, seated on a rocky ledge, a man in city clothes, intent on reading a book. The coincidence was so timely that it was not unwarranted to think of an extraterrestrial intervention.

"There's the book you're after," I said to those youngsters, handing them the spyglass trained on the stranger.

One by one they put an eye to the lens, then exchanged some looks, thanked me, and went out.

I have received a visit from a Reader, who came to submit to me a problem that upsets him: he has found two copies of my book *In a network of lines that et cetera,* identical on the outside, but containing two different novels. One is the story of a professor who cannot bear to hear the telephone ring, the other is the story of a billionaire who collects kaleidoscopes. Unfortunately, he was unable to tell me much more, and he was unable to show me the volumes, because before he could finish them, both were stolen, the second less than a kilometer from here.

He was still distraught over this strange episode; he told me that before presenting himself at my home he wanted to make sure I was in, and at the same time he wanted to continue reading the book, in order to discuss it with me with complete self-confidence; so with the book in his hand he had sat down on a rocky ledge from which he could keep an eye on my chalet. At a certain point he found himself surrounded by a troop of lunatics who flung themselves on the book. Around this book his insane captors improvised a kind of ritual, one of them holding it up and the others contemplating it with profound devotion. Heedless of his protests, they then ran off into the wood, taking the volume with them.

"These valleys teem with odd characters," I said to him, to calm him. "Don't give that book any more thought, sir; you haven't lost anything important: it was a fake, produced in Japan. To exploit illegally the success that my novels enjoy in the world, an unscrupulous Japanese firm disseminates books with my name on the cover which, however, are really plagiarisms from little-known Japanese authors of novels that, having had no success, were sent to be pulped. After much investigation, I have managed to unmask this fraud of which both I and the plagiarized authors are the victims."

"Actually, I rather liked that novel I was reading," the Reader confesses, "and I regret not having been able to follow the story to the end."

"If that's your only problem, I can tell you the source:

it is a Japanese novel, summarily adapted, with Western names given to true characters and places. The original is *On the carpet of leaves illuminated by the moon* by Takakumi Ikoka, an author, for that matter, who is more than worthy. I can give you an English translation, to compensate you for your loss."

I picked up the volume, which was on my desk, and gave it to him, after sealing it in an envelope, so he would not be tempted to leaf through it and thus would not immediately realize it had nothing in common with *In a network of lines that intersect* or with any other novel of mine, apocryphal or genuine.

"I knew there were false Flannerys around," the Reader said, "and I was already convinced that at least one of those two was a fake. But what can you tell me about the other?"

Perhaps it was unwise for me to go on informing this man of my problems. I tried to save the situation with a witticism: "The only books I recognize as mine are those I must still write."

The Reader confined himself to a polite little smile, then turned grave again and said, "Mr. Flannery, I know who's behind this business: it's not the Japanese, it's a certain Ermes Marana, who has started the whole thing from jealousy over a young woman whom you know, Ludmilla Vipiteno."

"Why have you come to see me, then?" I replied. "Go to that gentleman and ask him how things stand." I began to suspect that between the Reader and Ludmilla there was a bond, and this was enough to make my voice take on a hostile tone.

"I have no choice," the Reader agreed. "I have, in fact, the opportunity to make a business trip to the area where he is, in South America, and I will take advantage of it to look for him."

I was not interested in informing him that, to my

knowledge, Ermes Marana works for the Japanese and the headquarters of his apocrypha is in Japan. For me the important thing was for this nuisance to go as far away as possible from Ludmilla: so I encouraged him to make his trip and to undertake the most careful search until he found the ghost translator.

The Reader is beset by mysterious coincidences. He told me that, for some time, and for the most disparate reasons, he has had to interrupt his reading of novels after a few pages.

"Perhaps they bore you," I said, with my usual tendency toward pessimism.

"On the contrary, I am forced to stop reading just when they become most gripping. I can't wait to resume, but when I think I am reopening the book I began, I find a completely different book before me. . . ."

"Which instead is terribly boring," I suggest.

"No, even more gripping. But I can't manage to finish this one, either. And so on."

"Your case gives me new hope," I said to him. "With me, more and more often I happen to pick up a novel that has just appeared and I find myself reading the same book I have read a hundred times."

I have pondered my last conversation with that Reader. Perhaps his reading is so intense that it consumes all the substance of the novel at the start, so nothing remains for the rest. This happens to me in writing: for some time now, every novel I begin writing is exhausted shortly after the beginning, as if I had already said everything I have to say.

I have had the idea of writing a novel composed only of beginnings of novels. The protagonist could be a Reader who is continually interrupted. The Reader buys the new novel A by the author Z. But it is a defective copy, he can't go beyond the beginning. . . . He returns to the bookshop to have the volume exchanged. . . .

I could write it all in the second person: you, Reader . . . I could also introduce a young lady, the Other Reader, and a counterfeiter-translator, and an old writer who keeps a diary like this diary. . . .

But I wouldn't want the young lady Reader, in escaping the Counterfeiter, to end up in the arms of the Reader. I will see to it that the Reader sets out on the trail of the Counterfeiter, hiding in some very distant country, so the Writer can remain alone with the young lady, the Other Reader.

To be sure, without a female character, the Reader's journey would lose liveliness: he must encounter some other woman on his way. Perhaps the Other Reader could have a sister. . . .

Actually, it seems the Reader really is about to leave. He will take with him *On the carpet of leaves illuminated by the moon* by Takakumi Ikoka, to read on his journey.

On the carpet of leaves illuminated by the moon

The ginkgo leaves fell like fine rain from the boughs and dotted the lawn with yellow. I was walking with Mr. Okeda on the path of smooth stones. I said I would like to distinguish the sensation of each single ginkgo leaf from the sensation of all the others, but I was wondering if it would be possible. Mr. Okeda said it was possible. The premises from which I set out, and which Mr. Okeda considered well founded, were the following. If from the ginkgo tree a single little yellow leaf falls and rests on the lawn, the sensation felt in looking at it is that of a single yellow leaf. If two leaves descend from the tree, the eye follows the twirling of the two leaves as they move closer, then separate in the air, like two butterflies chasing each other, then glide finally to the grass, one here, one there. And so with three, with four, even with five; as the number of leaves spinning in the air increases further, the sensations corresponding to each of them are summed up, creating a general sensation like that of a silent rain, and —if the slightest breath of wind slows their descent—that of wings suspended in the air, and then that of a scattering of little luminous spots, when you lower your gaze to the lawn. Now, without losing anything of these pleasant general sensations, I would like to maintain distinct, not confusing it with the others, the individual image of each leaf from the moment it enters the visual field, and follow it in its aerial dance until it comes to rest on the blades of grass. Mr. Okeda's approval encouraged me to persevere in this purpose. Perhaps—I added, contemplating the form of the ginkgo leaf, a little yellow fan with scalloped edges—I could succeed in keeping distinct in the sensation of every leaf the sensation of every lobe of the leaf. On this point Mr. Okeda would not commit himself; at other times in the past his silence had served me as a warning not to let myself go in hasty conjectures, skipping a series of stages not yet checked. Bearing this lesson in mind, I began to concentrate my attention on capturing the tiniest sensations at the moment of their delineation, when their clarity was not yet mingled with a sheaf of diffused impressions.

Makiko, the youngest Okeda daughter, came to serve the tea, with her self-possessed movements and her still slightly childish grace. As she bent over, I saw on her bare nape, below her gathered hair, a fine black down which seemed to continue along the line of her back. I was concentrated on looking at it when I felt on me Mr. Okeda's motionless eye, examining me. Certainly he realized I was practicing on his daughter's neck my ability to isolate sensations. I did not look away, both because the impression of that tender down on the pale skin had overpowered me imperiously, and because, though it would have been easy for Mr. Okeda to direct my attention elsewhere with some common remark, he had not done so. In any event, Makiko soon finished serving the tea and rose again. I stared at a mole she had above her lip, to the left, and that brought back to me something of the earlier sensation, but more faintly. Makiko at first looked at me, upset, then lowered her eyes.

In the afternoon there was a moment I shall not easily forget, though I realize how trivial it seems in the telling. We were strolling on the bank of the little northern lake, with Makiko and her mother, Madame Miyagi. Mr. Okeda was walking ahead by himself, leaning on a long cane of white maple. In the center of the lake, two fleshy flowers of an autumn-blooming water lily had opened, and Madame Miyagi expressed the wish to pick them, one for herself and one for her daughter. Madame Miyagi had her usual frowning and slightly weary expression, but with that hint of stern obstinacy which made me suspect that in the long story of her troubled relations with her husband, about which there was so much gossip, her role was not merely that of the victim; and in truth, between Mr. Okeda's icy detachment and her own stubborn determination, I could not say who finally got the better. As for Makiko, she always displayed the gay and carefree air with which certain children who grow up amid bitter family dissension defend themselves against their surroundings, and she had borne it within her, growing up, and now faced the world of outsiders with it as if taking refuge behind the shield of an unripened and elusive bliss.

Kneeling on a rock at the bank, I leaned out until I could grasp the nearest shoot of the floating water lily, and I tugged at it gently, careful not to break it, to make the whole plant float toward the shore. Madame Miyagi and her daughter also knelt and stretched their hands out toward the water, ready to grasp the flowers when they came within reach. The bank of the little lake was low and sloping; to lean forward without too much risk, the two women remained behind my back, stretching out their arms, mother on one side, daughter on the other. At a certain moment I felt a contact in a precise point, between arm and back, at the level of the first ribs; or, rather, two different contacts, to the left and to the right. On Miss Makiko's side, it was a tense and almost throb-

bing tip, whereas on Madame Miyagi's side, an insinuating, grazing pressure. I realized that, through a rare and
sweet chance, I had been grazed at the same moment by
the left nipple of the daughter and the right nipple of the
mother, and that I must bend every effort not to lose that
chance contact and to appreciate the two simultaneous
sensations, distinguishing them and comparing their
spells.

"Push the leaves away," Mr. Okeda said, "and the stem
of the flowers will bend toward your hands." He was
standing over the group of the three of us as we leaned
toward the water lilies. In his hand he had the long cane
with which it would have been easy for him to pull the
aquatic plant close to the shore; instead he confined himself to advising the two women to perform the movement
that prolonged the pressure of their bodies against mine.

The two water lilies had almost reached the hands of
Miyagi and Makiko. I rapidly calculated that at the moment of the last yank, by raising my right elbow and immediately pressing it again to my side, I could squeeze
Makiko's tiny, firm breast, whole. But the triumph of the
water lilies' capture upset the order of our movements,
and so my right arm closed over a void, whereas my left
hand, which had abandoned its hold on the shoot, fell
back and encountered the lap of Madame Miyagi, who
seemed prepared to receive it and almost hold it, with a
yielding start which was communicated to my whole person. At this moment something was determined that later
had incalculable consequences, as I will recount in time.

Passing again beneath the ginkgo, I said to Mr. Okeda
that in the contemplation of the shower of leaves the fun-
damental thing was not so much the perception of each of
the leaves as of the distance between one leaf and another, the empty air that separated them. What I seemed
to have understood was this: an absence of sensations
over a broad part of the perceptive field is the condition

necessary for our sensitivity to concentrate locally and temporally, just as in music a basic silence is necessary so that the notes will stand out against it.

Mr. Okeda said that in tactile sensations this was certainly true; I was much amazed by his reply, because I had indeed thought of my contact with the bodies of his daughter and wife while I was communicating to him my observations on the leaves. Mr. Okeda continued talking about tactile sensations with great naturalness, as if it were understood that my discourse had had no other subject.

To shift the conversation to different ground, I tried to make the comparison with the reading of a novel in which a very calm narrative pace, all on the same subdued note, serves to enforce some subtle and precise sensations to which the writer wishes to call the reader's attention; but in the case of the novel you must consider that in the succession of sentences only one sensation can pass at a time, whether it be individual or general, whereas the breadth of the visual field and the auditory field allows the simultaneous recording of a much richer and more complex whole. The reader's receptivity with respect to the collection of sensations that the novel wants to direct at him is found to be much reduced, first by the fact that his often hasty and absent reading does not catch or neglects a certain number of signals and intentions actually contained in the text, and second because there is always something essential that remains outside the written sentence; indeed, the things that the novel does not say are necessarily more numerous than those it does say, and only a special halo around what is written can give the illusion that you are reading also what is unwritten. At all these reflections of mine, Mr. Okeda remained silent, as he does always when I happen to talk too much and am unable finally to extricate myself from my tangled reasoning.

On the carpet of leaves illuminated by the moon

In the following days I happened to find myself very often alone in the house with the two women, because Mr. Okeda had decided to carry out personally the library research that until then had been my chief task, and he preferred instead for me to remain in his study, putting his monumental card file in order. I had well-founded fears that Mr. Okeda had got wind of my conversations with Professor Kawasaki and had guessed my intention to break away from his school to approach academic circles that would guarantee my future prospects. Certainly, remaining too long under Mr. Okeda's intellectual tutelage was harming me: I could sense it from the sarcastic remarks Professor Kawasaki's assistants made about me, though they were not aloof to all relations with other tendencies, as my fellow students were. There was no doubt that Mr. Okeda wanted to keep me all day at his house to prevent me from spreading my wings, to curb my freedom of thought as he had done with his other students, who were by now reduced to spying on one another and denouncing one another for the slightest deviation from absolute subjection to the master's authority. I had to make up my mind as soon as possible and take my leave of Mr. Okeda; and if I postponed it, this was only because the mornings at his house during his absence produced in me a mental state of pleasant excitement, though of scant profit to my work.

In fact, in my work I was often distracted; I sought every pretext to go into the other rooms, where I might come upon Makiko, catch her in her privacy during the various situations of the day. But more often I found Madame Miyagi in my path, and I lingered with her, because, with the mother, opportunities for conversation— and also for sly joking, though often tinged with bitterness —arose more easily than with the daughter.

At supper in the evening, around the piping-hot suki-yaki, Mr. Okeda examined our faces as if the secrets of the day were written there, the network of desires, distinct and yet interconnected, in which I felt myself wrapped and from which I would not have liked to free myself before having satisfied them one by one. And so from week to week I postponed my decision to take leave of him and my poorly paid job with no prospects of a career, and I realized that it was he, Mr. Okeda, who kept tightening, strand by strand, the net that held me.

It was a serene autumn. As the November full moon approached, I found myself conversing one afternoon with Makiko about the most suitable place for observing the moon through the branches of the trees. I insisted that on the path under the ginkgo tree the carpet of fallen leaves would spread the moon's reflected glow in a suspended luminosity. There was a definite intention in what I said: to propose to Makiko a meeting under the ginkgo that same night. The girl answered that the lake was preferable, since the autumn moon, when the season is cold and dry, is reflected in the water with sharper outlines than the moon of summer, often shrouded in mists.

"I agree," I said hastily. "I can't wait to be with you on the shore at the moonrise. Especially"—I added—"since the lake stirs delicate sensations in my memory."

Perhaps as I uttered that sentence the contact of Makiko's breast returned to my memory too vividly, and my voice sounded aroused, alarming her. The fact is that Makiko frowned and remained a moment in silence. To dispel this awkwardness which I did not want to have interrupt the amorous daydreaming to which I was abandoning myself, I made an unwise and involuntary movement of the mouth: I bared and clenched my teeth as if to bite. Instinctively Makiko jumped back with an expression of sudden pain, as if she had really been given a bite at some sensitive spot. She recovered herself at once and left the room. I prepared to follow her.

Madame Miyagi was in the next room, sitting on a mat

on the floor, carefully arranging flowers and autumn branches in a pot. Advancing like a sleepwalker, unaware, I found her crouched at my feet, and I stopped just in time to avoid hitting her and knocking over the branches, striking them with my legs. Makiko's movement had roused in me an immediate stimulation, and this condition of mine did not escape Madame Miyagi, since my careless steps had brought me upon her in that way. In any case, the lady, without raising her eyes, shook against me the camellia blossom she was arranging in the pot, as if she wanted to hit or thrust back that part of me extending over her or even toy with it, provoke it, arouse it with a striking caress. I lowered my hands to try to save from disorder the arrangement of the leaves and flowers; meanwhile, she was also dealing with the branches, leaning forward; and it so happened that at the very moment when one of my hands slipped in confusion between Madame Miyagi's kimono and her bare skin and found itself clasping a soft and warm breast, elongated in form, one of the lady's hands, from among the branches of the *keiyaki* [*translator's note:* in Europe called Caucasian elm], had reached my member and was holding it in a firm, frank grasp, drawing it from my garments as if she were performing the operation of stripping away leaves.

What aroused my interest in Madame Miyagi's breast was the circle of prominent papillae, of a thick or minute grain, scattered on the surface of an areola of considerable extension, thicker at the edge but with outposts all the way to the tip. Presumably each of these papillae commanded sensations more or less sharp in the receptivity of Madame Miyagi, a phenomenon I could easily verify by subjecting them to slight pressure, localized as much as possible, at intervals of about a second, while observing the direct reactions in the nipple and the indirect ones in the lady's general behavior, and also my own reactions, since a certain reciprocity had clearly been established

between her sensitivity and mine. I conducted this delicate tactile reconnaissance not only with my fingertips but
also by arranging in the most suitable fashion for my
member to glide over her bosom with a grazing and encir-
cling caress, since the position in which we had happened
to find ourselves favored the encounter of these diversely
erogenous zones of ours, and since she indicated her liking
and her encouragement by authoritatively guiding these
routes. It so happens that my skin also, along the course of
the member and especially in the protuberant part of its
culmination, has points and passages of special sensitivity
that range from the extremely pleasant to the enjoyable to
the scratchy to the painful, just as there are points and
passages that are toneless or deaf. The fortuitous or calculated encounter of the different sensitive or hypersensi-
tive terminations, hers and mine, prompted an array of
various reactions, whose inventory looked to be extremely
laborious for us both.

We were intent on these exercises when, rapidly, from
the opening of the sliding door, Makiko's form appeared.
Obviously the girl had remained in expectation of my
pursuit and was now coming to see what obstacle had
delayed me. She realized at once and vanished, but not so
quickly as not to allow me time to notice that something
in her dress had changed: she had replaced her tight
sweater with a silk dressing gown which seemed made
purposely to keep falling open, to become loosened by the
internal pressure of what was flowering in her, to slide
over her smooth skin at the first attack of that greed for
contact which that smooth skin of hers could not fail, in
fact, to arouse.

"Makiko!" I cried, because I wanted to explain to her
(but really I would not have known where to begin) that
the position in which she had surprised me with her
mother was due only to a casual confluence of circumstances that had routed along detours a desire which was

unmistakably directed at her, Makiko. Desire that her silk robe, loosened or waiting to be loosened, now heightened and rewarded as in an explicit offer, so that with Makiko's apparition in my eyes and Madame Miyagi's contact on my skin I was about to be overcome by voluptuousness.

Madame Miyagi must have become clearly aware of this, for, grasping my back, she pulled me down with her on the mat and with rapid twitches of her whole person she slipped her moist and prehensile sex under mine, which without a false move was swallowed as if by a sucker, while her thin naked legs clutched my hips. She was of a sharp agility, Madame Miyagi: her feet in their white cotton socks crossed at my sacroiliac, holding me as if in a vise.

My appeal to Makiko had not gone unheard. Behind the paper panel of the sliding door there was the outline of the girl, kneeling on the mat, moving her head forward, and now from the doorway her face appeared, contracted in a breathless expression, her lips parted, her eyes widened, following her mother's and my starts with attraction and disgust. But she was not alone: beyond the corridor, in the opening of another door, a man's form was standing motionless. I have no idea how long Mr. Okeda had been there. He was staring hard, not at his wife and me but at his daughter watching us. In his cold pupil, in the firm twist of his lips, was reflected Madame Miyagi's orgasm reflected in her daughter's gaze.

He saw that I was seeing. He did not move. I realized at that moment that he would not interrupt me, nor would he drive me from the house, that he would never refer to this episode or to others that might take place and be repeated; I realized also that this connivance would give me no power over him, nor would it make my submission less burdensome. It was a secret that bound me to him but not him to me: I could reveal to no one what he was watching without admitting an indecorous complicity on my part.

On the carpet of leaves illuminated by the moon

What could I do now? I was destined to become more and more ensnared in a tangle of misunderstandings, because now Makiko considered me one of her mother's numerous lovers and Miyagi knew that I lived only for her daughter, and both would make me pay cruelly, whereas the gossip of the academic community, so quick to spread, nourished by the malice of my fellow students, ready to help also in this way their master's calculations, would throw a slanderous light on my frequent presence in the Okeda home, discrediting me in the eyes of the university professors on whom I most counted to change my situation.

Though tormented by these circumstances, I managed to concentrate and subdivide the generic sensation of my sex pressed by the sex of Madame Miyagi into the compartmented sensations of the individual points of me and of her, progressively subjected to pressure by my sliding movements and her convulsive contractions. This application especially helped me to prolong the state necessary to the observation itself, delaying the precipitation of the final crisis by evincing moments of insensitivity or partial sensitivity, which in their turn merely enhanced immeasurably the immediate return of voluptuous stimuli, distributed in an unpredictable fashion in space and time. "Makiko! Makiko!" I moaned in Madame Miyagi's ear, associating convulsively those instants of hypersensitivity with the image of her daughter and the range of sensations incomparably different which I imagined she could arouse in me. And to maintain control of my reactions I thought of the description I would make of them that same evening to Mr. Okeda: the shower of little ginkgo leaves is characterized by the fact that in each moment each leaf that is falling is found at a different altitude from the others, whereby the empty and insensitive space in which the visual sensations are situated can be subdivided into a succession of levels in each of which we find one little leaf twirling and one alone.

[9]

You fasten your seatbelt. The plane is landing. To fly is the opposite of traveling: you cross a gap in space, you vanish into the void, you accept not being in any place for a duration that is itself a kind of void in time; then you reappear, in a place and in a moment with no relation to the where and the when in which you vanished. Meanwhile, what do you do? How do you occupy this absence of yourself from the world and of the world from you? You read; you do not raise your eyes from the book between one airport and the other, because beyond the page there is the void, the anonymity of stopovers, of the metallic uterus that contains you and nourishes you, of the passing crowd always different and always the same. You might as well stick with this other abstraction of travel, accomplished by the anonymous uniformity of typographical characters: here, too, it is the evocative power of the names that persuades you that you are flying over something and not nothingness. You realize that it takes considerable heedlessness to entrust yourself to unsure instruments, handled with approximation; or perhaps this demonstrates an invincible tendency to passivity, to regression, to infantile dependence. (But are you reflecting on the air journey or on reading?)

The plane is landing; you have not managed to finish the novel *On the carpet of leaves illuminated by the moon* by Takakumi Ikoka. You continue reading as you come down the steps, sit in the bus that crosses the field, stand in the line at passport control and at customs. You are moving forward, holding the book open in front of your eyes, when someone slips it out of your hand, and as if at the rising of a curtain you see policemen arrayed before you, draped in leather cartridge belts, rattling with automatic weapons, gilded with eagles and epaulets.

Chapter nine

"But my book . . ." you complain, extending with an infant's gesture an unarmed hand toward that authoritative barrier of glistening buttons and weapon muzzles.

"Confiscated, sir. This book cannot enter Ataguitania. It's a banned book."

"But how can that be . . . ? A book on autumn leaves . . . ? What gives you the right . . . ?"

"It's on the list of books to be confiscated. These are our laws. Are you trying to teach us our job?" Rapidly, from one word to the next, from one syllable to the next, the tone shifts from dry to curt, from curt to intimidating, from intimidating to threatening.

"But I . . . I had almost finished. . . ."

"Forget it," a voice behind you whispers. "Don't start anything, not with these guys. Don't worry about the book; I have a copy, too. We'll talk about it later. . . ."

It is a woman traveler, looking self-assured, skinny in slacks, wearing big sunglasses, loaded with packages, who goes past the controls like someone accustomed to it all. Do you know her? Even if it seems to you that you do know her, act as if nothing has happened: certainly she doesn't want to be seen talking to you. She has signaled you to follow her: don't lose sight of her. Outside the airport she climbs into a taxi and motions you to take the taxi after hers. In the open countryside her taxi stops; she gets out with all her packages and climbs into yours. If it weren't for her very short hair and the huge eyeglasses, you would say she resembles Lotaria.

You venture to say, "But you're—"

"Corinna. Call me Corinna."

After rummaging in her bags, Corinna pulls out a book and gives it to you.

"But this isn't it," you say, seeing on the cover an unknown title and the name of an unknown author: *Around an empty grave* by Calixto Bandera. "The book they confiscated was by Ikoka!"

"That's what I've given you. In Ataguitania books can circulate only with fake dust jackets."

As the taxi moves at top speed through the dusty, smelly outskirts, you cannot resist the temptation to open the book and see whether Corinna has given you the real one. Fat chance. It is a book you are seeing for the first time, and it does not look the least bit like a Japanese novel: it begins with a man riding across a mesa among the agaves, and he sees some predatory birds, called *zopi-lotes,* flying overhead.

"If the dust jacket's a fake," you remark, "the text is a fake, too."

"What were you expecting?" Corinna says. "Once the process of falsification is set in motion, it won't stop. We're in a country where everything that can be falsified has been falsified: paintings in museums, gold ingots, bus tickets. The counterrevolution and the revolution fight with salvos of falsification: the result is that nobody can be sure what is true and what is false, the political police simulate revolutionary actions and the revolutionaries disguise themselves as policemen."

"And who gains by it, in the end?"

"It's too soon to say. We have to see who can best exploit the falsifications, their own and those of the others: whether it's the police or our organization."

The taxi driver is pricking up his ears. You motion Corinna to restrain herself from making unwise remarks.

But she says, "Don't be afraid. This is a fake taxi. What really alarms me, though, is that there's another taxi following us."

"Fake or real?"

"Fake, certainly, but I don't know whether it belongs to the police or to us."

You peep back along the road. "But," you cry, "there's a third taxi following the second. . . ."

"That could be our people checking the movements of

the police, but it could also be the police on the trail of our people. . . ."

The second taxi passes you, stops; some armed men leap out and make you get out of your taxi. "Police! You're under arrest!" All three of you are handcuffed and forced into the second taxi: you, Corinna, and your driver.

Corinna, calm and smiling, greets the policemen: "I'm Gertrude. This is a friend. Take us to headquarters."

Are you gaping? Corinna-Gertrude whispers to you, in your language, "Don't be afraid. They're fake policemen: actually they are our men."

You have barely driven off again when the third taxi forces the second to stop. More armed men jump out of it, their faces hidden; they disarm the policemen, remove your and Corinna's handcuffs, handcuff the policemen, and fling all of you into their taxi.

Corinna-Gertrude seems indifferent. "Thanks, friends," she says. "I'm Ingrid, and this man is one of us. Are you taking us to the command post?"

"Shut up, you!" says one who seems the leader. "Don't try acting smart, you two! Now we have to blindfold you. You're our hostages."

You don't know what to think any more, also because Corinna-Gertrude-Ingrid has been taken away in the other taxi. When you are again allowed to use your limbs and your eyes, you find yourself in a police inspector's office or in a barracks. Noncoms in uniform photograph you, full-face and profile; they take your fingerprints. An officer calls, "Alfonsina!"

You see Gertrude-Ingrid-Corinna come in, also in uniform; she hands the officer a folder of documents to sign.

Meanwhile, you follow the routine from one desk to another: one policeman takes your documents into custody, another your money, a third your clothes, which are replaced with a prisoner's overalls.

"What sort of trap is this?" you manage to ask Ingrid-

Chapter nine

Gertrude-Alfonsina, who has come over to you at a moment when your guards have their backs turned.

"Among the revolutionaries there are some counterrevolutionary infiltrators who have made us fall into a police ambush. But luckily there are also many revolutionaries who have infiltrated the police, and they have pretended to recognize me as a functionary of this command. As for you, they'll send you to a fake prison, or rather, to a real state prison that is, however, controlled not by them but by us."

You can't help thinking of Marana. Who, if not he, can have invented such a machination?

"I seem to recognize your chief's style," you say to Alfonsina.

"Who our chief is doesn't matter. He could also be a fake chief, pretending to work for the revolution for the sole purpose of favoring the counterrevolution, or one who works openly for the counterrevolution, convinced that doing so will open the way for the revolution."

"And you are collaborating with him?"

"My case is different. I'm an infiltrator, a real revolutionary infiltrated into the ranks of the false revolutionaries. But to avoid being discovered, I have to pretend to be a counterrevolutionary infiltrated among the true revolutionaries. And, in fact, I am, inasmuch as I take orders from the police; but not from the real ones, because I report to the revolutionaries infiltrated among the counterrevolutionary infiltrators."

"If I understand correctly, here everybody has infiltrated: in the police and in the revolution. But how can you tell one from the other?"

"With each person you have to discover who are the infiltrators that had him infiltrate. And even before that, you have to know who infiltrated the infiltrators."

"And you go on fighting to the last drop of blood, even knowing that nobody is what he says he is?"

"What's that got to do with it? Everybody has to do his part to the end."

"What is my part?"

"Stay calm and wait. Go on reading your book."

"Damn! I lost it when they liberated me, I mean, when they arrested me. . . ."

"No matter. The place where you're going now is a model prison; it has a library stocked with all the latest books."

"What about the banned books?"

"Where should banned books be found if not in prison?"

(You have come all the way to Ataguitania to hunt a counterfeiter of novels, and you find yourself prisoner of a system in which every aspect of life is counterfeit, a fake. Or, rather: you were determined to venture into forests, prairies, mesas, cordilleras on the trail of the explorer Marana, lost certainly while seeking the source of the oceanic novel, but you bang your head against the bars of the prison society which stretches all over the planet, confining adventure within its mean corridors, always the same. . . . Is this still your story, Reader? The itinerary you have followed for love of Ludmilla has carried you so far from her that you have lost sight of her: if she no longer is leading you, you can only entrust yourself to her diametric mirror image, Lotaria. . . .

But can it truly be Lotaria? "I don't know who you've got it in for. You mention names I don't know," she answers you every time you try to refer to past episodes. Can it be the rule of the underground that imposes it on her? To tell the truth, you are not at all sure of the identification. . . . Can she be a false Corinna or a false Lotaria? The only thing you know for sure is that her function in your story is similar to Lotaria's, so the name that fits her is Lotaria, and you would not be able to call her anything else.

"Do you mean to deny you have a sister?"

"I have a sister, but I don't see what that has to do with anything."

"A sister who loves novels with characters whose psychology is upsetting and complicated?"

"My sister always says she loves novels where you feel an elemental strength, primordial, telluric. That's exactly what she says: telluric.")

"You made a complaint to the prison library, on account of a defective volume," says the high official seated behind a high desk.

You heave a sigh of relief. Ever since a guard came to your cell to summon you, and made you follow corridors, go down stairs, walk through underground passages, climb more stairs, cross antechambers and offices, your apprehension has made you shudder, has given you flashes of fever. Instead, they simply wanted to process your complaint about *Around an empty grave* by Calixto Bandera! In the place of your anxiety, you feel reawaken in you the dismay that seized you when you saw in your hand an unglued binding that held together a few tattered, worn quires.

"Of course I complained!" you answer. "You boast so much, you people, about your model library in your model prison, and then when a person goes and asks for a book that has a proper card in the catalogue, he finds a handful of torn pages! Now I ask you how you can think of re-educating prisoners with systems like that!"

The man at the desk slowly takes off his eyeglasses. He shakes his head with a sad look. "I won't go into the details of your complaint. That's not my job. Our office, though it has close contacts both with prisons and with libraries, deals with broader problems. We sent for you, knowing you are a reader of novels, because we need advice. The forces of order—army, police, magistrature—

have always had difficulty judging whether a novel should be banned or allowed: lack of time for extensive reading, uncertainty of aesthetic and philosophical criteria on which to base the opinion. . . . No, don't fear that we want to force you to assist us in our censorship work. Modern technology will soon put us in a position to perform those tasks with rapidity and efficiency. We have machines capable of reading, analyzing, judging any written text. But it is precisely the reliability of the instruments on which we must run some checks. In our files you are listed as a reader of the sort corresponding to the average, and we see that you have read, at least in part, *Around an empty grave* by Calixto Bandera. We feel it would be opportune to compare your impressions of your reading with the results of a reading machine."

He has you taken into the machine room. "Allow me to introduce our programmer, Sheila."

Before you, in a white smock buttoned up to the neck, you see Corinna-Gertrude-Alfonsina, who is tending a battery of smooth metallic appliances, like dishwashers. "These are the memory units that have stored the whole text of *Around an empty grave*. The terminal is a printing apparatus that, as you see, can reproduce the novel word for word from the beginning to the end," the officer says. A long sheet unrolls from a kind of typewriter which, with machine-gun speed, is covering it with cold capital letters.

"Now, then, if you'll allow me, I'll take advantage of this opportunity to collect the chapters I still haven't read," you say, grazing with a shy caress the dense river of writing in which you recognize the prose that has kept you company in your prisoner's hours.

"Help yourself," the officer says. "I'll leave you with Sheila, who will insert the program we want."

Reader, you have found again the book you were seeking; now you can pick up the broken thread; the smile returns to your lips. But do you imagine it can go on in this way, this story? No, not that of the novel! Yours! How long are you going to let yourself be dragged passively by the plot? You had flung yourself into the action, filled with adventurous impulses: and then? Your function was quickly reduced to that of one who records situations decided by others, who submits to whims, finds himself involved in events that elude his control. Then what use is your role as protagonist to you? If you continue lending yourself to this game, it means that you, too, are an accomplice of the general mystification.

You grab the girl by the wrist. "Enough of these disguises, Lotaria! How long are you going to continue letting yourself be exploited by a police regime?"

This time Sheila-Ingrid-Corinna cannot conceal a certain uneasiness. She frees her wrist from your grasp. "I don't understand who you're accusing, I don't know anything about your stories. I follow a very clear strategy. The counterpower must infiltrate the mechanisms of power in order to overthrow it."

"And then reproduce it, identically! It's no use your camouflaging yourself, Lotaria! If you unbutton one uniform, there's always another uniform underneath!"

Sheila looks at you with an air of challenge. "Unbutton . . . ? Just you try. . . ."

Now that you have decided to fight, you can't draw back. With a frantic hand you unbutton the white smock of Sheila the programmer and you discover the police uniform of Alfonsina; you rip Alfonsina's gold buttons away and you find Corinna's anorak; you pull the zipper of Corinna and you see the chevrons of Ingrid. . . .

It is she herself who tears off the clothes that remain on her. A pair of breasts appear, firm, melon-shaped, a slightly concave stomach, the full hips of a *fausse maigre,* a proud pubes, two long and solid thighs.

"And this? Is this a uniform?" Sheila exclaims.

You have remained upset. "No, this, no . . ." you murmur.

"Yes, it is!" Sheila cries. "The body is a uniform! The body is armed militia! The body is violent action! The body claims power! The body's at war! The body declares itself subject! The body is an end and not a means! The body signifies! Communicates! Shouts! Protests! Subverts!"

With this, Sheila-Alfonsina-Gertrude has thrown herself on you, torn off your prisoner's trousers; your naked limbs mingle under the closets of electronic memories.

Reader, what are you doing? Aren't you going to resist? Aren't you going to escape? Ah, you are participating. . . . Ah, you fling yourself into it, too. . . . You're the absolute protagonist of this book, very well; but do you believe that gives you the right to have carnal relations with all the female characters? Like this, without any preparation . . . Wasn't your story with Ludmilla enough to give the plot the warmth and grace of a love story? What need do you have to go also with her sister (or with somebody you identify with her sister), with this Lotaria-Corinna-Sheila, who, when you think about it, you've never even liked. . . . It's natural for you to want to get even, after you have followed events of pages and pages with passive resignation, but does this seem the right way to you? Or are you trying to say that even in this situation you find yourself involved, despite yourself? You know very well that this girl always acts with her head, what she thinks in theory she does in practice, to the ultimate consequences. . . . It was an ideological demonstration she wanted to give you, nothing else. . . . Why, this time, do you allow yourself to be convinced immediately by her arguments? Watch out, Reader; here everything is different from what it seems, everything is two-faced. . . .

The flash of a bulb and the repeated click of a camera devour the whiteness of your convulsed, superimposed nudity.

"Once again, Captain Alexandra, I catch you naked in a prisoner's arms!" the invisible photographer reprimands.

"These snapshots will enrich your personal dossier. . . ." And the voice drifts off, with a sneer.

Alfonsina-Sheila-Alexandra pulls herself up, covers herself, gives a bored look. "They never leave me in peace a moment," she huffs. "Working at the same time for two secret services fighting between themselves has this drawback: both of them constantly try to blackmail you."

You start to get up, too, and you find you are wrapped in the rolls of the printout: the beginning of the novel is unfurling on the ground like a cat that wants to play. Now it is the stories you live that break off at the climactic moment: perhaps now you will be allowed to follow the novels you read all the way to the end. . . .

Alexandra-Sheila-Corinna, absorbed, has started pressing keys again. She has resumed her diligent manner, the kind of girl who puts her whole soul into everything she does. "There's something not working," she murmurs. "By now all of it should have come out. . . . What's wrong with it?"

You had already realized she's having a slightly nervous day today, Gertrude-Alfonsina; at a certain point she must have pressed the wrong key. The order of the words in the text of Calixto Bandera, preserved in the electronic memory to be brought again to light at any moment, has been erased in an instant demagnetization of the circuits. The multicolored wires now grind out the dust of dissolved words: the the the, of of of of, from from from from, that that that that, in columns according to their respective frequency. The book has been crumbled, dissolved, can no longer be recomposed, like a sand dune blown away by the wind.

Around an empty grave

When the vultures rise it's a sign the night is about to end, my father had told me. And I could hear the heavy wings flapping in the dark sky, and I could see their shadow obscure the green stars. It was a toilsome flight, which did not immediately break free of the earth, of the shadows of the bushes, as if only in flight did the feathers become convinced they were feathers and not prickly leaves. When the captors had flown off, the stars reappeared, gray, and the sky green. It was dawn, and I was riding along the deserted roads in the direction of the village of Oquedal.

"Nacho," my father had said, "as soon as I die, take my horse, my carbine, food for three days, and follow the dry bed of the stream above San Ireneo, until you see the smoke rising from the terraces of Oquedal."

"Why Oquedal?" I asked him. "Who is at Oquedal? Who should I look for?"

My father's voice became more and more faint and slow, his face more and more purple. "I must reveal to you a secret I have kept for many years. . . . It is a long story. . . ."

In those words my father was spending the last breath of his mortal agony, and I, knowing his tendency to digress, to lard all his talk with divagations, glosses, parentheses, and flashbacks, was afraid he would never arrive at communicating the essential thing to me. "Hurry, Father, tell me the name of the person I am to ask for on arriving at Oquedal. . . ."

"Your mother . . . Your mother, whom you do not know, lives at Oquedal. . . . Your mother, who has not seen you since you were in swaddling clothes . . ."

I had known that before dying he would talk to me about my mother. He owed it to me, after having made me live through my childhood and adolescence without knowing what she looked like or what name she had, the woman who had borne me, or why he had torn me from that breast when I was still sucking its milk, to drag me after him in his vagabond, fugitive life. "Who is my mother? Tell me her name!" About my mother he had told me many stories, at the time when I had not yet tired of asking about her, but they were stories, inventions, and each contradicted the others: at one time she was a poor beggar, at another a foreign lady traveling in a red automobile, once a cloistered nun, and once a circus rider; in one story she died giving birth to me, in another she was lost in an earthquake. And so the day came when I decided I would ask no more questions and would wait until he spoke to me of her. I had just turned sixteen when my father was stricken with yellow fever.

"Let me tell it from the beginning," he said, gasping. "When you have got to Oquedal, and have said: I am Nacho, son of Don Anastasio Zamora, you will have to hear many things about me, untrue stories, lies, calumny. I want you to know. . . ."

"The name! My mother's name! Quickly!"

"Now. The moment has come for you to know. . . ."

No, that moment did not come. After having rambled in

vain prefaces, my father's speech was lost in a death rattle and was extinguished forever. The young man who was now riding in the darkness along the steep roads above San Ireneo was still ignorant of the origins with which he was about to be reunited.

I had taken the road that flanks the deep chasm, high above the dry stream. The dawn, which remained suspended over the jagged edges of the forest, seemed to open to me not a new day but a day that came before all the other days, new in the sense of the time when days were still new, like the first day when men understood what a day was.

And as the day grew bright enough for me to see the other side of the chasm, I realized that a road ran along there, too, and a man on horseback was proceeding parallel to me, in the same direction, with a long-barreled army rifle hanging over one shoulder.

"Hey!" I shouted. "How far are we from Oquedal?"

He didn't even turn around; or, rather, worse than that: for an instant my voice made him move his head (otherwise I might have believed he was deaf) but he immediately returned his gaze to the road before him and went on riding without deigning me an answer or a sign of greeting.

"Hey! I asked you a question! Are you deaf? Are you dumb?" I shouted, as he continued swaying in his saddle with the gait of his black horse.

There was no knowing how long we had been advancing in the night, paired like this, separated by the steep chasm of the stream. What had seemed to me the irregular echo of my mare's hoofs resounding from the rough limestone of the other bank was, in reality, the clatter of those hoofs accompanying me.

He was a young man, all back and neck, with a tattered straw hat. Offended by his inhospitable behavior, I spurred on my mare, to leave him behind, to remove him from my sight. I had barely passed him when for some unknown reason I was inspired to turn my head toward him. He had slipped the rifle from his shoulder and was raising it to aim it at me. I immediately dropped my hand to the butt of my carbine, stuck in the saddle holster. He slung his rifle over his shoulder again as if nothing had happened. From that moment on, we proceeded at the same pace, on opposite banks, keeping an eye on each other, careful not to turn our backs. It was my mare who adjusted her gait to that of the black stallion, as if she had understood.

The story adjusts its gait to the slow progress of the iron-bound hoofs on climbing paths, toward a place that contains the secret of the past and of the future, which contains time coiled around itself like a lasso hanging from the pommel of a saddle. I already know that the long road leading me to Oquedal will be less long than the one left for me to follow once I have reached that last village at the frontier of the inhabited world, at the frontier of the time of my life.

"I am Nacho, son of Don Anastasio Zamora," I said to the old Indian huddled against the wall of the church. "Where is the house?"

Perhaps he knows, I was thinking.

The old man raised his red eyelids, gnarled as a turkey's. One finger—a finger as thin as the twigs they use to light the fire—emerged from beneath the poncho and pointed toward the palace of the Alvarado family, the only palace in that heap of clotted mud that is the village of Oquedal: a baroque façade that seems to have happened there by mistake, like a piece of scenery in an abandoned theater. Someone many centuries ago must have believed that this was the land of gold; and when he realized his error, for the palace, barely built, began the slow destiny of ruins.

Following the steps of a servant who has taken my

224

horse into his keeping, I pass through a series of places that ought to be more and more interior, whereas instead I find myself more and more outside; from one courtyard I move to another courtyard, as if in this palace all the doors served only for leaving and never for entering. The story should give the sense of disorientation in places that I am seeing for the first time but also places that have left in my memory not a recollection but a void. Now the images try to reoccupy these voids but achieve nothing except to assume also the hue of dreams forgotten the instant they appear.

In sequence, there are a courtyard where carpets are hung out for beating (I am seeking in my memory recollections of a cradle in a sumptuous dwelling), a second courtyard cluttered with sacks of alfalfa (I try to awaken recollections of an estate in my early childhood), a third courtyard with the stables opening off it (was I born among the stalls?). It ought to be broad daylight and yet the shadow that envelops the story shows no sign of brightening, it does not transmit messages that the visual imagination can complete with sharply defined figures, it does not record spoken words but only confused voices, muffled songs.

It is in the third courtyard that the sensations begin to assume form. First the smells, the flavors, then the sight of a flame that illuminates the ageless faces of the Indians gathered in the vast kitchen of Anacleta Higueras, their smooth skin, which could be very old or adolescent: perhaps they were already old men in the time when my father was here, perhaps they are the children of his contemporaries, who now look at his son the way their fathers looked at him, as a stranger who arrived one morning with his horse and his gun.

Against the background of the black fireplace and the flames, the tall form of a woman is outlined, wrapped in a blanket with ocher and pink stripes. Anacleta Higueras is preparing me a dish of spiced meatballs. "Eat, son, you've been traveling sixteen years finding your way home," she says, and I wonder whether "son" is the appellative an older woman always uses in addressing a youth or whether instead it means what the word means. And my lips are burning from the hot spices Anacleta has used to flavor her dish, as if that flavor should contain all flavors carried to their extreme, flavors I cannot distinguish or name, which now mingle on my palate like bursts of fire. I review all the flavors I have tasted in my life to try to recognize this multiple flavor, and I arrive at an opposite but perhaps equivalent sensation which is that of the milk for an infant, since as the first flavor it contains all flavor.

I look at Anacleta's face, the handsome Indian countenance which age has barely thickened without carving a single wrinkle on it; I look at the vast body wrapped in the blanket, and I wonder if it was to the high terrace of her now sloping bosom that I clung as a baby.

"You knew my father, then, Anacleta?"

"If only I had never known him, Nacho. It was not a good day, the day when he set foot in Oquedal. . . ."

"Why not, Anacleta?"

"From him nothing but evil came to the Indian people . . . and good did not come to the white people, either. . . . Then he disappeared. . . . But the day when he left Oquedal was not a good day, either. . . ."

All the Indians have their eyes glued on me, eyes that, like those of children, look at an eternal present without forgiveness.

Amaranta is the daughter of Anacleta Higueras. Her eyes are slanting, broad, her nose fine and taut at the nostrils, lips thick in a curving line. I have eyes like hers, the same nose, identical lips. "Is it true that we look alike, Amaranta and I?" I ask Anacleta.

"All those born in Oquedal look alike. Indians and whites have faces that can be confused. We are in a village of a few families, isolated in the mountains. For centuries we have married among ourselves."

"My father came from outside. . . ."

"Yes. If we do not love foreigners we have our reasons."

The mouths of the Indians open in a slow sigh, mouths with few teeth and no gums, rotting and decrepit, skeletons' mouths.

There is a portrait I saw in passing through the second courtyard, the olive-colored photograph of a young man, surrounded by wreaths of flowers and illuminated by a little oil lamp. "The dead man in that portrait also looks like one of the family," I say to Anacleta.

"That is Faustino Higueras, may God keep him in the shining glory of His archangels!" Anacleta says, and a murmur of prayers rises from among the Indians.

"Was he your husband, Anacleta?" I ask.

"My brother he was, the sword and the shield of our house and of our people, until the enemy crossed his path. . . ."

"We have the same eyes," I say to Amaranta, overtaking her among the sacks in the second courtyard.

"No, mine are bigger," she says.

"The only thing to do is to measure them." And I move my face to her face so that the arcs of our eyebrows meet; then, pressing one of my eyebrows against hers, I move my face so our temples and cheeks and cheekbones press together. "You see? The corners of our eyes end at the same point."

"I can't see anything," Amaranta says, but she doesn't move her face.

"And our noses," I say, putting my nose against hers, a bit sideways, trying to make our profiles coincide, "and our lips . . ." I groan, mouth closed, because now our lips are also attached, or, rather, half of my mouth and half of hers.

"You're hurting me," Amaranta says as I press her whole body against the sacks and feel the tips of her budding breasts and the wriggle of her belly.

"Swine! Animal! This is why you've come to Oquedal! Your father's son, all right!" Anacleta's voice thunders in my ears, and her hands have seized me by the hair and slam me against the columns, as Amaranta, struck by a backhand slap, moans, flung on the sacks. "You're not touching this daughter of mine, and you will never touch her in your life!"

"Why never in my life? What could prevent us?" I protest. "I'm a man, and she's a woman. . . . If destiny decided we were to like each other, not today, someday, who knows? Why couldn't I ask her to be my wife?"

"Curse you!" Anacleta shouts. "It can't be! You can't even think of it: you understand?"

Is she my sister, then?—I ask myself. What keeps Anacleta from admitting she's my mother? And I say to her, "Why are you shouting so much, Anacleta? Is there perhaps some blood tie between us?"

"Blood?" Anacleta recovers herself; the edges of the blanket rise until her eyes are covered. "Your father came from far away. . . . What blood tie can he have with us?"

"But I was born in Oquedal . . . of a woman from here. . . ."

"Go and look elsewhere for your blood ties, not among us poor Indians. . . . Didn't your father tell you?"

"He never told me anything, I swear, Anacleta. I don't know who my mother is. . . ."

Anacleta raises her hand and points toward the first courtyard. "Why wouldn't the mistress receive you? Why did she make you sleep down here with the servants? It was to her your father sent you, not to us. Go and present yourself to Doña Jazmina, say to her: I am Nacho Zamora y Alvarado, my father sent me to kneel at your feet."

Here the story should portray my spirit shaken as if by a hurricane at the revelation that the half of my name always hidden from me was that of the masters of Oquedal, and that estancias vast as provinces belonged to my family. Instead it is as if my journey backward in time merely coils me in a dark vortex where the successive courtyards of the Alvarado palace appear, one set in the other, equally familiar and alien to my deserted memory. The first thought that comes to my mind is the one I proclaim to Anacleta, grabbing her daughter by a braid. "Then I am your master, the master of your daughter, and I will take her when I please!"

"No!" Anacleta shouts. "Before you touch Amaranta I'll kill you!" And Amaranta draws away with a grimace that bares her teeth, whether in a moan or a smile I do not know.

The dining room of the Alvarados is dimly lighted by candlesticks encrusted with the wax of years, perhaps so that the peeling stucco decorations and the tattered lace of the hangings cannot be noted. I have been invited to supper by the mistress. Doña Jazmina's face is covered by a cake of powder that seems on the verge of coming loose and falling into the plate. She is also an Indian, under her hair, dyed a copper color and waved with a curling iron. Her heavy bracelets glitter at every spoonful. Jacinta, her daughter, was reared in a boarding school and wears a white tennis sweater but is like the Indian girls in her glances and movements.

"In this room at that time there were gaming tables," Doña Jazmina relates. "At this hour the games began and could even last all night. Some men lost whole estancias. Don Anastasio Zamora had settled here for the gambling, for no other reason. He always won, and the rumor had spread among us that he was a cheat."

"But he never won any estancia," I feel obliged to point out.

"Your father was the sort of man who, no matter what he had won during the night, had already lost it at dawn. And besides, with all his messes with women, it didn't take him long to go through what little he had left."

"Did he have affairs in this house, affairs with women . . . ?" I venture to ask her.

"There, down there, in the other courtyard, he went hunting for them, at night . . ." Doña Jazmina says, pointing toward the Indians' quarters.

Jacinta bursts out laughing, hiding her mouth with her hands. I realize at this moment that she looks exactly like Amaranta, even if she is dressed and has her hair fixed in an entirely different fashion.

"Everybody resembles everybody else, in Oquedal," I say. "There is a portrait in the second courtyard that could be the portrait of all. . . ."

They look at me, a bit upset. The mother says: "That was Faustino Higueras. . . . By blood he was only half Indian; the other half was white. In spirit, however, he was all Indian. He was with them, he took their side . . . and so he met his end."

"Was he white on his father's side, or his mother's?"

"You ask a lot of questions. . . ."

"Are all the stories of Oquedal like this?" I say. "White men who go with Indian women . . . Indian men with white women . . ."

"Whites and Indians in Oquedal resemble one another. The blood has been mixed since the time of the Conquest. But masters should not go with servants. We can all do as we want, our class, with anyone of our own kind, but not with them . . . never. . . . Don Anastasio was born of a landowning family, even if he was poorer than a beggar. . . ."

"What does my father have to do with all of this?"

"Ask them to explain to you the song the Indians sing: After Zamora passes . . . the score is even. . . . A baby in the cradle . . . and a dead man in the grave . . ."

"Did you hear what your mother said?" I say to Jacinta, as soon as we can talk by ourselves. "You and I can do anything we want."

"If we wanted. But we don't want."

"I might want to do something."

"What?"

"Bite you."

"As for that, I could gnaw you clean as a bone." And she bares her teeth.

In the room there is a bed with white sheets; it is not clear whether it is unmade or has been turned down for the night, shrouded in the thick mosquito net that hangs from a canopy. I thrust Jacinta among the folds of the gauze, and it is not clear whether she is resisting me or drawing me on; I try to pull up her clothes; she defends herself, ripping away my buckles and buttons.

"Oh, you have a mole there, too! Just like me! Look!"

At that moment a hailstorm of blows rains down on my head and shoulders, and Doña Jazmina is on us like a fury. "Let go of each other, for God's sake! Don't do it! You can't! Separate! You don't know what you're doing! You're a scoundrel, like your father!"

I pull myself together as best I can. "Why, Doña Jazmina? What do you mean? Who did my father do it with? With you?"

"Lout! Go to the servants! Out of our sight! With the servant women, like your father! Go back to your mother! Go on!"

"Who is my mother?"

"Anacleta Higueras, even if she doesn't want to admit it, since Faustino died."

* * *

Around an empty grave

The houses of Oquedal at night huddle against the earth, as if they felt pressing on them the weight of the moon, low and shrouded in unhealthy mists.

"What is this song they sing about my father, Anacleta?" I ask the woman standing motionless in a doorway like a statue in a niche of a church. "It mentions a dead man, a grave. . . ."

Anacleta takes down the lantern. Together we cross the cornfields.

"In this field your father and Faustino Higueras had a quarrel," Anacleta explains, "and decided that the two of them were one too many for this world, and they dug a grave together. Once they had decided they had to fight to the death, it was as if the hatred between them were spent: and they worked in harmony, digging the ditch. Then they stood there, one on one side of the ditch, one on the other, each grasping a knife in his right hand, with the left wrapped in his poncho. And one of them, in turn, would leap over the grave and attack the other with blows of the knife, and the other would defend himself with the poncho and try to make his enemy fall into the grave. They fought like that till dawn, and no dust rose any more from the ground around the grave because it was so soaked with blood. All the Indians of Oquedal formed a circle around the empty grave and around the two young men, gasping and blood-stained, and they all were silent and motionless so as not to disturb the judgment of God, on whom the entire fate of them all depended, not just that of Faustino Higueras and Nacho Zamora."

"But . . . I am Nacho Zamora. . . ."

"Your father, too, at that time was called Nacho."

"And who won, Anacleta?"

"How can you ask me that, boy? Zamora: no one can judge the ways of the Lord. Faustino was buried in this same earth. But for your father it was a bitter victory, since that same night he left and was never seen again at Oquedal."

"What are you telling me, Anacleta? This grave is empty!"

In the days that followed, the Indians of the villages near and far came in procession to the grave of Faustino Higueras. They were setting off for the revolution, and they would ask me for relics to carry in a gold box at the head of their regiments in battle: a lock of hair, a scrap of the poncho, a clot of blood from a wound. But Faustino was not there, his grave was empty. From that day on many legends have been born: some say they have seen him at night running over the mountain on his coal-black horse, keeping watch over the sleeping Indians; some say he will not be seen again until the day when the Indians go down to the plain, and he will be riding at the head of the columns. . . ."

Then it was Faustino! I saw him!—I want to say, but I am too overwhelmed to utter a word.

The Indians have silently approached with their torches and now form a circle around the open grave.

From their midst a young man with a thick neck comes forward, a tattered straw hat on his head. His features are similar to those of many here in Oquedal—I mean the slant of the eyes, the line of the nose, the curve of the lips that all resemble mine.

"What gave you the right, Nacho Zamora, to lay your hands on my sister?" he says, and a blade gleams in his right hand. His poncho is wrapped around his left forearm and one end of it trails to the ground.

A sound comes from the mouths of the Indians, which is not a murmur but rather a truncated sigh.

"Who are you?"

"I am Faustino Higueras. Defend yourself."

I stand beyond the grave, I wrap my poncho around my left arm, I grasp my knife.

[10]

You are taking tea with Arkadian Porphyrich, one of the most intellectually refined people in Ircania, who deservedly occupies the position of Director General of the State Police Archives. He is the person you have been ordered to contact first, the moment you arrive in Ircania on the mission assigned you by the Ataguitanian High Command. He has received you in the hospitable rooms of his office library, "the most complete and up-to-date in Ircania," as he told you at once, "where confiscated books are classified, catalogued, microfilmed, and preserved, whether they are printed works or mimeographed or typewritten or manuscript."

When the Ataguitanian authorities, who were holding you prisoner, promised you liberation provided you would agree to carry out a mission in a distant country ("official mission with secret aspects as well as secret mission with official aspects"), your first reaction was to refuse. Your scant inclination for government assignments, your lack of vocation for the profession of secret agent, and the obscure and tortuous way in which the duties you would have to fulfill were outlined, were sufficient reasons to make you prefer your cell in the model prison to the incognito of a journey in the boreal tundras of Ircania. But the thought that if you remained in their hands you could expect the worst, your curiosity about this assignment "which we believe may interest you, as a reader," the calculation that you could pretend to become involved and then foil their plan, persuaded you to accept.

Director General Arkadian Porphyrich, who seems perfectly aware of your situation, even its psychological aspects, speaks to you in an encouraging and didactic tone. "The first thing we must never lose sight of is this: the police are the great unifying power in a world otherwise doomed to fall apart. It is natural that the police forces of different and even opposing regimes should recognize common interests on which to collaborate. In the field of the circulation of books . . ."

"Will they achieve a uniformity in censorship methods among the various regimes?"

"Not uniformity. They will create a system in which the methods support and balance one another in turn. . . ."

The Director General invites you to examine the planisphere hanging on the wall. The varied color scheme indicates:

the countries where all books are systematically confiscated;

the countries where only books published or approved by the State may circulate;

the countries where existing censorship is crude, approximate, and unpredictable;

the countries where the censorship is subtle, informed, sensitive to implications and allusions, managed by meticulous and sly intellectuals;

the countries where there are two networks of dissemination: one legal and one clandestine;

the countries where there is no censorship because there are no books, but there are many potential readers;

the countries where there are no books and nobody complains about their absence;

the countries, finally, in which every day books are produced for all tastes and all ideas, amid general indifference.

"Nobody these days holds the written word in such high esteem as police states do," Arkadian Porphyrich says. "What statistic allows one to identify the nations where literature enjoys true consideration better than the sums appropriated for controlling it and suppressing it? Where it is the object of such attentions, literature gains an extraordinary authority, inconceivable in countries where it is allowed to vegetate as an innocuous pastime, without risks. To be sure, repression must also allow an occasional breathing space, must close an eye every now and then, alternate indulgence with abuse, with a certain unpredictability in its caprices; otherwise, if nothing more remains to be repressed, the whole system rusts and wears down. Let's be frank: every regime, even the most authoritarian, survives in a situation of unstable equilibrium, whereby it needs to justify constantly the existence of its repressive apparatus, therefore of something to repress. The wish to write things that irk the established authorities is one of the elements necessary to maintain this equilibrium. Therefore, by a secret treaty with the countries whose social regime is opposed to ours, we have created a common organization, with which you have intelligently agreed to collaborate, to export the books banned here and import the books banned there."

"This would seem to imply that the books banned here are allowed there, and vice versa. . . ."

"Not on your life. The books banned here are super-banned there, and the books banned there are ultra-banned here. But from exporting to the adversary regime one's own banned books and from importing theirs, each regime derives at least two important advantages: it encourages the opponents of the hostile regime and it establishes a useful exchange of experience between the police services."

"The assignment I have been given," you hasten to explain, "is limited to contacts with officials of the Ircanian police, because it is only through your channels that the opponents' writings can come into our hands." (I am careful not to tell him that the objectives of my mission also include direct relations with the clandestine network of the opposition, and, as the situations require, I can favor one side against the other or vice versa.)

236

Chapter ten

"Our archive is at your disposal," the Director General says. "I could show you some very rare manuscripts, the original drafts of works that reached the public only after having been sifted by four or five censorship committees and cut each time, modified, watered down, and finally published in a mutilated, edulcorated version, unrecognizable. For true reading one must come here, my dear sir."

"And do you read?"

"Do I read outside of my professional duties, you mean? Yes, I would say that every book, every document, every piece of evidence in this archive I read twice, two entirely different readings. The first, in haste, summarily, to know in which file I must keep the microfilm, under what heading it must be catalogued. Then, in the evening (I spend my evenings here, after the official office hours: the place is calm, relaxing, as you see), I stretch out on this sofa, I insert the film of some rare work in the reading machine, some secret dossier, and I enjoy the luxury of savoring it for my exclusive pleasure."

Arkadian Porphyrich crosses his legs in their boots, runs one finger between his neck and the collar of his uniform laden with decorations. He adds: "I don't know if you believe in the Spirit, sir. I believe in it. I believe in the dialogue that the Spirit conducts uninterruptedly with itself. And I feel that this dialogue is fulfilled as my gaze examines these forbidden pages. The Police is also Spirit, the State that I serve, the Censorship, like the texts on which our authority is exercised. The breath of the Spirit does not require a great audience to reveal itself; it flourishes in the shadow, in the obscure relationship perpetuated between the secrecy of the conspirators and the secrecy of the Police. To make it live, my reading, disinterested but always alert to every licit and illicit implication, is enough, in the glow of this lamp, in this great building with its deserted offices, the moment I can unbutton the tunic of my official's uniform and let myself be visited by the ghosts of the forbidden, which during daylight hours I must inflexibly keep at a distance. . . ."

You have to admit that the Director General's words give you a feeling of comfort. If this man continues to harbor a desire and a curiosity for reading, it means that in the written paper in circulation there is still something not fabricated or manipulated by the omnipotent bureaucracies, that outside these offices an outside still exists. . . .

"And what about the apocrypha conspiracy?" you ask, in a voice that tries to be coldly professional. "Are you informed about it?"

"Certainly. I have received a number of reports on the question. For a certain time we deceived ourselves, convinced we could keep everything under control. The secret services of the major powers went to great trouble to take over this organization, which seemed to have ramifications everywhere. . . . But the brains of the conspiracy, the Cagliostro of counterfeits, always eluded us. . . . Not that he was unknown to us: we had all his data in our files, he had long since been identified as an interfering swindler, a translator; but the true reasons for his activity remained obscure. He seemed to have no further relations with the various sects into which the conspiracy he had founded became divided, and yet he still exercised an indirect influence on their intrigues. . . . And when we man aged to get our hands on him, we realized it was not easy to bend him to our will. . . . His driving motive was not money, or power, or ambition. It seems he did everything for a woman, to win her back, or perhaps only to get even, to win a bet with her. It was that woman we had to understand if we wanted to succeed in following the moves of our Cagliostro. But we have not been able to discover who she is. It is only through a deductive process that I have managed to learn many things about her, things I could not communicate in any official report: our directive bodies are not capable of grasping certain subtleties. . . .

"For this woman," Arkadian Porphyrich continues, seeing how intently you are drinking in his words, "reading means stripping herself of every purpose, every foregone conclusion, to be ready to catch a voice that makes itself heard when you least expect it, a voice that comes from an unknown source, from somewhere beyond the book, beyond the author, beyond the conventions of writing: from the unsaid, from what the world has not yet said of itself and does not yet have the words to say. As for him, he wanted, on the contrary, to show her that behind the written page is the void: the world exists only as artifice, pretense, misunderstanding, falsehood. If this were all, we could easily give him the means to prove what he wanted; by we, I mean colleagues in the various countries and the various regimes, since there were many of us offering him our collaboration. And he didn't refuse it. On the contrary . . . But we could not manage to grasp whether he was joining in our game, or we were acting as pawns in his. . . . And what if it were simply a question of a madman? Only I could figure out his secret: I had him kidnapped by our agents, brought here, kept for a week in our solitary-confinement cells; then I interrogated him personally. His trouble was not madness, perhaps only desperation; the bet with the woman had long been lost; she was the winner, it was her always curious, always insatiable reading that managed to uncover truths hidden in the most barefaced fake, and falsity with no attenuating circumstances in words claiming to be the most truthful. What could our illusionist do? Rather than sever the last thread that tied him to her, he went on sowing confusion among titles, authors' names, pseudonyms, languages, translations, editions, jackets, title pages, chapters, beginnings, ends, so that she would be forced to recognize those signs of his presence, his greeting without hope of an answer. 'I have understood my limitations,' he said to me. 'In reading, something happens over which I have no power.' I could have told him that this is the limit that even the most omnipotent police force cannot broach. We can prevent reading: but in the decree that forbids reading there will be still read something of the truth that we would wish never to be read. . . ."

"And what became of him?" you ask with a concern perhaps no longer dictated by rivalry, but by solidarity and understanding.

"The man was finished; we could do what we liked with him: send him to forced labor or give him a routine job in our special service. Instead . . ."

"Instead . . ."

"I allowed him to escape. A fake escape, a fake clandestine expatriation, and his trail was lost again. I believe I recognize his hand, every now and then, in material I happen to see. . . . His quality has improved. . . . Now he practices mystification for mystification's sake. . . . Our power now has no more effect on him. Luckily . . ."

"Luckily?"

"Something must always remain that eludes us. . . . For power to have an object on which to be exercised, a space in which to stretch out its arms . . . As long as I know there exists in the world someone who does tricks only for the love of the trick, as long as I know there is a woman who loves reading for reading's sake, I can convince myself that the world continues. . . . And every evening I, too, abandon myself to reading, like that distant unknown woman. . . ."

Rapidly you wrest from your mind the inappropriate superimposition of the images of the Director General and Ludmilla, to enjoy the apotheosis of the Other Reader, radiant vision that rises from the disenchanted words of Arkadian Porphyrich, and you savor the certainty, confirmed by the omniscient Director, that between her and you there no longer exist obstacles or mysteries, whereas of the Cagliostro, your rival, only a pathetic shadow remains, more and more distant. . . .

But your satisfaction cannot be complete until the spell of the interrupted readings is broken. Here, too, you try to broach the subject with Arkadian Porphyrich. "As a contribution to your collection, we would have liked to offer you one of the banned books most in demand in Ataguitania—*Around an empty grave* by Calixto Bandera—but in an excess of zeal, our police sent the entire printing to be pulped. We have been informed, however, that an Ircanian translation of this novel is circulating secretly in your country, in a clandestine, mimeographed edition. Do you know anything about it?"

Arkadian Porphyrich gets up to consult a file. "By Calixto Bandera, did you say? Here it is: at the moment it doesn't seem to be available. But if you will be so patient as to wait a week, or two at most, I have an exquisite surprise in store for you. Our informers report that one of our most important banned authors, Anatoly Anatolin, has been working for some time on a version of Bandera's novel in an Ircanian setting. From other sources we know that Anatolin is about to finish a new novel entitled *What story down there awaits its end?*, for whose confiscation we have already arranged a surprise police action, so as to prevent the work from entering underground circulation. As soon as we have seized it, I will have a copy prepared for you urgently, and you will be able to decide for yourself whether it is the book you are hunting for."

In a trice you hatch your plan. You have ways of getting in contact directly with Anatoly Anatolin; you must beat the agents of Arkadian Porphyrich to the draw, gain possession of the manuscript before them, save it from confiscation, carry it to safety, and carry yourself also to safety, from both the Ircanian police and the Ataguitanian. . . .

That night you have a dream. You are in a train, a long train, which is crossing Ircania. All the travelers are reading thick bound volumes, something that happens more easily in countries where newspapers and periodicals are not very attractive. You get the idea that some of the travelers, or all, are reading one of the novels you have had to break off, indeed, that all those novels are to be found there in the compartment, translated into a language unknown to you. You make an effort to read what is written on the spine of the bindings, though you know it is useless, because for you the writing is undecipherable.

One traveler steps into the passage and leaves his volume on his seat to show it is occupied; there is a bookmark in the pages. The moment he has gone out, you reach both hands for the book, you skim through it, you are convinced it is the one you seek. At that moment you realize that all the other travelers are looking at you, their eyes filled with menacing disapproval of your indiscreet behavior.

To conceal your embarrassment, you stand up and lean out of the window, still holding the volume in your hand. The train has stopped amid tracks and signal poles, perhaps at a switch point outside some remote station. There is fog and snow, nothing can be seen. On the next track another train has stopped, headed in the opposite direction, all its windows frosted. At the window opposite yours, the circular movement of a gloved hand restores to the pane some of its transparency: a woman's form emerges, in a cloud of furs. "Ludmilla . . ." you call her. "Ludmilla, the book . . ." you try to tell her, more with gestures than with your voice, "the book you're looking for . . . I've found it, it's here. . . ." And you struggle to lower the window to pass it to her through the hard fringe of the ice that covers the train in a thick crust.

"The book I'm looking for," says the blurred figure, who holds out a volume similar to yours, "is the one that gives the sense of the world after the end of the world, the sense that the world is the end of everything that there is in the world, that the only thing there is in the world is the end of the world."

"That's not so!" you shout, and you hunt in the incomprehensible book for a sentence that can contradict Ludmilla's words. But the two trains depart, move off in opposite directions.

An icy wind sweeps the public gardens of the capital of Ircania. You are seated on a bench waiting for Anatoly Anatolin, who is to deliver to you the manuscript of his new novel, *What story down there awaits its end?* A young man with a long blond beard, a long black coat, and an oilcloth cap sits down beside you. "Act natural. The gardens are always under close observation."

A hedge protects you from alien eyes. A little bundle of pages passes from the inside pocket of Anatoly's long overcoat to the inside pocket of your short pea jacket. Anatoly Anatolin takes out more pages from the inside pocket of his jacket. "I had to divide the pages among my various pockets, so that the bulging wouldn't attract attention," he says, extracting a roll of pages from an inside pocket of his vest. The wind whips a page from his fingers; he rushes to retrieve it. He is about to produce another pack of pages from the rear pocket of his trousers, but two agents in civilian clothes spring from the hedge and arrest him.

What story
down there
awaits
its end?

Walking along the great Prospect of our city, I mentally erase the elements I have decided not to take into consideration. I pass a ministry building, whose façade is laden with caryatids, columns, balustrades, plinths, brackets, metopes; and I feel the need to reduce it to a smooth vertical surface, a slab of opaque glass, a partition that defines space without imposing itself on one's sight. But even simplified like this, the building still oppresses me: I decide to do away with it completely; in its place a milky sky rises over the bare ground. Similarly, I erase five more ministries, three banks, and a couple of skyscraper headquarters of big companies. The world is so complicated, tangled, and overloaded that to see into it with any clarity you must prune and prune.

In the bustle of the Prospect I keep meeting people the sight of whom, for various reasons, is unpleasant to me: my superiors, because they remind me of my inferior position; my inferiors, because I hate to feel possessed of an authority I consider petty, as petty as the envy, servility, and bitterness it inspires. I erase both categories, without any hesitation; out of the corner of my eye, I see them shrink and vanish in a faint wisp of fog.

In this operation I am careful to spare passersby, outsiders, strangers who have never bothered me; indeed, the faces of some of them, if I observe them objectively, seem worthy of sincere interest. But when a crowd of strangers is all that remains from the world surrounding me, I suddenly feel lonely and disoriented, so better to erase them as well, the whole lot, and forget it.

In a simplified world I have greater probabilities of meeting the few people I like to meet: Franziska, for example. Franziska is a friend, and when I run into her, I feel a great joy. We exchange witticisms, we laugh, we tell each other things, ordinary events but perhaps ones we do not tell other people, and when we discuss them together, they prove interesting to both of us, and before saying good-bye, we both insist we must meet again as soon as possible. Then months pass, until we run into each other in the street, by chance: festive cries, laughter, promises to get together again soon, but neither of us ever does anything to bring about a meeting; perhaps because we know that it would no longer be the same thing. In a reduced and simplified world, now that the air has been cleared of all those pre-established situations which would make the fact of my seeing Franziska more often suggest a relationship between us somehow requiring definition, perhaps eventual marriage, or, in any event, our being considered a couple, assuming a bond possibly extending to our respective families, to our forebears and descendants, to siblings and cousins, and a bond between the environment of our joint lives and our attachments in the sphere of incomes and possessions; now, having achieved the disappearance of these conditions which, all around us, silently, weighed on us and on our conversations, causing them never to last more than a few minutes, my meeting Franziska should be even more beautiful and enjoyable. So it is natural for me to try to create the circumstances most favorable to a crossing of our paths, such as the abolition of all young women wearing a pale fur like the one she wore last time, so that if I see her from a distance, I can be sure it is she, without any risk of misunderstandings or disappointments, and then the abolition of all young men who look as if they might be friends of Franziska and might conceivably be about to meet her, maybe intentionally, and delay her in pleasant conversation just when I should be the one to meet her, by chance.

I have gone into details of a personal nature, but this should not lead anyone to believe that my abolitions are inspired primarily by my own immediate, private interests; on the contrary, I try to act in the interest of the whole (and hence also my own, but indirectly). True, to begin somewhere, I made all the public buildings that occurred within my range disappear, with their broad steps and columned entrances and their corridors and waiting rooms, and files and circulars and dossiers, but also with their division chiefs, their director-generals, their vice-inspectors, their acting heads, their permanent and temporary staff; but I did this because I believe their existence is damaging or superfluous to the harmony of the whole.

It is that time of day when droves of employees leave the overheated offices, button up their overcoats with their fake-fur collars, and pile into buses. I blink, and they have vanished: only some scattered passersby can be discerned, far off, in the deserted streets from which I have also scrupulously eliminated automobiles and trucks and buses. I like to see the surface of the street bare and smooth as a bowling alley.

Then I abolish barracks, guard houses, police stations: all people in uniform vanish as if they had never existed. Perhaps I've let things get out of hand; I realize that firemen have suffered the same fate, and postmen, municipal streetcleaners, and other categories that might deservedly have hoped for a different treatment; but what's done is done: no use splitting hairs. To avoid trouble, I quickly abolish fires, garbage, and also mail, which after all never brings anything but problems.

I check to make sure that hospitals, clinics, rest homes have not been left standing: to erase doctors, nurses, patients seems to me the only possible health. Then courts, with their complement of magistrates, lawyers, defendants and injured parties; prisons, with prisoners and guards inside. Then I erase the university with the entire faculty, the academy of sciences, letters, and arts, the museum, the library, monuments and curators, theaters, movies, televisions, newspapers. If they think respect for culture is going to stop me, they're wrong.

Then come the economic structures, which for too long a time have continued to enforce their outrageous claim to decide our lives. What do they think they are? One by one, I dissolve all shops, beginning with the ones selling prime necessities and ending with those selling superfluities, luxuries: first I clear the display windows of goods, then I erase the counters, shelves, salesgirls, cashiers, floorwalkers. The crowd of customers is momentarily bewildered, hands extended into the void, as shopping carts evaporate; then the customers themselves are also swallowed up by the vacuum. From consumer I work back to producer: I abolish all industry, light and heavy, I wipe out raw materials and sources of energy. What about agriculture? Away with that, too! And to keep anyone from saying I want to regress toward primitive societies, I also eliminate hunting and fishing.

Nature . . . Aha! Don't think I haven't caught on. This nature business is another fine fraud: kill it! A layer of the earth's crust is all that has to remain, solid enough underfoot, and everywhere else, nothingness.

I continue my walk along the Prospect, which now cannot be distinguished from the endless plain, deserted and frozen. There are no more walls as far as the eye can see, no mountains or hills; not a river or a lake or a sea: only a flat, gray expanse of ice, as compact as basalt. Renouncing things is less difficult than people believe: it's all a matter of getting started. Once you've succeeded in dispensing with something you thought essential, you realize you can also do without something else, then without many other things. So here I am walking along this empty surface that is the world. There is a wind grazing the ground, dragging with flurries of fine snow the last residue of the vanished world: a bunch of ripe grapes which seems just picked from the vine, an infant's woolen bootee, a well-oiled hinge, a page that seems torn from a novel written in Spanish, with a woman's name: Amaranta. Was it a few seconds ago that everything ceased to exist, or many centuries? I've already lost any sense of time.

There, at the end of that strip of nothing I continue to call the Prospect, I see a slender form advancing, in a pale fur jacket: it's Franziska! I recognize her stride in her high boots, and the way she keeps her arms hidden in her muff, and the long striped scarf flapping after her. The cold air and the cleared terrain guarantee good visibility, but I wave my arms in vain, trying to attract her attention: she can't recognize me, we're still too far apart. I advance, hastening my steps; at least I think I'm advancing, but I lack any reference points. Now, on the line between me and Franziska, some shadows can be discerned: they are men, men in overcoats and hats. They are waiting for me. Who can they be?

When I have come close enough, I recognize them: they're the men from Section D. How is it they've remained here? What are they doing? I thought I had abolished them, too, when I erased the personnel of all the offices. Why have they placed themselves between me and Franziska? "Now I'll erase them!" I decide, and concentrate. Nothing doing: they're still there between us.

What story down there awaits its end?

"Well, here you are," they greet me. "Still one of us, are you? Good for you! You gave us a real hand, all right, and now everything is clean."

"What?" I exclaim. "Were you erasing as well?"

Now I can understand my sensation that, this time, I had ventured further than in my previous exercises of making the world around me disappear.

"But tell me something: weren't you the ones who were always talking of increment, of implementing, of expansion . . . ?"

"Well? There's no contradiction. . . . Everything is contemplated in the logic of projections. . . . The line of development starts again from zero. . . . You had also realized that the situation had come to a dead end . . . was deteriorating. . . The only thing was to help the process along. . . . Tendentially, something that might seem negative in the short run, in the long run can prove an incentive. . . ."

"But I didn't mean it the way you did. . . I had something else in mind. . . . I erase in a different way . . ." I protest, and I think: If they believe they can fit me into their plans, they're wrong!

I can't wait to go into reverse, to make the things of the world exist again, one by one or all together, to set their variegated and tangible substance, like a compact wall, against the men's plans of general vacancy. I close my eyes and reopen them, sure of finding myself on the Prospect again, teeming with traffic, the street lamps lighted at this hour, and the final edition of the papers in the kiosks. But instead: nothing. The void all around us is more and more void, Franziska's form on the horizon comes forward slowly, as if she had to climb the curve of the earth's globe. Are we the only survivors? With mounting terror I begin to realize the truth: the world I believed erased by a decision of my mind that I could revoke at any moment is truly finished.

"You have to be realistic," the officials of Section D are

saying. "Just take a look around. The whole universe is . . . let's say it's in a transitional phase. . . ." And they point to the sky, where the constellations have become unrecognizable, here clotted, there rarefied, the celestial map in upheaval, stars exploding one after the other, while more stars emit a final flicker and die. "The important thing is that now, when the new ones arrive, they must find Section D in perfect working order, its cadres complete, its functional structures in operation. . . ."

"But who are the new ones? What do they do? What do they want?" I ask, and on the frozen surface that separates me from Franziska I see a fine crack, spreading like a mysterious trap.

"It's too early to say. For us to say it in our terms. At present we can't even see them. But we can be sure they're there, and for that matter, we had been informed, even before, that they were about to arrive. . . . But we're here, too, and they can't help knowing it, we who represent the only possible continuity with what there was before. . . . They need us. They have to turn to us, entrust to us the practical management of what remains. . . . The world will begin again the way we want it. . . ."

No, I think, the world that I would like to begin existing again around me and Franziska can't be yours; I would like to concentrate and think of a place in every detail, a setting where I would like to be with Franziska at this moment; for example, a café lined with mirrors, which reflect crystal chandeliers, and there is an orchestra playing waltzes and the strains of the violins flutter over the little marble tables and the steaming cups and the pastries with whipped cream. While outside, beyond the frosted windows, the world full of people and of things would make its presence felt: the presence of the world, friendly and hostile, things to rejoice in or to combat. . . . I think this with all my strength, but by now I know my strength isn't enough to make it exist: nothingness is stronger and has occupied the whole earth.

"To work out a relationship with them won't be easy," the Section D men continue, "and we'll have to be on our toes, not make mistakes, not allow them to cut us out. We had you in mind, to win the new ones' confidence. You've proved your ability in the liquidation phase, and of all of us you're the least compromised with the old administration. You'll have to introduce yourself, explain what the Section is, how they can use it, for urgent, indispensable jobs. . . . Well, you'll figure out the way to make things look best. . . ."

"I should be going, then. I'll go look for them . . ." I hasten to say, because I realize that if I don't make my escape now, if I don't reach Franziska immediately and save her, in a minute it will be too late; the trap is about to be sprung. I run off before the Section D men can hold me, ask me questions, give me instructions. I advance over the frozen crust toward her. The world is reduced to a sheet of paper on which nothing can be written except abstract words, as if all concrete nouns were finished; if one could only succeed in writing the word "chair," then it would be possible to write also "spoon," "gravy," "stove," but the stylistic formula of the text prohibits it.

On the ground that separates me from Franziska I see some fissures open, some furrows, crevasses; at each moment one of my feet is about to be caught in a pitfall: these interstices widen, soon a chasm will yawn between me and Franziska, an abyss! I leap from one side to the other, and below I see no bottom, only nothingness which continues down to infinity; I run across pieces of world scattered in the void; the world is crumbling. . . . The men from Section D call me, they motion desperately for me to come back, not to risk going any farther. . . . Franziska! One more leap and I'll be with you!

She is here, she is opposite me, smiling, with that

What story down there awaits its end?

golden sparkle in her eyes, her small face a bit chapped from the cold. "Oh! It's really you! Every time I walk on the Prospect I run into you! Now, don't tell me you spend all your days out strolling! Listen: I know a café here at the corner, all lined with mirrors, and there's an orchestra that plays waltzes. Will you invite me there?"

[11]

Reader, it is time for your tempest-tossed vessel to come to port. What harbor can receive you more securely than a great library? Certainly there is one in the city from which you set out and to which you have returned after circling the world from book to book. You have one hope left, that the ten novels that evaporated in your hands the moment you began reading them can be found in this library.

Finally a free, calm day opens before you; you go to the library, consult the catalogue; you can hardly repress a cry of rejoicing, or, rather, ten cries; all the authors and the titles you are looking for appear in the catalogue, duly recorded.

You compile a first request form and hand it in; you are told that there must be an error of numbering in the catalogue; the book cannot be found; in any case, they will investigate. You immediately request another; they tell you it is out on loan, but they are unable to determine who took it out and when. The third you ask for is at the bindery; it will be back in a month. The fourth is kept in a wing of the library now closed for repairs. You keep filling out forms; for one reason or another, none of the books you ask for is available.

While the staff continues searching, you wait patiently, seated at a table along with other, more fortunate, readers, immersed in their volumes. You crane your neck to left and right, to peek at the others' books. Who knows? One of these people may be reading one of the books you are looking for.

The gaze of the reader opposite you, instead of resting on the book open in his hands, wanders in the air. But his eyes are not absent: a fixed intensity accompanies the movements of the blue irises. Every now and then your eyes meet. At a certain point he addresses you, or, rather, he speaks as if into the void, though certainly to you:

"Don't be amazed if you see my eyes always wandering. In fact, this is my way of reading, and it is only in this way that reading proves fruitful for me. If a book truly interests me, I cannot follow it for more than a few lines before my mind, having seized on a thought that the text suggests to it, or a feeling, or a question, or an image, goes off on a tangent and springs from thought to thought, from image to image, in an itinerary of reasonings and fantasies that I feel the need to pursue to the end, moving away from the book until I have lost sight of it. The stimulus of reading is indispensable to me, and of meaty reading, even if, of every book, I manage to read no more than a few pages. But those few pages already enclose for me whole universes, which I can never exhaust."

"I understand you perfectly," another reader interjects, raising his waxen face and reddened eyes from his volume. "Reading is a discontinuous and fragmentary operation. Or, rather, the object of reading is a punctiform and pulviscular material. In the spreading expanse of the writing, the reader's attention isolates some minimal segments, juxtapositions of words, metaphors, syntactic nexuses, logical passages, lexical peculiarities that prove to possess an extremely concentrated density of meaning. They are like elemental particles making up the work's nucleus, around which all the rest revolves. Or else like the void at the bottom of a vortex which sucks in and swallows currents. It is through these apertures that, in barely perceptible flashes, the truth the book may bear is revealed, its ultimate substance. Myths and mysteries consist of impalpable little granules, like the pollen that sticks to the butterfly's legs; only those who have realized this can expect revelations and illuminations. This is why my attention, in contrast to what you, sir, were saying, cannot be detached from the written lines even for an instant. I must not be distracted if I do not wish to miss some valuable clue. Every time I come upon one of these clumps of meaning I must go on digging around to see if the nugget extends into a vein. This is why my reading has no end: I read and reread, each time seeking the confirmation of a new discovery among the folds of the sentences."

"I, too, feel the need to reread the books I have already read," a third reader says, "but at every rereading I seem to be reading a new book, for the first time. Is it I who keep changing and seeing new things of which I was not previously aware? Or is reading a construction that assumes form, assembling a great number of variables, and therefore something that cannot be repeated twice according to the same pattern? Every time I seek to relive the emotion of a previous reading, I experience different and unexpected impressions, and do not find again those of before. At certain moments it seems to me that between one reading and the next there is a progression: in the sense, for example, of penetrating further into the spirit of the text, or of increasing my critical detachment. At other moments, on the contrary, I seem to retain the memory of the readings of a single book one next to another, enthusiastic or cold or hostile, scattered in time without a perspective, without a thread that ties them together. The conclusion I have reached is that reading is an operation without object; or that its true object is itself. The book is an accessory aid, or even a pretext."

A fourth speaks up: "If you mean to insist on the subjectivity of reading, then I agree with you, but not in the centrifugal sense you attribute to it. Every new book I read comes to be a part of that overall and unitary book that is the sum of my readings. This does not come about without some effort: to compose that general book, each individual book must be transformed, enter into a relationship with the books I have read previously, become their corollary or development or confutation or gloss or reference text. For years I have been coming to this library, and I explore it volume by volume, shelf by shelf, but I could demonstrate to you that I have done nothing but continue the reading of a single book."

"In my case, too, all the books I read are leading to a single book," a fifth reader says, sticking his face out from behind a pile of bound volumes, "but it is a book remote in time, which barely surfaces from my memories. There is a story that for me comes before all other stories and of which all the stories I read seem to carry an echo, immediately lost. In my readings I do nothing but seek that book read in my childhood, but what I remember of it is too little to enable me to find it again."

A sixth reader, who was standing, examining the shelves with his nose in the air, approaches the table. "The moment that counts most for me is the one that precedes reading. At times a title is enough to kindle in me the desire for a book that perhaps does not exist. At times it is the *incipit* of the book, the first sentences. . . . In other words: if you need little to set the imagination going, I require even less: the promise of reading is enough."

"For me, on the other hand, it is the end that counts," a seventh says, "but the true end, final, concealed in the darkness, the goal to which the book wants to carry you. I also seek openings in reading," he says, nodding toward the man with the bleary eyes, "but my gaze digs between the words to try to discern what is outlined in the distance, in the spaces that extend beyond the words 'the end.' "

The moment has come for you to speak. "Gentlemen, first I must say that in books I like to read only what is written, and to connect the details with the whole, and to consider certain readings as definitive; and I like to keep one book distinct from the other, each for what it has that

Chapter eleven

is different and new; and I especially like books to be read from beginning to end. For a while now, everything has been going wrong for me: it seems to me that in the world there now exist only stories that remain suspended or get lost along the way."

The fifth reader answers you: "That story of which I spoke—I, too, remember the beginning well, but I have forgotten all the rest. It must be a story of the *Arabian Nights*. I am collating the various editions, the translations in all languages. Similar stories are numerous and there are many variants, but none is that story. Can I have dreamed it? And yet I know I will have no peace until I have found it and find out how it ends."

"The Caliph Harun-al-Rashid"—this is the beginning of the story that, seeing your curiosity, he agrees to tell— "one night, in the grip of insomnia, disguises himself as a merchant and goes out into the streets of Baghdad. A boat carries him along the waters of the Tigris to the gate of a garden. At the edge of a pool a maiden beautiful as the moon is singing, accompanying herself on the lute. A slave girl admits Harun to the palace and makes him put on a saffron-colored cloak. The maiden who was singing in the garden is seated on a silver chair. On cushions around her are seated seven men wrapped in saffron-colored cloaks. 'Only you were missing,' the maiden says, 'you are late'; and she invites him to sit on a cushion at her side. 'Noble sirs, you have sworn to obey me blindly, and now the moment has come to put you to the test.' And from around her throat the maiden takes a pearl necklace. 'This necklace has seven white pearls and one black pearl. Now I will break its string and drop the pearls into an onyx cup. He who draws, by lot, the black pearl must kill the Caliph Harun-al-Rashid and bring me his head. As a reward I will give myself to him. But if he should refuse to kill the Caliph, he will be killed by the other seven, who will repeat the drawing of lots for the black pearl.' With a shudder Harun-al-Rashid opens his hand, sees the black pearl, and speaks to the maiden. 'I will obey the command of fate and yours, on condition that you tell me what offense of the Caliph has provoked your hatred,' he asks, anxious to hear the story."

This relic of some childish reading should also be included in your list of interrupted books. But what title does it have?

"If it had a title I have forgotten that, too. Give it one yourself."

The words with which the story breaks off seem to you to express well the spirit of the *Arabian Nights*. You write, then, *He asks, anxious to hear the story* in the list of titles you have asked for in vain at the library.

"May I see?" the sixth reader asks, taking the list of titles. He removes his nearsighted glasses, puts them in their case, opens another case, takes out his farsighted glasses, and reads aloud:

"*If on a winter's night a traveler, outside the town of Malbork, leaning from the steep slope without fear of wind or vertigo, looks down in the gathering shadow in a network of lines that enlace, in a network of lines that intersect, on the carpet of leaves illuminated by the moon around an empty grave— What story down there awaits its end?—he asks, anxious to hear the story.*"

He pushes his eyeglasses up on his brow. "Yes, a novel that begins like that . . ." he says, "I could swear I've read it. . . . You have only this beginning and would like to find the continuation, is that true? The trouble is that once upon a time they all began like that, all novels. There was somebody who went along a lonely street and saw something that attracted his attention, something that seemed to conceal a mystery, or a premonition; then he asked for explanations and they told him a long story. . . ."

"But, look here, there's a misunderstanding," you try to warn him. "This isn't a book . . . these are only titles . . . the *Traveler* . . ."

Chapter eleven

"Oh, the traveler always appeared only in the first pages and then was never mentioned again—he had fulfilled his function, the novel wasn't his story. . . ."

"But this isn't the story whose continuation I want to know. . . ."

The seventh reader interrupts you: "Do you believe that every story must have a beginning and an end? In ancient times a story could end only in two ways: having passed all the tests, the hero and the heroine married, or else they died. The ultimate meaning to which all stories refer has two faces: the continuity of life, the inevitability of death."

You stop for a moment to reflect on these words. Then, in a flash, you decide you want to marry Ludmilla.

[12]

Now you are man and wife, Reader and Reader. A great double bed receives your parallel readings.

Ludmilla closes her book, turns off her light, puts her head back against the pillow, and says, "Turn off your light, too. Aren't you tired of reading?"

And you say, "Just a moment, I've almost finished *If on a winter's night a traveler* by Italo Calvino."

A Selected List of Classics Available from Minerva

While every effort is made to keep prices low, it is sometimes necessary to increase prices at short notice. Mandarin Paperbacks reserves the right to show new retail prices on covers which may differ from those previously advertised in the text or elsewhere.

The prices shown below were correct at the time of going to press.

☐	7493 9933 3	**Complete Short Stories**	Bertolt Brecht	£5.99
☐	7493 9934 1	**Adam, One Afternoon**	Italo Calvino	£5.99
☐	7493 9923 6	**If on a Winter's Night a Traveller**	Italo Calvino	£6.99
☐	7493 9878 7	**The Call of the Toad**	Günter Grass	£6.99
☐	7493 9702 0	**Berlin Novels**	Christopher Isherwood	£9.99
☐	7493 9054 9	**Goodbye to Berlin**	Christopher Isherwood	£6.99
☐	7493 8681 9	**Mr Norris Changes Trains**	Christopher Isherwood	£6.99
☐	7493 9952 X	**The Castle**	Franz Kafka	£5.99
☐	7493 9953 8	**The Metamorphosis**	Franz Kafka	£6.99
☐	7493 9955 4	**The Trial**	Franz Kafka	£6.99
☐	7493 9808 6	**To Kill a Mockingbird**	Harper Lee	£7.99
☐	7493 8647 9	**Buddenbrooks**	Thomas Mann	£8.99
☐	7493 8623 1	**Death in Venice and Other Stories**	Thomas Mann	£5.99
☐	7493 8657 6	**Doctor Faustus**	Thomas Mann	£7.99
☐	7493 8642 8	**The Magic Mountain**	Thomas Mann	£8.99
☐	7493 8662 2	**Mario and the Magician**	Thomas Mann	£6.99
☐	7493 8682 7	**Royal Highness**	Thomas Mann	£6.99
☐	7493 9757 8	**Short Stories**	W. Somerset Maugham	£8.99
☐	7493 9155 3	**The Grapes of Wrath**	John Steinbeck	£8.99

All these books are available at your bookshop or newsagent, or can be ordered direct from the address below. Just tick the titles you want and fill in the form below.

Cash Sales Department, PO Box 5, Rushden, Northants NN10 6YX.
Phone: 01933 414000 : Fax: 01933 414047.

Please send cheque, payable to 'Reed Book Services Ltd.', or postal order for purchase price quoted and allow the following for postage and packing:

£1.00 for the first book, 50p for the second; **FREE POSTAGE AND PACKING FOR THREE BOOKS OR MORE PER ORDER.**

NAME (Block letters)...

ADDRESS...

....

☐ I enclose my remittance for ....

☐ I wish to pay by Access/Visa Card Number ☐☐☐☐☐☐☐☐☐☐☐☐☐☐☐☐

Expiry Date ☐☐☐☐

Signature ....

Please quote our reference: MAND